Painted Walls

Bureau Novel #2

Megan Mitcham

Copyright Warning

Published by MM Publishing LLC

Edited by Lacey Thacker

Cover Design by Deranged Doctor Designs

First electronic publication: October 2015
First print publication: October 2015

Digital ISBN: 978-1-941899-15-1

Print ISBN: 978-1-941899-16-8

Praise for the Base Branch Series

"Megan Mitcham's books are well-paced, well-plotted suspense novels edged with stunning sensual intensity. Her lovers are cold and deadly--except when they are skin-to-skin. I can't wait for the next book in the series!"

- **DELILAH DEVLIN**
New York Times and USA Today bestselling author

"Nail-biter all the way to the end."

- **Michelle**, MsRomanticReads
Adult Romance & Erotic Book Reviews

"This is a fresh and exciting story with lots of great characters."

- **5 Star Amazon Review**, Enemy Mine

"Megan now joins my elite team of must read authors. I fell in love with her work in *Enemy Mine*, and it just gets better the more I read."

- **TNT Reviews**

BOOKS BY MEGAN MITCHAM

BASE BRANCH NOVELS
ENEMY MINE
JUSTICE MINE
STRANGER MINE
WARRIOR MINE
DANGER MINE
PRISONER MINE
SURVIVOR MINE - 2017

BASE BRANCH SUBSERIES
VERSIONS - updated 2016
VIRTUES - 2016
VARIATIONS - 2016

BUREAU NOVELS
FOR ALL TO SEE
PAINTED WALLS

ANTHOLOGIES
ANTICIPATION
CONQUESTS
ROGUE HEARTS - 2016
SEX OBJECTS - 2016
COWBOY HEAT
HIGH OCTANE HEROES
WILD AT HEART VOLUME II
benefiting Turpentine Creek Wildlife Refuge

BOX SET
HEARTS IN DANGER
benefiting The American Heart Association

To the broken ones. And really, aren't we all beautifully broken at some point in our lives?

1986

Sarah shuffled through the family room with a large basket of folded clothes on her hip. The familiar electronic chime of the nightly news intro caught her attention. Determined to complete the job she'd begun before taking in the broadcast, she continued on toward the hallway. Two hours obsessing over the four large carpet samples that lined the far wall had eaten her free time for the day. And she still couldn't decide between sea foam green and boring beige.

Tom Brokaw's ominous lilt hit her ears. "Good evening. A gruesome discovery in Monroe, Louisiana today."

Her feet sank into the plush shag, stalling her progress. She turned toward the television. The static-laced picture on the screen beckoned. Sarah sank to the bright orange carpet. She released the plastic hamper and hugged her middle without sparing the flooring another thought.

Her eyes locked onto the scene outside a suburban home similar to her own. A trim green lawn edged the ranch-style house. Vibrant flowers and orderly beds garnished the brick. A garden gnome peeked around the square hedges. The sharp arch of a swing set loomed over the tall white fence. The starkest contrast, though, was the whirling red and blue lights atop the line of police cars that rimmed the yard.

Her stomach shimmied.

The camera angle shifted left, revealing a young reporter in a tan suit and maroon tie. He cleared his throat, lifted his chin, and gave a carnival mask of concern. His eyes held the glimmer of excitement.

"Authorities have found the body of a young mother slain in her home. Officials have yet to release the victim's name or the circumstances behind her death, but, Tom, this is believed to be the work of the Blood Red Killer."

The scene shrank to a small window above the anchor's side-swept hair.

"The murderer's signature is clear. For more than a decade he has killed young women in their homes, drained their bodies of blood, and painted an entire wall with it. And yet, droves of evidence haven't helped authorities capture this monster. No significant leads have been pursued in the south's string of terror killings." His head shook and his lips pursed. "We'll have more on this story later in the broadcast."

Sarah made the sign of the cross and prayed for the young woman's soul. She also offered a plea of safety for herself and her young daughter. Living in Louisiana, the epicenter of this madman's death field, made these prayers habitual. Ten years of fear and nightly prayers hadn't stopped the killings. What ever would?

An engine roared into the driveway. She couldn't see through the drawn curtains, but she jumped so high at the rumbling horses she nearly levitated above the hideous carpet. Her hand clutched her churning heart.

Sarah's gaze jumped to the waxed shine of the grandfather clock, to the open corridor leading to the bedrooms, and then back to the ticking hands. The ornate gold arms showed the time. Five thirty-four.

Her fingers relaxed. She forced a long, weighty breath through her lips and chuckled at her fluttering nerves. Of course it was five-thirty. The news cast had just started. Of course a car rumbled in the driveway. It was five-thirty. The end of another long week of single parenting. It seemed every time her husband came home from a business trip she had another murder to tell him about. But she wouldn't open with sad news. They had so much to be happy about.

A smile spread across Sarah's face. She scrambled to her feet and turned away from the television, the horrors forgotten for now. "Daddy's home!"

Light, yet fiercely rapid, footfalls echoed down the hall. Her daughter breached the living room at a sprint. Chubby legs pumped small bare feet toward the front door, not sparing her a glance. Giddy laughter sang from her angel's bright pink lips. Sarah's breath caught in equal parts awe and irritation. Two smears of purple colored her daughter's lids.

"Race you," the little one challenged over one shoulder as she zipped past.

"Miss." Sarah popped both hands onto her hips. Those little feet slowed. "I told you last time not to get into my makeup."

Her daughter snapped her head around so quickly that the long, vibrant red ponytail Sarah had pulled back that morning smacked her daughter on the cheek. "I didn't." Miniature hands showed major exacerbation, stretching wide and spearing toward the parquet floor at the foyer.

"I know your eyelids weren't purple at birth."

A crinkle appeared between her light red brows. Her lips puckered. "Momma, what's burf?"

"Never mind that. Why did you get into my cosmetics bag after I told you not—"

An exaggerated sigh cut her off. Knobby shoulders drooped. "It's markers. Not your cosmics."

Sarah bit her lips together to keep from smiling. The girl had a point. She hadn't told her daughter not to color her face. "We'll talk about this in a few minutes. Right now, let's go greet your daddy."

Once again, Sarah found herself left in the dust as her growing tot rocketed to the sturdy oak door. Her dainty hands gripped the fat golden knob. Sarah hurried over. She reached out a hand in assistance.

"I do it myself!" her stubborn child admonished with a cut of her green eyes and a tone that told Sarah she'd done a fine job chastising her daughter when the need arose.

"All right. All right." She retracted her hand. "Do it yourself. Women should be independent." Yeah, just like she was...not. She'd had plans to continue on for her master's degree, and even bigger plans for her career, but she'd met James Red Hardy her senior year at Louisiana State University. Somehow, she'd managed to get married, and then pregnant, all within a month of graduation.

Doggedly, her daughter maneuvered the handle this way and that, tugging and grunting with all her might. Sarah waited with false patience to watch her daughter solve the puzzle. Because planned or not, her family was the very best thing in her life—and the thought of having them all under one roof transformed her into an atomic bomb of glee...at least until her husband's next business trip. Single parenting was hard work.

It took one more attempt before the girl realized she had to twist the lock in order to successfully open the door. With a three-year-old it was particularly important to keep the chain on the door at all times. If it wasn't for this sadistic killer on the loose, the thoughts of even locking the front door would have never occurred to Sarah.

They lived in a post-WWII subdivision of lovely ranch-style homes in a crush of old gentry—the land of green lawns and fancy cars, where the men and women constantly tried to outdo one another with the newest gadgetry and fashions. It was a place where everybody knew your name, your parents' names, and where you went to school and church. And of course, they also gossiped about your latest news long before it was public.

The girls hustled down the short concrete path to the driveway where the shiny grey Oldsmobile had parked. The driver swung the heavy door wide and bolted like a track star to the little girl. He scooped her into his arms and kept coming until he reached Sarah. His muscled arms wrapped around her waist and the ground disappeared under her feet.

James spun them around and around. Laughter and giggles filled the neatly-manicured lawn. Sarah buried her face against his neck and inhaled. "I'm so glad you're home," she moaned.

He pulled back and his green gaze danced between her and their beautiful girl. A smile curved his full lips. "Oh, my girls, I've missed y'all!"

"I miss you so much, Daddy." Their daughter's bow mouth plumped into a pout.

His hold tightened around Sarah's middle. "What would you say if I quit my job and stayed home with you girls all the time?"

Sarah shook her head while her daughter's bobbed with abandon. "Oh no you don't. If you stayed home I'd never get any hugs from her," she said, tickling tiny ribs. "That girl has you up on a pedestal."

"Well you do too," James pointed out with a waggle of a brow.

"Yeah," she smiled. "I understand her feelings. I just don't like being the leftovers."

"Daddy! I drive." The little one wiggled in his arms.

"Anything you want, Ruby Slippers," James drawled. He set those tiny feet on the concrete walkway and they pattered the short distance to the car.

"That's why I'm second fiddle," Sarah explained. "You let her get away with murder." She gently pinched his firm pectoral for emphasis.

His gaze snapped from their daughter to her. He leaned over, tipping her back at the middle. Sarah's fingers tightened on the lapel of his suit. His mouth connected with hers and pressed a near punishing kiss onto her lips.

"You're not second fiddle or leftovers," he growled. "You're ripe and fresh." She clung to him, pulling him closer. He nibbled a trail along her jaw. When his voice reached her ear it was gruff. "And I plan to have my fill shortly."

A zing of anticipation pierced her belly.

After another kiss, James righted them. They shared a stare that chased away the memory of five cold nights spent alone. Then he turned his attention to the car. "My Ruby." He spoke with a quiet reverence as he looked at his daughter. James kissed her cheek. "I'll be right back." He hurried to the trunk, extricated his suitcase, and closed the trunk. Suitcase in hand, he rounded the car and gave his Ruby a wide sweep of his arm. "Come over here and tell me about your week." She bailed from the door and charged. He stepped back several feet and dropped his bag, allowing her to reach maximum velocity.

All Sarah could see was her precious daughter tripping and planting her baby teeth into the concrete. She closed her eyes until an uproarious giggle filled the air—along with Ruby. Her father tossed her into the stratosphere and caught her with tender hands. James kissed her nose, plucked his suitcase off the ground, and headed her way.

Sarah hugged herself to keep her swelling heart inside her chest.

"You coming, gorgeous?" James winked as he walked past her.

She turned toward him. "I'll close the car door, grab the mail, and meet you two inside. Oh, ask her about her H-O-R-S-E."

His eyes shot wide. "We don't have one in the backyard, do we?"

"No, silly. She drew one at story time this week."

"Ooh!" That small, but effective, mouth shouted. "We read *Bonny's Day* at the library." Her daughter clapped.

"*Bonny's Big Day*," Sarah corrected.

Soft red waves shook vigorously. "Yeah, Bonny is a horse. It's a white one. I want Bonny. She's pretty."

"You do, huh?" James grinned.

The two headed for the house with their foreheads together in serious conference. One small hand splayed on his handsome face while the other repeatedly smoothed over his blazing red hair.

Sarah sighed and headed for the sedan. Several feet away new car scent wafted from the interior. Three years old and the thing still looked as though it belonged on a dealer's show floor.

If only he'd attend the inside of the house with such gusto.

She chuckled. That'd be the day. The day that rain fell up, the moon rose in the morning, and the sun appeared at night.

She shoved the door with her hip to avoid smudges on the waxed paint. A loud thud echoed in the bustling neighborhood and blended in with a thousand other noises. Across the street, the Wooldridge's contractor hammered the last of the wood siding on their new addition. Three houses down, a gangly teenager dribbled a basketball up the driveway to the rim attached above the garage. Somewhere a mower hacked at the grass that perpetually strived for the height of pine trees.

No one noticed the resounding gong her hips created, but Sarah heard the message loud and clear.

Lay off the beignets.

With a grumble she walked faster than usual to the mailbox and swung her arms for added calorie burning. Like a one-thousandth of a mile walk would do any good. Like she should care. Her husband loved her soft curves and so did she.

Sarah yanked open the small metal door to retrieve a water bill and one leaflet for Fortress Insurance. Why they sent promo to their own customers and—even better—an employee was beyond her comprehension. She shrugged, closed the box, and headed up the drive.

As she neared James' car the stench of bleach stung her nostrils and yanked her attention from the stupid pamphlet. A slit of grey peeked out from the trunk's interior. When he'd fetched his suitcase the lid must not have latched.

She hurried forward to secure the hatch, but again a punch of bleach gagged her. Sarah glanced left and right, looking for the source of the stench, but found none.

Her fingers grazed the cool metal and her muscles contracted to slam the top. Again the bleach singed her nostrils. Sara's gaze narrowed on the trunk.

There was clean, and there was overboard.

An alien emotion coiled around her spine. Despite the glaring sun and soaring temperatures, goose flesh spread across her skin. Instinct pumped the blood in her veins at a frantic pace, telling her to run.

One inch at a time she lifted the lid.

Bleach stung her eyes. She blinked and turned her chin until James' red car-washing bucket snagged her gaze. A terrycloth washrag and bottle of bleach were nestled in the bucket.

Sarah lifted the terrycloth. Her heart plummeted onto the driveway and rolled to the street. Maybe a passing car would put her out of her misery.

A short stack of Polaroids stood maybe ten deep. She could easily make out the woman's long, lean legs, her bare breasts, and hair flowing over the edge of a bed.

How? Why? Who was she?

Irrational rationalization explained away the pictures in a manner of seconds. He wouldn't cheat on her. He wouldn't destroy their family over a roll in the sheets. She trusted him. For the five years they'd been married she hadn't once questioned his business trips. Jealousy hadn't once tainted her mind or emotions.

Trembling fingers eased the photos from the trunk. And then everything in a thousand-mile area screeched to a halt.

Dead eyes stared into the camera. Severed skin flayed wide on the woman's neck and dripped into a bucket—James' red car wash bucket.

Sarah stumbled backward. Her knees hit the driveway. She looked to the house where inside the most notorious serial killer talked horses with her daughter. The pictures scattered along with her life.

Chapter One

Shopping bags crackled against the heavy door of Ava Shepherd's apartment building. She pressed her backside onto the glass and held it open for her friend. Annelise Braden hoisted the black garment bags into the air to keep the bottom from dragging the ground. At barely five feet the tea-length dress Ava had chosen at Neiman Marcus hit her petite partner-in-crime at the ankles.

"It's a good thing I work out." A sheen of sweat glistened above the woman's red lips in the portico's light. She dabbed at it with the back of her free hand and sauntered through the entry on classic black pumps that matched her classic black suit. The neon-rainbow blouse underneath, however, muted the ensemble's timeless appeal. "Otherwise I'd have dropped your gorgeous coral dress three blocks ago."

"I'll send your personal trainer flowers." Ava grinned.

"Forget Frank." Her hand swatted the air. "Send them to me."

"As long as Fiona doesn't get jealous," she said, falling into step with her one friend in all the world. Their heels clacked against the gray-tiled floor.

"Please." She flipped her long blonde hair off of her face. "You like dick. Therefore, Fee has nothing to get jealous about." Annelise slowed and tossed a look over her shoulder. "You do like dick, don't you?" She shrugged. "I mean," she lowered her voice conspiratorially, "you haven't exactly been on the prowl for a guy, but I still know you're not a lesbian."

"How do you know?" Ava asked with a hitched brow and a fat grin on her lips.

"Because I'm the hottest piece of muff-munchin' snatch around the office, we're friends, and you've never made a move or given me the signal to make one."

Ava's laugh sprung from her chest and bounced around the glass coffee tables, arched ceiling, and decadent chandeliers in the entryway. Two men in suits eyed them as though they might yank their bras off and burn them in the lobby.

At a distance, Annelise appeared to be the picture of purity, with sharply tailored suits, pearls, and pearly whites. Her look was corporate chic, until you took into account the blouse she'd chosen to wear today—which was the parting blow of an argument she'd had with their boss the previous day. But share a coffee with her proper image and it morphed to less-than-conventional one foul word at a time.

"You're outrageous and I love you." Ava winked.

Annelise rolled her shoulder. "I love you, girly. Us outcasts have to stick together."

Ava didn't like to think she and Annie—as only she called her—were friends based on their taboo states in the social stratosphere, but it had brought them together. They were too complicated to sit at the cool-kids table at lunch. Though they'd each left high school behind over a decade ago, their independent stigmas stuck.

They split the circular table with its extra-large vase and fresh arrangement. Annelise stayed straight, aiming for the elevators, while Ava veered sharply toward the stairwell on the left.

"I thought you worked out?" This was their routine, but she loved giving her friend a hard time and no way would Ava take the elevator. She hated confined spaces.

"I do. Just not on your stairs." Annelise switched the hanger to her other hand and then pushed the call button for the car.

Ava backed into the stairwell and lifted her gaze. If she looked at the walls her insides quaked, slowly at first, but they gained strength with each additional second. As a functioning member of society she'd learned tricks for getting by without drawing more attention to herself than being *her* already did.

She jogged up the steps, her legs accustomed to the single flight of stairs multiple times per day. The five full bags in her hands made turning the knob difficult, but if she'd adapted to anything it was a challenge. After conquering the metal door, she crossed the hallway to her apartment and dropped the bags from her right hand to fish out her keys.

Her gaze slid up and down the corridor, eyeing each of the seven other doors in view. Ava's fingers grazed the simple silver baton on the end of her key chain and tugged it from the depths of her briefcase. She flipped past her car's key fob to the one for her home of six years and slid it into the deadbolt. Unease zapped her triumph over finding all the outfits she needed. Not even the extra 30 percent off she'd scored curbed her hesitance to twist the lock and open the door.

Maybe it won't be there today.

Yeah right.

The lock smacked into the mechanism. Ava braced herself with a deep breath and shoved the door wide. As it had been for the last four days, a newspaper lay on the tan wooden floor exactly six inches inside the threshold.

In all her time at the apartment she'd never ordered, nor ever paid, for a newspaper. She sure as hell hadn't requested one from 1989 announcing the ruling on James Bloody Red Hardy's trial.

A ding heralded the arrival of the elevator.

Ava scooped up the paper without reading the headline she knew by heart. Guilty on All Counts. She hurried between the bed on the right side of the room and the fancy bureau that housed a television she never watched. At the bedside table she folded the ancient print and stuffed it in the drawer with the others.

Annelise's heels clicked closer. Bags rustled. "So excited about your new shoes you forgot your makeup?"

Her friend stepped into the apartment, closed the door, and laid the bags she'd brought in from the hallway onto the bed. She spread the garment bag out next to them and sighed. Annie peeled out of her jacket and tossed it onto the bed too.

No denying it any longer. The taunts had started again. One of her neighbors must have found out who she was. It didn't have to be someone in the building, but it was the most likely scenario.

"That's better." Annelise stretched her bare arms wide and tilted her narrow face to the whirling fan. She sighed again. Her arms dropped to her sides. She straightened. Her gaze zeroed on Ava. "What's wrong? Having buyer's remorse? Or do you want me to go so you can use your swizzle stick?"

Annelise's finger glided through the air and pointed at the open nightstand.

The over-the-top comment scattered Ava's anxiety. She closed the drawer. "Uh, I don't have a swizzle stick."

Annie clutched her heart. "Oh my Lord." She plucked her jacket off the bed and dug through the bags for her purse.

"Where are you going?" Ava began unloading her evening's spoils. "Can't be my friend if I don't have a swizzle stick?"

"We are going shopping."

Ava grabbed a handful of clothes from the nearest bag and tossed them at Annelise. She swatted them onto the bed with a chuckle. "I don't need a...I don't need one of those."

"Holy shit." Annie slapped her palms together. "Please tell me you masturbate. If you deny it, we're going shopping immediately or taking you to St. Patrick's and enrolling you in the nunnery."

"Annelise!" She tried to wither her friend with a stern glare.

"What'll it be, Sister Serenity of the bored vagina?"

Ava tossed her hands into the air and growled. "Fine, I masturbate, daily, and my fingers do the job, every time."

The hand was back over Annie's heart, but this time soothing with gentle pats. "Thank goodness."

Ava laughed at her own heated face and her crazy-ass friend.

Annie joined in, but too soon her laughter died. She set her jacket down. "So, what's wrong?"

Ava shooed away her concern and headed through the seating area, into the dining nook, and into the kitchen. She grabbed two cups from the cabinet and filled them with water from the spout on the front of the refrigerator. Annelise rounded the corner and rooted a hand on the granite countertop.

"What did Dickey say about your shirt?" Ava asked.

"He growled, told me no matter what the Supreme Court decides, neither God nor nature support homosexuality. We should all be put on an island and the problem would be solved in one generation."

Ava choked on her water. "That narrow-minded horse's ass. What did you say?"

"That I don't believe in fairytales. That they could send their one-hundred fifty-million orphaned children to the island, we'd raise them to be kind, well-adjusted adults, and make the world a better place. And no, he couldn't visit."

"How is it that he gives us orders?" Ava abandoned her cup and shook her head. The end of her red ponytail caught on her collar. She slipped off her suit jacket, rounded Annie, and hung it on the back of a dining chair.

Annie scoffed. "Being the assistant to a pig-headed man like that..." She paused, inhaled deeply, and grinned. "It makes going to work every day a treat because I know I annoy him way more than he does me. Besides, he's all about work and only says something like that when I stick it to him."

She drank deeply, and then added, "And no one gives you orders. Hell, you haven't been in the office all week."

Their office was the National Center for the Analysis of Violent Crime at the FBI's facility on Quantico. And yes, she mostly did her own thing at work, since she did it so well. Dickey Greaves, their boss, had been the most renowned profiler the bureau had ever known, until—after more than seven years in the ranks—they'd finally given Ava a shot. In the first two years with the special unit she'd bested his record of unsubs apprehended through extensive profiling.

And you won so many friends in the process.

"I've been hosting the Crime Analysis Workshop at the Law Enforcement Convention in Alexandria all week. You knew that. It's why I could only go shopping this evening."

"I'll bet Stan was pissed Dickey picked you to host instead of him." Annelise's smile said how torn up she was about that.

"Ever the instigator, you." Ava wagged her finger.

"So, I shouldn't mention it to him?" She frowned.

Ava rolled her eyes and caught the numbers on the microwave's digital clock. "It's ten-thirty! I haven't even packed yet."

"Because you just bought clothes. Nothing like waiting till the last minute, sister girl."

"The conference," she reminded.

"What about last week or last month?"

"I still didn't know if I could go. I was working on the strangler case in Idaho."

She'd have hated to miss Nathan's wedding and the mini vacation she was forced to take because of it. Without that incentive she would've never touched the stack of leave she'd accumulated over the years.

"Idaho. Now that's a random place."

"What?" Ava asked, clueing back into the conversation.

"Idaho." Annie shrugged. "Who goes to Idaho? Arizona has the Grand Canyon. Nevada has Vegas. Wyoming has Yellowstone. What does Idaho have?" Ava thought about it for so long that Annelise wandered into the other room. "My point exactly."

"Potatoes," Ava countered.

Annie grabbed the most recent copy of *Time* from the coffee table and plopped onto the white couch. She absently rolled the magazine into a tube and pointed it at Ava. "Now, what were you all wigged out about?"

"You're a croc." Ava huffed. She marched past her friend and the mound of clothes on her bed to the open door on the far wall. A right turn brought her face to face with a nice walk-in closet full of clothes not suitable for a beach wedding on a tropical island.

"Full of shit?" Annelise hollered from the sofa. "You're not the first to say it."

"No. Not a crock of shit. A crocodile. Once your jaws clamp on an idea they never let it go." She hefted her small suitcase from the corner, rounded the wall, and tossed it onto the remaining space on her white comforter.

If Annie hadn't made her paint the kitchen a violet gray, the main room a pastel green, and her bathroom blue, everything in her life would be white, including half of her wardrobe. Yeah, when her shrink found out about her white obsession, the scholar had nearly come out of her armchair.

"Never." Annelise bobbed her head. "So you might as well tell me."

Ava knew she should tell someone about her anonymous heckler. But she hesitated. At thirty-two years old she'd seen a hell of a lot worse than musty newspapers. She'd seen the true nature of

God fearing, upstanding, well-meaning citizens and their offspring. Too often it had been hideous.

"Release the burden," Annie prodded. "You know you'll feel better."

"You know *you'll* feel better."

"Yes, because I'll have helped my friend work through something that's troubling her." Annelise toed off her shoes and tucked her bare feet under her bottom. She planted her elbows onto the arm of the white sofa. Her lids batted a thousand.

Ava turned away. She unzipped her suitcase, pulled off price tags, and blindly folded a pair of shorts, the bottoms of a bathing suit, a cover-up. There was something else she'd been agonizing over. She didn't want to say the words aloud, but she had to give Annie something or the woman would dig in her heel on the subject.

"He's going to be there," Ava whispered. The fact was a secret, a surprise for Nathan, but she'd found out from her mother, who was good friends with his mother, despite the time and distance that had been their undoing.

"You should've bought sexier panties."

"He's not going to see my panties."

"True. Commando. Always a good choice."

Ava smacked a lace sarong onto the stack of folded clothes and pivoted toward Annelise with folded arms.

"What?" Annie flipped her palms up at her lap as though she were flashing her panties. "Easy access."

"He's not getting access. He doesn't want access." Ava tossed her hands into the air. She dipped through the doorway, but veered left this time. The small bathroom with its sky-blue walls and white porcelain failed to ease the clench in her stomach. She yanked the extra toiletry kit she kept for trips from the cabinet without looking at her reflection in the mirror.

When she spun around Annelise stood in the large closet with hands on slight hips, accentuating her disproportionate D cups. "Oh, he wants access. You never forget a good piece of—"

"Don't say it," Ava interrupted.

"Pussy," Annie continued with a sinister grin. "I guarantee when he gets an eye full of you in that dress he'll fall at your feet, and that's a perfect height for fellatio."

Ava closed her eyes and slapped her hands over them. She listed onto the doorframe. A groan rumbled in her throat, taking with it the fight she clung to every day of her life. "Isn't Fiona waiting up for you or something?"

"Nope, she's on night shift at the hospital. Come here, let me prove my point, and then I'll stop."

On weary feet Ava shuffled forward.

"Open your eyes before you trip, break your nose, and make a good deep-throating session impossible. You can't breathe through a broken nose."

Ava dropped her hand and opened her eyes. "How do you know you have to breathe through your nose when giving head?"

"Believe it or not I tried to be normal for the first half of my life." Annelise took the travel pack from her hand and set it on a shelf.

"You, any other way than you are, would be abnormal."

"Which is why we're friends." Annie grinned. She placed a cold hand on Ava's shoulder and turned Ava away from her to face the bathroom. "Don't move."

She did as she was told, not even straightening the lilt of her head.

Annie skirted her and walked to the bathroom. Her hand grasped the knob and pulled it closed. Too late to bolt, Ava realized her friend's intent. The beveled mirror hanging on the outside of the door caught Ava's reflection. Her gaze jumped to Annie's.

"I might be small, but I'm deceptively strong," Annie said, pointing to the mirror. "Look at yourself or I'll make you."

Ava rolled her eyes. "I have a gun and I know how to use it."

"It's in your purse."

"Then let me amend that. I have guns and I know how to use them." Ava pulled out the top drawer of the built-in chest to her right.

"You're too moral to shoot me, especially when I'm trying to help you."

"Help me what?"

"Look in the mirror and you'll see."

Ava closed the drawer with a bit more force than necessary, and then used the mirror to stare into the center of her chest.

"Your tits are nice, but I want you to look higher."

She looked at the little mounds barely interrupting the hang of her powder pink silk blouse. "My breasts are hardly B cups."

"Perky B cups that won't hang to your knees in a few years. I'll have to get a lift before my fiftieth birthday because I refuse to wear a granny bra." Annie circled her index finger around her face several times. "Now higher."

Incrementally, her gaze rose to the hollow at the base of her pale throat, to the slant of her slender jaw, and then her wide peach-colored lips.

She stalled, not wanting to go higher. In the mornings, when getting ready for work, she could look at her features as nothing more than tools of a trade. In order to catch bad guys, she needed to be able to speak. She needed to see.

But in the evenings she became the legacy she couldn't deny, no matter how hard she tried.

Annelise's phone vibrated a second before Bruno Mars' *Count on Me* filled the intimate space. The first time Ava heard the poppy, heartfelt hit crooning from her friend's phone, her eyebrows nearly hid behind her hairline. Annie's preferred tunes ran toward the sexy beats of R & B. Her friend used the upbeat song sparingly, reserving it for her sister, and then six months ago, Ava.

"If it were anyone else I'd decline."

"If it were anyone else you'd answer and tell them to piss off."

"I only do that to telemarketers."

"My, how the years have tamed you."

Annelise pinched the phone from her skirt pocket, but pointed at Ava before answering. "This doesn't mean you're off the hook."

When her friend left the room Ava huffed and lifted her chin. Her gaze lanced into the clear green eyes in the mirror. The pit in her stomach yawned. She rubbed a hand over her belly, smoothing out the wrinkles of her tan pencil skirt. Fly-aways fanned her forehead in a ginger halo. After an eight-hour day lecturing groups of law enforcement professionals on the broad points of profiling and four hours of marathon shopping the strands had defected from her fishtail braid. She swatted them back and then ran a manicured finger over the sprinkle of pigment on her nose.

Ava toyed with the pearl button at the top of her blouse. Would it kill her to show a bit of skin?

Sure her top lacked sleeves, but the jacket she'd worn all day had them. She slipped the bead through the slit and flattened back the cool material. A small V of alabaster flesh peeked from the silk.

Her fingers slipped down to the next button and unveiled another inch of skin. Not scandalous by Catholic school standards. Not even outrageous by her own standards for anyone else. Nope. She held these standards for only herself ever since she'd been accepted into the FBI training program nearly ten years ago.

"You're so hard on yourself," Annie whispered. She leaned against the door frame and crossed her arms over her rainbow blouse. "You are a smart, loving, beautiful woman. Sure you made a mistake. It doesn't mean he doesn't still have feelings for you."

Well, that reaffirmed the steer-clear approach she'd plotted for the long weekend.

"I'm proud of you."

"For showing a hint of negative cleavage?"

Annelise chuckled. "Yes. Baby steps."

"Baby steps," she agreed. "How's Josie?"

"She's great. I'm keeping the baby this weekend so she and Trent can have some alone time. She swears they'll sleep the entire weekend, but I know better. They're gonna try to make Finn a sister."

"He's only six months old. And, no offense—"

"Don't you know by now, you can't offend me?"

"True enough. You're not exactly kid friendly. You sneer at them on the Metro."

"Kids are one step removed from bacteria, but babies are sunshine." When Ava didn't respond, she added, "My mom made me babysit for allowance. Josie got allowance for making her bed. I had to make my bed or get grounded."

Ava bracketed her face with her hands and gasped. "The horror."

"My point is, I know how to handle babies. Finny will be as happy as Kimmie K in an illicit video."

"Only you would compare the two."

"It's a gift." Annelise slipped the phone into her pocket and crossed the little room. She wrapped Ava in an impressive hug, considering her size. "Have fun and if you need anything tomorrow, call my cell. I'm taking off to stick it to Dickey and rest up before sunshine arrives."

***

Ava should've taken Friday off too. Annie was doing it. It would've given her more time to pack, time to sleep, and anger wouldn't be scorching the blood from her veins.

Q & A at any event was sketchy. The host was at the mercy of the crowd. Law enforcement conferences were especially hard for the FBI. Locals saw them as glory hogs, Big Brother, or worse, meaningless bureaucrats. The seminars were harder still for female experts, and only a small percentage of women ranked high enough to attend or sprinkle the crowds with estrogen.

Luckily the week had gone smoothly with her groups. The only minor dust-up she'd heard about involved an agent seated on a panel with two police chiefs discussing—of all things—teamwork at state borders.

"Please, if you have any questions, stand and make your way to the microphones at the bottom of either aisle."

The surly man who'd sneered at her every talking point and coughed up a lung at her heartfelt conclusion shot to his feet—as she knew he would. At one out of five events, there was someone who'd hated her from conception. Some blurted their ugly questions in the midst of her talk. Others tossed in a back-handed comment in transitions. The really callous ones used the microphones during Q & A to air their grievances for ultimate shock effect.

It no longer shocked her. It made her want to shove the mic up their asses and send them waddling back to their precincts. Ava placed her hands behind her back and clenched them. The handsome man—save for his scowl—inched his way down the row. His athletic build drew and held the gaze of the two women in the audience. One other member stood and hurried to the mic first.

Ava released her grip and smiled. "Yes, sir. Your name and question please."

"Um, my name is Leon. This is a silly question, but in light of the heaviness of our topic I figured why not?" He adjusted the belt below his paunch. "Has Hollywood ever contacted you to advise on a set, you know, on a movie about a serial killer?"

"No, not me personally, but the Bureau is contacted quite often with those type of requests. Most often they are referred to a retired expert on their particular topic of interest."

"Thank you." Leon nodded and scuttled to his seat. The guys around him snickered.

People were so cruel. No, the question wasn't relevant to the topic, but it was one he wanted answered and he had the guts to ask. What was wrong with that?

"Thank you, Leon." She gave him an exceptionally wide grin, and then turned to meet her fate.

Handsome, with jet black hair and eyes to match, stood in front of the microphone on the opposite aisle. His chest inflated with each breath.

Ava swallowed her rage. "Yes, sir. Your name and question please."

"Who the hell let you into the FBI?"

The room of full-grown men who'd seen mothers beat their children, husbands kill their wives, and the youth of America snort away their futures gasped like ladies gossiping on the back pew after church. They looked to the man. Then their heads snapped toward Ava. With wide eyes and gaping mouths they awaited her reaction.

Though she knew exactly where this venture led, she followed along. To do anything else would only fuel the fire. She gripped her smile with both hands and maintained the man's gaze.

"No one let me in. I graduated from Cornell with a bachelor's degree in biology and society with a minor in psychology. I received a master's degree in forensic science from John Jay College of Criminal Justice, while also garnering three years of professional experience as a researcher for the National Institute of Justice. I applied, like the other thousands of applicants, the month I turned twenty-three. Because of my test scores, I was given a provisional letter of appointment. After that I was further tested both mentally and physically. The Bureau ran a full background check. I passed the physical fitness requirements and medical examination."

Ava drew a breath. The first, it seemed, since he'd asked the question. "No one let me in. I made it impossible for them to keep me out. Now, I didn't catch your name."

Handsome's upper lip curled. The sides of his mouth arched toward the floor, distorting his pleasing features. "My name. How about your name?"

"You may call me Supervisory Special Agent Shepherd."

"Your real name." He snarled the words.

The audience's gazes flip-flopped between them.

"You mean the name I was given at birth?"

"That's right."

"Because you're a real cop—a man's man— you feel you've been duped. You feel you've uncovered a conspiracy too maniacal for words. Well, sir, how do you think a three-year-old would feel watching their father taken away in handcuffs? How do you think a six-year-old would feel learning —before they fully understood the concept of alive and dead—that their father was responsible for killing what is expected to be more than a hundred women?"

She clapped her hands in front of her. "The truth is, you have no idea. You've never taken a minute to put yourself in another's shoes, and until you do, you won't make chief."

"You don't know anything about me, Satan's Spawn."

The old nickname lanced her heart. After hearing it every day for the last twenty-nine years it still made her breath catch, her lungs burn, her heart ache.

A man from his row barked, "Sit down, Lieutenant Boston."

The no-longer-remotely handsome man's face reddened. His fists clenched. "We shouldn't take pointers from a mass murderer's kid." He stomped toward the door.

"He wasn't a mass murderer. He killed masses, but he was a signature...no, he was *the* signature serial killer. More notorious than Bundy or Cotton, Dammer, or Jack the Ripper."

The man stilled just before the door, listening.

"He killed young women, often mothers, in their homes. He drained their blood. He smeared it on a small portion of the wall above the victims' beds." Ava swung her gaze around the silent room, meeting as many gazes as would meet hers in return. "He gave me half of my genes, but he is not my father. And he is the reason I have sworn to stop as many killers as I possibly can." Again her gaze traveled the room. More looked back.

"Because of my work, forty-three repeat killers have been captured and prosecuted to the fullest extent of the law, stopping them from killing before they reach serial status. Hopefully you can look past the origins of the blood coursing through my veins and use the tools I've given you today to help me stop serial killers before they get their start. Thank you."

Ava gathered her notes from the podium and placed them inside her tote. She exited the stage and headed straight for Mr. Mouth for no other reason than to prove to everyone, especially herself, that his words wouldn't stall her quest to right her father's wrongs.

No applause broke out. The quiet of the dead followed her out the amphitheater, down the hallway, out a side door, and to her car. She should've checked out at the conferences' registration desk, but she couldn't stomach seeing the conspiratorial looks as news spread. Spread it would, just like a fire bomb on a hillside in the California summer.

When she reached her car, familiar cream paper with bold black letters lay sandwiched between her windshield and the driver's side wiper blade. She had a mind to go back in and track down the son of a bitch, Mr. Mouth. Maybe he was her home heckler too. But dammit, she had to get to the airport. The lines at Dulles usually doubled with weekend travelers.

Chapter Two

Thank goodness she'd decided to wear her hair in a low bun. With all the humidity, if she'd worn it down, she could've camouflaged herself as one of the red, pink, and orange tulle pompoms secured to the backs of the white wooden chairs that lined the aisle.

She'd hadn't expected such a turn out—the chairs were tucked together eight columns across and eight rows deep. Eager bottoms filled the majority. Given a choice Ava would've picked the aisle seat on the last row, not because she didn't want to see her cousin and his bride exchange vows, but because she wanted to see *him* coming.

Her mom and dad held each of her hands and towed her down the outside edge of the groom's side toward her aunt April in the front row, forcing her to switch tactics. She trained her gaze on her mother. "Where's Ford?"

Sarah Shepherd's mouth pressed into a line. Her eyes squinted, and she turned her gaze to the setting sun.

Ava tried her dad. Preston Shepherd grimaced. His deeply tanned cheeks wrinkled at the corners of his mouth. His free hand mussed neatly combed salt and pepper hair. "He needed a minute."

"The hostages died?" she whispered.

"No," he answered quietly. "They'll all make it, but one of the three who were shot in the rescue is paralyzed."

"It wasn't his fault," she said.

"No, but your brother listens about as well as you do when you don't get your man in the first forty-eight hours." They reached the aisle and her dad flourished his hand, ushering her mom in first.

Sarah Shepherd's fingers grazed her husband's clean-shaven cheek before she sauntered past. When April, her dad's sister, saw them coming she hurried to her feet and tossed her arms wide. The collective mood rose as the two women hugged and exchanged squeals, which were apparently a pre-wedding ritual. She'd heard more than three groups of women do it and she'd only arrived at the spectacular mansion situated on the strip of beach ten minutes ago.

"Aunt April, you look stunning." Ava leaned in and kissed her aunt's rosy cheek.

"It's this place," she explained. "Howard and I came down last Saturday and I swear these are rejuvenating waters."

"I'm glad to hear it. So sorry Ford and I were late getting in last night. This morning really," she amended. "I blame my brother."

"Brothers are good for blaming." She kissed Ava's cheek again, and then reached for her brother. While the siblings greeted each other with a bear hug, Ava surreptitiously glanced at her aunt's boyfriend of six months. She'd yet to meet the man, but she'd heard plenty about him. Well, not him exactly. More accurately, his age. Boy Toy, as Nathan called him, was precisely seven years to the day older than April's son.

Howard's athletic frame filled out a pale blue linen shirt that matched his date's thin strapped dress. *The water? Nope.* The man had done something to her aunt. It looked good on a woman who had seen the worst the world had to offer. Despite the age difference and probability that the romance wouldn't last longer than the green peas in her freezer, Ava caught her aunt's eye and nodded her approval.

They sat, her mother and father next to the mother of the groom, then Ava, with a seat saved for Ford. Ava had crowd watched before her training with the Bureau, but after, her gaze scanned a room like an old lady spying on her neighbors. To keep from accidentally spotting *him*, she pulled her phone from her white clutch. In seconds the crowd and gentle sway of the ocean faded into the background. The bloated inbox of her work email curbed the rising tempo of her heartbeats.

Time passed. Her list of emails pertaining to the strangler case shrank.

"Always working." An amused whisper fluttered over the shell of her ear and slipped down her neck.

She hadn't heard the voice in a decade. In that time it had grown more potent. Deeper. Sexier. Whiskey and syrup tones melded in just two words. Her heart leapt and then settled in her stomach, while her traitorous nipples lunged toward the seductive sound.

Ava's suddenly unsteady fingers volleyed her phone. The thin case slipped through her hands and bounced on the fitted coral skirt of her sleeveless dress.

Kenneth Hunt's large hand bolted toward her. Strong fingers pinned the phone to her outer thigh. "Whoa there. I didn't mean to startle you."

His touch burned through the material and seared her skin. Ava clamped her lips together to keep from crying out in ecstasy or misery. Her gaze jumped to his face. That damn smile she'd relied upon to brighten her world grinned, friendly and open, as though the past didn't sit in the inches between them, sucking the oxygen from his lungs like it did hers. Of course, he'd probably moved on years ago. A man with his looks and charm wouldn't last long in the store front of the singles boutique. There'd probably been a riot for his attention.

Hot fingertips brushed up her thigh. The heat they created collected on her cheeks. Thank goodness a ginger could blame the redness on the distant sun and warm temperatures. But her mouth refused to move.

He must have taken her silence as acquiescence. He plucked the clutch from her lap, slipped her phone inside, snapped the clasp, and then replaced it. "You don't want to drop that in the sand. You'd never get all the grains out." His index finger indicated the crowd behind them. "Besides, I think this thing is about to get underway. I saw a little girl in a pink dress psyching herself up to bomb the aisle with rose petals."

In spite of the tingle in Ava's unmentionables and the hundreds of questions pinging around her brain, a giggle rumbled in the back of her throat. She swallowed and found her voice. "Bomb the isle?"

Keen's sky-blue eyes sparkled. His full mouth pursed and his head bobbed. "Oh yeah. The girl could pitch for the Marlins, judging by her practice petal-toss."

"The Marlins suck," Ford's burly voice intruded. Her brother sat on the other side of Keen, leaned forward, and tweaked his wrist. "She puts the perfect amount of twist on her release. That little girl could start for the Braves."

Both men wore tan suits with blue ties. Keen had also donned a blue button-down that complimented his eyes. They were both in the neighborhood of six foot two with solid frames. They both had blond hair, but the tones and lengths split the spectrum. Her brother's dark shag hung near his dark brows. Since she'd last seen Keen he'd shorn his locks to a near buzz. Still, his close crop of hair matched the faint yellow rays of the sun. The cut sharpened his bad-boy image, which hadn't needed a lick of help with his dimpled chin, chiseled cheekbones, and laser gaze.

She waited for the men to change seats. Instead, they exchanged a handshake, and then turned toward the house. A string quartet situated on the far side of an elegant arbor, strung with ivory lace and a magnificent spray of red Gerber daisies, peach roses, and white and pink flowers she couldn't name, struck the first few notes of La Rejouissance.

Ava twisted toward her father—not Keen—to see this flower girl the boys talked about. Ava's hands shook as though she'd come face to face with the Ghost of Christmas Past. And hadn't she? She wrapped one hand around the clutch in her lap and the other gripped the seat back as though the force of his presence would sweep her out to sea. The last thing Ava wanted was for the man who'd been nicknamed Keen, not just for its similarity to Ken,

but because it perfectly described his shrewd
acumen, to notice his effect on her.

Though she kept her gaze on a petite girl with
tight dark spirals of hair and a basket full of rose
petals, Ava caught movement in her periphery. Ford
leaned over and whispered something into Keen's
ear. The men chuckled under their breath. A wide
smile spread across Keen's mouth.

Regret stung her reserve. Not so very long
ago, but a lifetime ago in other respects, she'd been
the one to make him smile, to make him laugh. And
now it seemed anyone could accomplish the task.

Keen's elbow nudged her shoulder—like she
was just one of the guys. His chin lifted toward the
back of the aisle, from where her gaze had drifted
with her thoughts. The flower girl wound up. She
pelted a man in the front row with a handful of
multicolored petals. The burst exploded against his
chest, flying in every direction.

The crowd's laughter floated up on an earnest
breeze. As though she were a veteran who suffered
post-traumatic stress disorder, Ava saw blood
where silken, harmless bits of flowers rained. She
shut her eyes and honed in on Keen's laugh. The
sound hurt. It helped too. It helped erase the
ugliness of her job, the ugliness of her world.

When the music changed tempo Ava opened
her eyes and found Nathan strolling between the
clumps of petals just behind the minister toward
the arbor. His pink tie would earn him a lifetime's
worth of ribbing from the two behind her. But
combined with his tan suit and cream shirt it
transformed the kid she'd picked on for years into a
devilishly handsome man.

The minister centered the spray of flowers
and then faced the congregation. His gray hair
contrasted with his milky black skin. He clutched a

Bible to his white button down and nodded at
Nathan. Her cousin reciprocated before stepping to
the man's left side and facing the music.

Again the music morphed. A melodic wedding
march swelled with the rhythm of the ocean.
Goosebumps swept across Ava's arms. The eager
throng rose. She used the back of the chair and
stood on weak knees. This many years later and
proximity to Keen still wreaked havoc on her
autonomic system. The realization stiffened her
back. The time had come for her to face the past.

First though, she wanted to look to the
future...her cousin's future anyway. Too bad her
height gave her an awesome view of people's
shoulder blades. She stretched onto tiptoes, but her
feet sank farther into the sand.

"Give her a boost," Ford whispered.

Keen's hands bracketed her waist.

Breath surged into Ava's lungs. Before she
could think to protest her feet left the sand. Her
hands doubled their grip on the clutch. She
clamped her lips together to keep from squealing
her dissent. The solid wood of the seat met the
soles of her feet. Keen's hands slipped slowly off her
hips.

She didn't dare turn toward him to beg him
to put his hands back or to yell at him for the
privilege he took with her body. Judging by the heat
in her cheeks, her face likely matched her hair
perfectly. From years of embarrassment Ava found
the wherewithal to lift her chin and otherwise act as
though she didn't want to bury herself in the sand.

The added height brought Nathan's bride into
view. The radiant brunette, in an ivory dress worth
weeping over, trained her gaze on Nathan. A
gigantic smile lit her entire face and showed just
how excited she was to be closing the distance

between them. Ava didn't do marriage or happily ever after, but now she was old enough that the cynic in her head was drowned out by the strings vibrato.

When Madelyn reached the third row from the front Ava stepped down from the chair in self-preservation. She spared Keen a sideways glance and found him absently rubbing his left shoulder. They'd almost lost him. The memory of that phone call coiled her stomach.

Ava met his gaze and mouthed, *Are you okay?* For being as smart as she was sometimes she was so magically stupid.

As though he'd been caught with his hand in the till, Keen straightened. He jerked a curt nod and lifted his gaze over her head to the couple.

Her gaze darted to them as well, but didn't register them until the kiss heard round the world. Really. It bordered on obscene. Nathan dipped his bride low and cupped her with his body. Ava felt the heat rising in her cheeks again.

Why had Keen chosen to sit next to her?

Ford whooped into her ear. Ava whipped her head around to find him in Keen's place and the man for which she blushed, gone.

***

Ava stood next to the dance floor watching her brother dance away his troubles with two caramel-skinned beauties. Across the room her dad ushered her mom to an uncluttered corner and whipped her into a sassy foxtrot. She hadn't seen Keen since he opened the doors to announce the couple. And that was for the best.

A group of kids to her left—maybe high-school aged—rushed the dance floor. Their absence revealed the newest member of her family. One she'd yet to meet. Madelyn stared at the gyrating bodies and smiled. When her gaze snagged on Ava's parents her grin doubled.

"Don't look too long, or else they'll have you out there dancing until your feet fall off," Ava warned.

Madelyn turned toward Ava and her eyes widened for just a second. Ava didn't fault her. Her particular color of red caught people off guard on a regular basis. She recovered quickly. "Thanks for the tip. My dance card is about full, especially in these heels." The edge of a cream stiletto peeped out from the edge of ruffles. No wonder she towered over Ava. "Barefoot on the beach was the way to go."

"It was a lovely ceremony. I can't believe you lived here and gave it up for my smelly cousin." Ava offered her hand. "I'm Ava Shepherd."

"Madelyn Gar...Brewer. Well, that's going to take some getting used to."

"I can't even imagine." Technically she could imagine getting used to a new name, but not for wedding bells and babies.

"It's so nice to meet you." Madelyn gave a firm shake. "I'm glad you were able to make it."

"I'm just sorry we missed the rehearsal dinner. It's Ford's fault. I missed my flight waiting for him to show. I swear, I don't know how my brother is so good at his job when he can't get anywhere on time."

"It's because I'm so good at my job that I can't get anywhere on time." Ford bumped Ava's shoulder, jarring her thoughts for a second.

"Always so humble." Ava rolled her eyes and inwardly groaned.

"Wife, I see you've met the hell raisers of my youth." Nathan stepped behind Madelyn and wrapped his bride in his arms.

Madelyn harrumphed. "I think they're still perfectly capable of raising hell."

If she only knew.

"I like her already." Ford winked and held out his hand. "Welcome to the family." He patted the back of her hand.

"What kept you from free steak and lobster?" Nathan asked.

"A loony with a pipe bomb and four hostages." Ford crossed his arms as casually as if he were talking about a shot off the back nine.

"You're in law enforcement too?" Madelyn awed.

"I can't believe they let him in either, Madelyn." Keen stepped into the circle. He held his hand flat at about crotch level. Ava stared at his crotch for several beats too long, and then looked at the string of lights overhead. "Yeah, they lowered the bar the day they let this kid join."

Ava looked back in time to see the ultra-slow-mo punches to the kidney and jaw Keen and Ford exchanged.

Classin' it up one day at a time.

"Wow, the mean age just dropped a few decades." Ava narrowed her gaze at them.

"Oh, come on," Keen scoffed.

"Don't make me make you squawk like a chicken in front of all these people," Ford warned.

Absolutely not. They wouldn't dare.

"What was that?" Keen put his hand to his ear. "The sun's rising? The roosters are crowing."

They stalked toward her one step.

Not after all these years. Not here. Not now. Please no.

"I swear, I deal with psychopaths all day." Ava glared. "I don't need crazies while I'm on vacation."

They took another step toward her. It was official. She was one of the guys again. The newsflash should make her happy.

"I'll hold her. You tickle her." Ford nodded at Keen.

She looked back and forth between them, hoping her expression conveyed ample warning.

"No way. Last time, I held her and got clobbered in the goods, while you ran away like a sissy." Keen put up his hands.

Nathan laughed at that, not stopping until tears ran down his cheeks. "He ran," Nathan wheezed out the words, "because Ava...threatened to tell Aunt Sarah...where he kept his girlie mags."

Ava's gaze swung around the group. Ford and Keen had backed off and both wrestled with their own fits of laughter. A flutter of giggles caught her unaware.

"How old were y'all?" Madelyn asked.

"College." Ava clamped her lips together, fighting back an all-out laugh.

Keen and Ford both doubled over.

"So, Ava, what do you do that you deal with psychopaths all day?" Madelyn asked innocently.

That took the giggle right out of her. She maintained her smile. "The Bureau."

"Seriously? Did y'all make a pact as kids or something?" Madelyn put her hands on her hips and looked at them each in turn.

Seriously, did she not know?

Nathan wove his fingers in between his wife's. "We all have our own reasons for joining."

"Okay, I know why Nathan joined the Bureau. And I'm 98 percent certain you two boys joined so you could shoot bad guys. But Ava, what made you join the FBI?"

Ava struggled to bury her surprise. "I assumed you knew."

Nathan's gaze met hers full on. "It's your story to tell, Av, not mine."

Ava stood with her mouth gaping, without a clue of what to say. This wasn't exactly first meet conversation nor wedding talk. Nathan turned his bride around and whispered something that had Madelyn gooey-eyed. They kissed...again.

With no safe place to look, habit had Ava reaching for her phone. A banner across the top alerted her to a missed call from Annelise. She needed to return a phone call. They couldn't have planned a better exit strategy if they'd tried. But that's how it was with Annie. Their friendship, as odd as it seemed to some, just clicked.

Ava lifted her chin to address the group and found a giant had entered the circle.

"Everyone, I'd like you to meet my dear friend, Amadi." Madelyn clung to Nathan's side, but used her free hand to point. "This is Kenneth Hunt, Nathan's partner."

He leaned in, shook Keen's hand, and then turned to Nathan. "I thought Dick was your partner." The man said it in a straight face, but Ava saw the twinkle in his intelligent eyes.

"You better be glad you're a gigantic ninja master because you deserve an ass kicking for that." Nathan nodded.

Amadi's rigid jaw cracked, revealing a brilliant smile between full midnight-black lips.

"And," Madelyn continued, "These are Nathan's cousins, Ford and Ava Shepherd."

He shook Ford's hand, and then turned his shrewd gaze on Ava. When someone made her brother and cousin look short, they made her look like a child. Visions of Jack and the Giant, David and Goliath, and the lion and the mouse flashed in her mind. But Amadi's calm, sure demeanor drew her.

The giant spoke to her cousin, but held Ava's gaze. "Nathan, if you think I need a whooping for that, what will you think about this? Ava, might I have the pleasure of this dance?"

She could stay in the awkward circle of Keen, two love birds, and her brother, or go with a veritable stranger. Oddly enough, she preferred the company of people who didn't know her all that well. With strangers she could be the Bureau agent who'd put away a bunch of bad guys. With strangers she could be the fun girl who doesn't sleep around. With strangers she could be the best portions of herself and forget the rest.

Until they found out.

Ava was countries away and on vacation. *Why not?* "I'd love to."

He grabbed her clutch from her hand and thrust it at Ford. "You're going to need both hands for this."

"Oh Lord," she giggled.

Amadi dragged her onto the dance floor which had swollen with twirling, whirling, and writhing bodies since the sun had set. His wide frame cleared a path. At the center, in the safety of numbers, he turned and held gently to both her hands. His hips swaggered and rolled easily. Seductively. Her gaze flew to his face. The gentle smile remained on his lips and abated her unease... with him. If only she could get past her unease with herself.

"Relax your shoulders." Amadi bicycled her hands in a large circle. "Feel the music." He moved her hands side to side. Her hips followed the motion. She caught the beat of the drums. "That's it. Let your troubles go for now. For the night. For your time on the island."

"Is it that obvious I'm troubled?" she asked with a fraudulent laugh.

"Not to most. But then most are oblivious, lost in their own highs and lows." He lifted her hands above her head. His curling hips encouraged her own to move in turn.

"So you're not lost in your own highs and lows?" Ava closed her eyes. She let the music seep into her skin, into her bones, to the marrow.

"No. I absorb the good, release the bad, and enjoy the present." Amadi turned her to face away from him. He stayed back allowing her room to arch and sway to the beat of the band.

Keen's laugh cut though her euphoric haze. Her eyes bolted open. She found him and Ford grinding on either side of the two island beauties. The music drummed on without her.

Amadi curled an arm around her middle, turned her once more, dipped her back, and then twirled her up to face him. She blinked into his amber eyes.

"If you're in love with him, why aren't you with him?"

"Has anyone ever told you, you need to work for the Bureau?"

"Only your cousin and only about thirty times." He grinned, but held her gaze.

She poked him in the rib. "Fine. We were young. I was scared."

"And now?"

"I'm just scared."

He swayed her into the music again and studied her. "Do you love yourself?"

"What?" It took effort not to jar the pace he'd set.

"It's a simple question. The answer is often not so simple." Amadi spun her. "Most people love parts of themselves, but rarely the whole enough to answer unequivocally yes."

"Good to know I'm not the only one." She grimaced. "What are you, the island shrink? You're way cheaper and more effective than mine."

"Figure out what you have to do to love yourself, and then you can really love him."

"I need a drink."

"Nah, I need to shut up and you need to dance."

Chapter Three

"Holy shit. I don't fucking believe it." Her brother's voice boomed over the distance he closed.

Ava levered herself up from the beach towel. "Will you watch your mouth? There are kids around."

"Ahhh, they don't speak English." He plopped onto the sand next to her.

"You don't know that."

"Sure do. See that kid over there?" He pointed to a toddler playing in the sand. "Well that's his nanny." His finger trailed over to a voluptuous beauty lying next to the kid on her towel. Her fully exposed rump clad in a G-string bikini bottom gleamed under the Caribbean sun.

Ford grinned.

"I went to Paradise Bar with Ekene and a few others last night. She was there. There was a language barrier, but we got through it."

The woman with the bare bottom shifted off of her stomach and onto her finely-formed rump. She arched her back and raised her arms toward the sky, stretching in the sexiest way Ava had ever seen. Ava's palms dampened and she swallowed hard at the lusty sight. When the woman's arms returned to her side she cocked one behind her and turned her gaze on Ford. She gave him a flirtatious glance before returning her watchfulness to the kid.

Ava smacked her brother in the gut, his gut being a chiseled eight-pack. "You are incorrigible."

His smile widened. Ava remembered back to his infancy, when that smile actually held innocence. After age one the kid had been pure mischief. Now that he was a man, the only thing that had changed was the definition of his jaw and body hair.

Ava shook her head at him. "What is so fucking unbelievable?"

"Wow! Besides the fact that my goodie two shoes little sister just used the f-bomb?"

Her gaze narrowed to evil slits. "Don't patronize me with the little sister routine. I'm older than you, not that I'll be admitting it for much longer."

"My you're feisty today. It doesn't have anything to do with seeing a certain someone yesterday, does it?"

Ava's body hummed at the thought of that someone. She wiped her sweaty palms onto the towel, yanked her knees up to her chest, and hugged them.

"Did you come out here just to ruin my tiny excuse for a vacation?"

"You know, he left this morning."

Ava took the blow to the center of her chest without falling over. "If I had my gun, I'd shoot you in the pinkie toe."

He threw his sand-covered hands into the air. "Okay. Okay. I'm done. I just came to visit with my favorite sister before I leave for the airport. I was pretty freakin' surprised you're actually relaxing on the beach, no laptop in sight, no file or phone in your hand. It's a first in...I don't know how many years."

"I finished up the two reports I brought with me on the flight here. Since you weren't on the flight to talk to me."

Ford didn't say anything, but his lips scrunched to one side.

"And," Ava continued, "I have an analysis to complete on the return flight. But...I'm trying to take Amadi's advice and find my center. Besides, you're one to talk. You're leaving paradise today."

Her arm swept through the air. From the light sapphire ocean to the lush green vegetation, vibrant colors pleased the eye. Who in their right mind would ever want to leave this place?

"And you're leaving tomorrow," he countered.

"I know. I have work to do."

"Ava, there will always be work for you and me. We have job security. You need to learn that there's more to life than the job."

"Everybody's a shrink now." Her eyes rolled of their own volition. "Like what?"

"Fun. Food. The world. Adventure. Sex."

If he was going to point out her short comings, turnabout was only fair play. "What about love? Commitment? A family?"

"Point taken." Ford cleared the air between them with a swipe of his hand. "Forget I said anything." His phone buzzed. He pulled it from his pocket and examined the screen. "My cab is on its way."

"Can I borrow your phone for a second?" Ava extended her hand.

"As long as you don't call Keen just to hear the sound of his voice, and then hang up."

She yanked the phone from his hand and shoved his chest. "Shut up. That was a lifetime ago."

"And I'll never let you live it down."

"No kidding." She smiled in spite of her herself. "I'm trying to call Annie back. She called last night, but I haven't been able to get in touch with her this morning."

"She probably wanted to see if you'd gotten laid, and then remembered who you were and that it was a waste of time. You can always tell her I got laid. So you'll have something to talk about."

"You ass." Ava ignored him as best she could and dialed. Again the line rang once, and then went to voicemail. She depressed the end button, instead of adding to her previous three messages.

"Nothing?"

"Straight to voicemail."

"She probably got laid last night and is sleeping it off." Ford leaned in, kissed her cheek, and plucked his phone from her fingers. "I'm sure everything is fine. I love you. Take care of yourself."

"Back at ya, brother." She kissed his forehead. He rose, but she stopped him with a tug on the hand. "Hey, I know you were going to stay longer. What came up?"

"Negotiations out of a federal building in Los Angeles are tanking. We're going in." We, meaning Ford and the other members of the FBI's hostage rescue team.

"How many hostages?"

"Fifty-four hostages. Six takers."

"And they need the best."

He put a palm up and shrugged.

"Did you tell the parents goodbye?"

"I went to their villa, but there were some funny noises. I didn't want to disturb them."

"Oh come on," Ava hollered. She crinkled her face and shooed him away.

"Yeah, I think that's what they were trying to do."

"You're sick."

"I hope you have a nice dinner with them this evening."

"You're just messing with my mind, again."

He shrugged his shoulders, gave her a salute, and headed off to save the world.

***

An alarm blared loudly enough that it wouldn't surprise her to open her eyes and find a police cruiser and fire engine parked in her bedroom. Ava cracked an eye lid. The world before her blurred. She blinked. Once. Twice. A room not her own came into focus. Panic seized her for a split second before she remembered she was in her suit at a swank complex in the British Virgin Islands.

The light on the clock across the room blinked four-thirty a.m. Ava stumbled out of bed, realizing too late that the sheets were entwined around her legs. She pitched forward. Her head smacked the doorframe of the bathroom. Twinkling lights danced in the blackness. With a grunt she gripped the wood and propped against the wall for balance. She kicked the sheets from her feet. Free-footed, she turned and felt along the interior of the bathroom wall for the light switch.

The image the mirror shot back in the light frightened her as much as any mugshot she'd ever seen. The hand rubbing the sting out of her forehead covered half of her face, but one bloodshot green eye squinted back at her. Pillow crease lines decorated the visible half of her lightly sunburned face. Her hair was tousled from the fitful hours of sleep she'd claimed.

Two hours of sleep. She remembered seeing two a.m. not long ago. Why'd she even bother going to sleep? She should've just stayed up.

"Are you all right?" The deep rumble sent her reeling again.

Ava's fight or flight instinct kicked into over drive. From the size of the blurred movement she picked up in the mirror she chose flight. She hurled herself inside the bathroom door, slammed it shut, and locked it with lightning speed. She lunged for the window above the toilet and wrung on the latch. Then the intruder's words re-replayed in her head.

Are you all right?

Realization sank slowly through the fog of beer and sleep.

"Ava?" The thick voice came through the door. "It's Amadi. I didn't mean to frighten you. I just heard a loud noise and wanted to make sure you were okay."

She opened the door, then sank onto the closed toilet seat. Her head plunged into the well of her hands. Embarrassment and nausea nibbled on her insides.

"You don't remember we decided I would stay here and get some sleep before driving you to the airport this morning?"

There were no words adequate enough to articulate her awkwardness. So she didn't try.

His chuckle filled the tiny room. "I guess you had more to drink last night than normal."

"I don't drink," she whispered.

She liked control. Too much for most people. Her family and Annie had always been after her to let loose, to take risks in love and life. But it wasn't in her to be free. She was forever bound to her past. Forever raging against it.

"Oh? Well you did last night. So did your parents. Lushes, the lot of you."

She lifted her head slightly and glared at him. After taking in the view, Ava had to laugh at herself.

How could anyone forget when a person the size of
a small mountain occupied space in your villa.

Amadi took up the entire doorway. He leaned
against the door frame. His bare chest rippled in a
relaxed state. Midnight skin wrapped smooth as
silk over his chest and bulging arms. Khaki pants
covered long and well-muscled legs, while one bare
foot rested atop the other.

Why couldn't she be in lust with him? He was
lust worthy, if ever anyone was. Ava moaned and
face planted into her palms.

"Are you packed? It looks like you did most of
it before dinner last night."

"Packed?" she mumbled against her hands.

"Yes. Home. Airport. Flight. DC. Any of this
ringing a bell?"

"Oh no." Of all the times to let loose. "Oh
Lord." She jerked upright. Her hands fell to her
sides. "We didn't..." She trailed off, unable to
fathom the thought, much less speak the words.

Amadi grinned. He folded his arms over his
chest and stared at her for several seconds. When
she was at the brink of bursting he gave a tiny
shake of his head. "No. I like my women coherent."

Though she'd known the answer, hearing it
released the pressurized air trapped in her lungs.
She sagged against the tank. "This is all your fault."

"Do you love yourself yet?" His head canted in
question.

"I kind of hate myself right now."

"Good."

Her mouth hung in a gape for a minute. "How
is that good?"

"It's progress."

"Making a total ass of myself is progress?"

"You didn't make an ass of yourself. You had
a good time." He knelt in front of her. "There's

nothing wrong with letting go, even if you have a flight at dawn." Amadi tugged a lock of her hair. "You might throw up on the person sitting next to you, but you will make it, if we hurry."

"What about hating *you*? Is that progress?"

***

After a five-hour delay—in Miami of all places —and ten hours on various planes, Ava's stomach no longer rebelled against her fruity freedom cocktails. But she'd miss her morning run... all week maybe. Her head pounded. Her body ached with each turn of the wheel. She crossed the Potomac on George Washington Memorial Parkway, skirted the waterfront, and then hooked Washington Circle Park headed into the heart of DC.

Eight minutes later she pulled into a miracle spot only a block from the front door of her building. She'd purchased the simple condo eleven years ago for the proximity to the office when she'd been assigned to the FBI headquarters. When starting with the Bureau, the National Center for the Analysis of Violent Crime had been her goal. Seven long years later, she was recruited into the NCAVC and transferred to Quantico, giving her a two-hour commute. Most days she welcomed it. Some of her best analysis had been accomplished in bumper to bumper traffic along I-95.

Ava pulled the keys from the ignition and slumped against the seat. The leather creaked.

So close, and yet so far away.

A bag. A briefcase. A hanging bag. A purse. Zero will to move. Ava's eyes closed. When the universe didn't spin backward she cheered somewhere deep inside. Her limbs grew heavy and the six-year-old coupe's seat became unusually comfortable.

The sensible side of Ava rebelled. She was doing everything she warned people not to do. Her fingers slid across the smooth wood grain at the door handle, up the pleated leather, and onto the ledge. The metal door lock barely stood out from the hard sill. Of course she'd already locked the doors. She sighed. Her hand slipped down to the door rest.

A loud thud rippled through the car's interior and Ava's body. Her heart rammed headlong into her sternum and collapsed before jumping again. A gigantic newspaper with an all-too-familiar headline landed on her windshield...at least, her sleep-deprived brain thought that's what it was.

She blinked wildly in search of the offender while she reached for her sidearm. A sidearm not attached to the waist of her blue jean shorts. The damn thing sat inside her suitcase in the trunk of her car.

When she looked back to the windshield, instead of a newspaper, Ava found a thick manila folder with a Bureau issued case number penciled on the tab.

A new case.

Past the folder Special Agent Winslow Gray stood in the muggy night with his free fist at the ready. The beefy points struck the glass. The window held through four obnoxious smacks of his heavy hand, but just barely. Shards of sound splintered the car's quiet interior.

Ava sighed in relief and braced her shaking palms on the steering wheel. Breaths inflated and deflated her lungs like she'd just run a marathon, or worse. Their gazes connected. His scrutiny lanced more violently than ever before. That said something. The man's hazel eyes scored metal and hardened criminals on a daily basis.

Per usual, Ava blinked first. To offset the loss she searched the street and sidewalk for his partner. Special Agent Lara Abbott leaned a shoulder on a light pole five feet from the front of Ava's car. The woman's model-long legs crossed at the ankle. A sleeveless blouse displayed her defined arms and belied her casual stance. One hand rested on the butt of her pistol. The other gripped the top of the cellphone clipped to the belt of her gray slacks.

The heavy knuckles pounded a dull four-beat again. "Come on, Shepherd. Open up."

She'd worked long and damn hard for the title in front of her name. Some people nipped the seniority off her name because of ignorance. A few did it out of spite. Gray nor Abbott ever had, and this wasn't the night to start. Especially if they wanted her input on a case.

Ava unlocked the doors and shoved hers open. "Supervisory Special Agent Shepherd," she corrected.

Gray's heavy arm shot out and grabbed the door. "You look like hell, Shepherd."

His flagrant disrespect evaporated her fatigue. Her teeth ground together. She kicked her legs out onto the asphalt and stood. "Thank you, Gray. You sure know how to make a girl feel special."

"You're always put together. Why not now?" He gestured at her wrinkled linen blouse, jean shorts, and flip flops.

Her mouth hung wide for a beat too long, showing her utter shock at the direction of this conversation. In the year and a half she'd sporadically worked with the hard-boiled duo Ava had never witnessed this kind of role reversal. Despite Gray and Abbott's vast size difference and the societal presumption that a man the size of a Sherman Tank would take the lead Abbott was always the mouthy muscle and Gray was the quiet analyst. But even then their exchanges were always professional.

"I don't mean to be rude, which apparently you have no problem with tonight, but we're going to have to do this another time. I just got off a plane and I'm not feeling well."

"No." Gray's massive bald head shook. "We're doing this now. In fact, you're going to have to come with us."

The filling in Ava's back left molar throbbed. Something wasn't right. The NCAVC office assigned her cases. Agents didn't order her around. If anything it was the other way around.

Ava squared her shoulders to the juggernaut of a man. "What the hell is going on here?"

Abbott straightened and walked to the front of the car. "We're going to need you to come with us. We have to ask you some questions in regards to a murder." Her tone was too conciliatory. Too not-Abbott.

Ava's muscles were on vacation, her head pounded, and the queasiness settled back in her stomach. "Look, call and talk to the NCAVC director. I'm not doing this right now. If your case is urgent he can assign you someone else immediately."

"You don't understand." Abbott inhaled deeply. "You're our number one suspect."

Chapter Four

The woman ran screaming down the stairs of the opulent St. Petersburg, Florida mansion barreling in Keen's direction. Familiarity kept him from diving behind the car and drawing his weapon. If the wail came from anyone else, he'd have measured the scene, identified the threat, the innocents, calculated the odds, and plotted his next move.

His mom crashed into his open arms. Her cheers melted into ardent sobs. Keen breathed in the familiar scent of rosin, Opium perfume, and hairspray. How many times had she held him through the years as he cried out his juvenile troubles? Far more than he cared to remember. Growing up as the only boy in his school—and probably a five-hundred-mile radius—that could dance the Nutcracker or even say the word without hysterical laughter, lent itself to a world of angst.

Keen tightened his hold and let her exhaust her worries and fear on his shirt in the safety of his arms. A smile curved one side of his mouth. There was no humor in it. He had always been the comforted, now he was the comforter. What a paradigm shift.

His mother's sobs abated and still he kept her cradled in his arms. After her death grip

loosened at his waist he eased her back with the
length of his arms.

"I'm fine, Mom. Really." When the crease of
her brow remained he released her and stepped
back. He danced a small jig and shook his arms
about. "See?"

"Don't you give me that smile." She shook her
head. The chignon pinned at the back of her hair
didn't budge.

"What smile?"

"The one that's sweet enough to make sugar
jealous. The one you give when you're trying to get
out of something." Her long fingers pinched her
slender hips, made more dramatic by the black
leotard and sheer skirt at her waist.

"I don't know about all that." He laughed
despite the fire that scorched a path down his arm
and across his chest. Keen grabbed his mother's
hand and hummed the first few bars of the intro to
Swan Lake.

The woman morphed from mom into the
world-renowned prima ballerina Jillian Hunt, now
Jillian H. Wright, with the point of her toes. Keen
led her into the turns, braced her on the
extensions, and then braced himself for the simple
lift. Pain tore at the gnarled tendons in his shoulder
as though the bullet were still firmly lodged inside,
tearing and consuming his abilities with each
motion.

He set her gently on the cobblestone drive
and bowed at their imaginary audience. Her wide
smile took the edge off the ache.

"Such pain and such joy you bring me." She
cupped his cheek. "I am so grateful to have you in
my life. You test the durability of my heart and
nerves, but I wouldn't trade you in for a more docile

version. No, not for all the reassurances in the world."

"I love you too."

"Now grab your bags and I'll show you to your suite."

"Yes, ma'am." He nodded, hurried to the open trunk, and then ducked his head behind the open lid. Keen exhaled. His eyes threatened to roll into his head from the ache.

"Why don't you let me buy this car from you once and for all?" His mom propped her hand on the pointed fin at the back of the vintage, mint condition, 1976 Ferrari 330 GT.

Keen pulled on his happy face, yanked his duffle bag from the interior, and closed the top, careful not to catch his mom's fingers. "If you'd cherish it like I do, I'd give it to you, but I know you."

His mom flashed a stage smile and covered her heart with her hand. "Why, me? I'm an angel fallen from the heavens."

"That reviewer was talking about your dancing ability. They never lived with you, or crossed you."

"True." She fell into step with him and they climbed a ridiculous number of steps to reach the front door. "But how I would cherish ramming it into a brick wall." Her arms stretched wide. "A really thick, large brick wall."

They wouldn't talk about his father. They wouldn't talk about how much his abandoning them when he was four hurt. They wouldn't talk about the amount of resentment they harbored for Richard Dean Hunt and his other families. But they would talk about that damn car.

The classic was the only thing beside good genes his father had ever given him. Any other man, with the amount of pride Keen possessed, would have balked at the gift from a man who gave no time or apparent care to his only son. Any other man would have walked away from the gift with his head held high. Not Keen. His pride had fallen away at the sight of the classic artistry of the precision interment. At his college graduation he accepted the gift with a smile and nod from the man who sired him, the man he had only seen a handful of times in his life. The man, who apparently understood beauty.

"You have to let it go, Mom."

"Maybe when I die." She bounced a narrow shoulder.

"But probably not."

She grinned, opened a twelve-foot door, and ushered him inside her regal home and through to the back door. This wasn't the home he'd grown up in, but that didn't matter. With the help of the United States Armed Forces he'd learned home was where his head rested. His home tonight was a pool house that tripled his Miami apartment in size and spectacle.

What a world away from the gritty mud huts outside Ramadi.

"You have to be tired." His mom gestured to the bed through the pool house's glass front wall. "Regina freshened the linens. We haven't had a guest in there since we moved in. Denny's happy to get some use out of the thing."

"Where is ole Denny?"

"He's not old."

"Compared to Juan..." He raised his brows and let the sentence fall off.

"Oh you, hush." She swatted his behind. Her elegant fingers stung through his khakis.

"Ouch." He tossed his bag onto the threshold and rubbed his cheek. "Fine. No more about him." Add her third and significantly younger husband to the list of things they wouldn't talk about. "I drove all this way to see you, not sleep on your fancy bed. Come and sit with me."

Keen led the way to two plush lounge chairs on the patio beside the single lane Olympic-length pool. He held her hand until she sat, and then walked to the other one and collapsed onto it. The days drained off him one droplet at a time. Two long days actually that included a flight, seeing Ava, a wedding, a reception, seeing Ava dance with another man, staying up all night thinking about Ava sleeping with said man, a flight, and then the drive.

Ritzy boats eased past in the choppy bay. A steady breeze blew off the water holding the humidity and temperature in check. Pelicans perched on the end of the dock. A big one spread his wings and flapped into the headwind. The bird glided through the air, making the wind do the work. He hovered, his wing-tips nearly touching the water until he soared, and then dove. His neck stretched long. His wings stretched back. The pelican hit the surface like a missile. Deadly precision combined with grace.

"Did you see that?" His mother awed.

"Pretty amazing." Keen inhaled the salty air, and then slowly let it out. "Did I mess you up coming in early?" He pointed to her ballet slippers.

"Not at all. I'm so happy you're here. I'll have to go into the studio for a couple of hours."

"If you need to be there, go. I'll be fine."

"I needed to be here. I needed to see you. To know you're whole. Even if the scene out front hurt you like hell."

Leave it to Mom to call him out on his BS.

"I thought I played it off pretty well."

"Yes. To anyone else, Kenneth Richmond Hunt, you look like a man in top physical condition. But I'm your mother and I know better. There's pain in your shoulder, restlessness in your mind, and heaviness in your heart. Want to talk about it?"

Keen tossed an arm over his eyes and yawned. "Wow. Would you look at that? I'm suddenly exhausted."

"All right. I'll talk. You can listen."

He made a sincere effort to stifle his groan. It didn't work. His mother—like most mothers—was not easily deterred. She ignored his fit.

"Three times. You've been shot three times in the last seven years. Have you stopped to think about why it is you've been shot so many times?"

He let his arm fall from his eyes and looked at her. His mouth parted, but she propelled on without waiting for a reply.

"I'll tell you why. You're relentless in your work, doing it all so you can take the burden off of others. You're brash. Always the first to react. The first to move. You're cocky as hell, and you don't have a healthy level of fear."

He opened his mouth wider to speak, but she jumped him again.

"Oh, I know there's a little fear in there," she said pointing to his chest. "But it's only enough to give you a damn rush."

"You're restless because you know you can't keep going like you've been going. You know you need a change. You just don't know what the change should be. And since I'm your mother, and am immensely more experienced in life, I'm going to tell you what you need."

Keen propped his elbow on the armrest and settled his chin on top. "I was afraid you were going to keep all the wisdom to yourself." He knew exactly where this train headed. If he were wise he'd jump now and deal with the fall.

"Wise-ass."

"Better than a dumb-ass." Which he sincerely was for letting her continue.

She harrumphed. "You need a woman."

"Well, Mom, I don't have a problem getting one, or two, or three. Though, sometimes they're hesitant about being there at the same time. Some of them anyway. Not all of them."

"Little shit." Her nose scrunched, but her smile shined through her ire. "Let me rephrase. You need a wife. You need to start a family." His smug smile fell away. "You need something to anchor you to this life. You need something worth living for, worth fighting for."

"And I thought I just needed a vacation."

"One certainly won't hurt."

"Okay then." He stood, grabbed his mother's hand, and helped her up. "Get to work and I'll start vacationing." He'd heard the phone tucked into the pocket of her skirt vibrate six times since they'd been sitting.

She sighed, but kissed his cheek and eased toward the main house.

"Go. I'll see you at dinner?"

"Absolutely," she beamed. "I'm happy you're here."

He was too. Wasn't he?

As if the voice inside his head wasn't enough, now his mother's chimed in to the incessant loop of questions trampling his brain. Keen wandered into the pool house. He steered clear of the sparkling crystal on the wet bar. That wouldn't help the situation. He also gave the smattering of paint on an extra-large canvas a wide berth. The thing probably cost more money than he'd accumulate in his entire life.

Playing it safe for the first time in a long time, he stripped, and then pulled on one of the twenty or so pairs of swim trunks in the dresser. Keen made thirty-three laps in the pool before the voices echoing in his head were drowned out by the screaming pain in his shoulder. No longer did he hear his own thoughts or his mother's helpful advice about his life, about his love, a love buried so deep inside because it hurt to even acknowledge its existence. When the words and thoughts were quiet he lifted himself out of the pool, stripped out of his swim trunks just inside the pool house door, rubbed off the excess water with a towel, then dropped onto the bed.

***

A tap on the door woke Keen what seemed like ten minutes later. He levered onto his elbows, craned his head, and blinked his mom's silhouette into view.

"Shit." He scrambled for the covers he'd kicked off the bed during his nap and wrestled them across his glaring white backside. By the time he covered and found a pair of shorts from his bag his mother stood facing the water. He hurried to the door. "Sorry. I'm not used to sleeping in plain view."

Little peals of laughter spilled in from the open door. She turned and aimed her gaze on his. "It's nothing I haven't seen or spanked before."

"I know it. You swatted me a few hours ago."

A dimple creased her forehead. Her lips formed a line that waggled back and forth.

"What?" Keen checked his zipper.

"You're covered and it's no big deal, but it's been more than a few hours."

"What time is it?"

"Two something."

"You should've woken me sooner. I sure as hel...I didn't mean to sleep an entire day away."

"You needed your rest. Besides, I was late getting back from the studio and I had to check on a few things this morning. Get dressed and come eat a late lunch with me." She motioned to the patio area where their food was ready and waiting.

"Yes ma'am."

"Oh and the vertical button on the small white remote controls the shades." She pressed a smile between her lips, turned, and headed for the table.

Good to know.

He hurried inside, tugged on a shirt, and joined her in short order.

She surveyed his frayed khaki shorts and grease stained T-shirt. "You're so unassuming at times. The boy who had the world at his feet matured into the man before me."

"I look homeless huh?"

"No. You look like a man who forged his own path in life with little help from anyone."

"You helped me."

"Helped you? I don't count buying you a meal when I visited helping."

"I did."

"That's one of the things I love about you."

"Don't list them. I'll get a fat head."

"Already have one. Why do you think I went with the big doors?"

His shoulders shook. It hurt, but the laugh felt good. He guessed she was right. His dad—the man he knew as Dad, her second husband and still

business partner—would have put him through
school at his alma mater, Harvard. Instead, Keen
got a scholarship to Florida State where he first met
and became friends with Nathan Brewer. Then he
worked his way through law school at the
University of Mississippi as a mechanic. He learned
most of the trade helping his mother's father out in
his garage. After college the army had been his
escape from reality, from the crumble of the world
he'd known, from the reality he wasn't ready to deal
with.

Jillian H. Wright lifted her water glass toward
him. "Bon appétit."

"Bon appétit, maman." After his mother lifted
her fork and took a bite he did the same, but
devoured much more of the Mediterranean salad
and chicken panini in far fewer bites. He wiped his
mouth. "So, how's the studio? How are the girls in
tutus?"

"Two of my girls in tutus just received their
acceptances into the American Ballet Theatre."

"Nice."

"Nice? It's amazing. One was chosen as a
principle. She's young, talented, but mostly she's
unbelievably dedicated to her craft. She'll have an
amazing career. They both will."

He caught the wistful quality in her voice. It
bore into his gut and stayed. Dance had been her
life since she could walk. He'd seen the pictures to
prove it. She was once the young, talented,
dedicated principle. She had literally danced the
world over. She'd had a career most dancers dream
of, but never realize. Her time was cut short
because of love, because of him. He realized longing
when he saw it. He knew what it was to long for
something unattainable.

"I'm sorry, Mom."

"Oh, dear." She shooed him with a waving hand. "I'm not and you shouldn't be. I do miss it. The stage. The lights. The roaring applause. But I still have dance which is what I loved more than any of the other. Most importantly, I have you."

"What do you say we go to dinner and dancing tonight? You, me, and Denny?"

She cupped a hand over her smile. "Oh, I'd love to."

"Great."

"Let me text Denny and make sure it works with his schedule. He's been in court non-stop for the past week." She grabbed the phone from the pocket of her slacks and pecked out a message.

"On a divorce case?" His mother met Dennis while she was on the market for a top-notch divorce attorney from husband number three. "I thought those things hardly ever went to court."

"They usually settle before then, but the ones that don't are beasts."

"Ah, amour."

They finished their food, and then talked about everything and nothing in particular until her phone chimed nearly two hours later.

"Denny can't make it. He'll be in depositions for another two and a half hours."

"We can wait. I'm not particularly hungry, though, I could always eat."

"Always." She nodded. "I'll let him know."

Her finger ticked away at the phone's screen. Almost immediately after she finished, the thing chimed. She squinted at the screen and stretched her arms just a bit. Her mouth stretched wide. A hand clutched at her stomach. His mother doubled over in hysterics.

"What is it?"

Several seconds later she panted a few breaths. "I'll read his text verbatim. It's too ridiculous. He says, 'Truth time. I'll be done in an hour, but I hate dancing. You two go without me. I look like a jackass with its tail on fire.'"

"Truer words." Keen shrugged. "I was at your wedding."

Her mouth dropped open.

"Tell him we both could use a good laugh and to get his ass home ASAP."

"All right." She hung her head and typed with a huge grin on her face.

"Don't forget the ass," he cautioned.

"I would never." After pressing send she set the phone on the table like it were a live explosive. When it buzzed she shoved it at him and laughed. "You look."

Keen grabbed the phone. "I'm not scared." He read the text and groaned. "But maybe I should've been." *Only if your mom promises to back that ass up on me.* His stomach roiled and he tossed the phone to his mother.

Her gaze scanned the text and she nearly fell off the chair.

"It's not funny." He frowned. "Tell him he's no longer allowed to go with us."

"Pff." His mother hunched over the phone and typed with the sudden speed of a middle-schooler. "Heck yes, he's coming tonight."

Keen didn't know if she meant the comment as a double entendre and he hated his brain for going there. "I'm going to barf. I need to go for a run, then shower." He jumped up from the seat and collected the dishes.

"I'll get those."

"Thanks for lunch."

Her giggle followed him into the pool house. "Ugh, at least they're happy." He dressed and headed to the main road in record time. The image of his mom and...ugh. He had to erase that from his gray matter. After a three mile run out and back, Keen showered and dressed.

He grabbed his phone off the night stand, where it had been all day, and checked it out of habit. Typically the thing was on him at all times, but not on vacation. The screen lit and the notifications practically bitched him out. He scrolled through. Nine missed calls.

"Shit." Not even a full day back in the States and already work was hounding him. Didn't they know he'd only been released from the slammer—wound rehab—a few days ago?

He couldn't cave. Not tonight. It was his only night with his mother. She deserved his full attention. He squeezed the phone in frustration. The device almost disappeared in his large fist.

A sense of duty played on his consciousness like a Kentucky fiddler. He tossed it onto the bed. "Sorry, boys, you're going to have to figure it out on your own." He'd done more than his fair share for his country. They could hang one more night.

Keen headed for the door. As he reached for the handle *Return of the Mac* blasted the room. He looked at the door knob and then back at the phone.

Responsibility jumped onto his shoulders. It weighed a thousand pounds and made it impossible to turn the knob. At the very least he needed to see who called at a stalker-like frequency.

A defeated growl left his throat and echoed inside the large room. Just a quick check, and then off to dinner. He picked up the phone and barked, "Hunt."

The feminine voice on the other end sobbed. "Oh! Thank God. Thank you, God in heaven! Keen?"

He answered tentatively to the familiar, yet undistinguishable voice on the other end of the line. "Yes."

"I'm sorry. I know my hysterics don't help, but I just...I'm so thankful you answered. It's Sarah."

"Mrs. Shepherd?" He recognized Ava's mother's voice now that she spoke instead of wailed into the phone. "Are you okay? What's wrong?"

"No one is hurt. We're all okay, but I need your help. Ava needs your help. We're still in the islands and won't be able to make it to DC until tomorrow evening at the earliest, and it might be later than that. There's a storm threatening and the airport has canceled all fights in and out until further notice."

Keen's stomach lurched. He couldn't take the suspense any longer. "Sarah, what's the problem? Why does Ava need help?"

"She...she's suspected of murder. The Bureau brought her in for questioning."

"What? That's..."

"I know, impossible. She arrived home a few hours ago and they demanded she come in for questioning. She called us on the way to headquarters. We told her not to answer any questions until her lawyer arrived, but she believes in the system, and in herself."

"Damnit, Ava," he cursed mostly to himself.

"Preston called in a favor to one of his associates in DC and he'll arrive shortly to help on the legal side, but we need you to go. Keen, we're stuck. Ford is on the job. Nathan is unreachable, sailing somewhere in the ocean with his new bride.

You know the Bureau inside and out. We trust you. She trusts you."

Chapter Five

Three strident knocks shook the interrogation room door. Special Agent Lara Abbott's eyes turned to molten pits ready to incinerate Ava. Like she'd knocked on the damn thing. She hadn't, but she knew who did because he'd done it five times already. Which meant she'd been in the eight-by-twelve windowless room for five hours and counting.

Abbott pressed forward. Any bit of softness Ava had perceived from the agent vanished the moment they'd set foot in the room so long ago. Her fingers, splayed on the metal table between them, turned white. She crowded Ava's space so much that Ava thought the muscled woman might crawl across the unyielding table and strangle the truth from her.

"Put me in cuffs, Winslow, or else I'm going to kill that man. Enough with the damn knocking already." Abbott shoved off the table and stalked to the door, her striated muscles showing with every movement.

"Go ahead. I didn't see anything." Winslow Gray kept his hands interlaced behind his big head and reclined farther into the chair next to the one Abbott didn't bother using. "One less defense attorney in the world." His upper lip wrinkled.

"Makes it a better place in my opinion. What do you think, Ava?"

She held her tongue and Gray's gaze. They didn't need to know she'd thought the whole thing was an elaborate and truly awful practical joke. They didn't need to know the muscles above her shoulder blade knotted so tightly that mariners could use her to secure their sails in gale force winds. They didn't need to know a trail of sweat ran from her armpits to the waist band of her shorts, but they could probably see that for themselves. They didn't need to know that she was closer to breaking than she'd ever been.

Childhood. Adolescence. FBI training. Her first year on the job. Her reoccurring nightmares. All as the daughter of the Blood Red Killer. Those trials. Those triumphs had tempered the steel in her spine. Those wins had prepared her for the next challenge.

But she couldn't see around this, through this, past this.

She sat on the other side of the table being questioned in a murder.

After nearly five hours she didn't know any more about the crime she supposedly committed than when she walked in the room.

Abbott ripped the door open. "If you knock on this door again, I'm putting you in handcuffs." Abbott propped her hand on her hip and stared up at a man who looked eerily similar to Keen. So much that Ava had thought Keen had gone wild with a box of ink black Clairol in the last two days.

"You just gave me incentive, Special Agent Abbott." Thick lips spread over a sweeter than honey smile that she'd seen before. His gaze locked on Abbott's. Ava swallowed past the sexual tension that sparked in the confined space, thankful to have something else to think about than her impending doom. "I just needed to ask my client if she's come to her senses and decided to let me in the room."

Abbott growled, folded her arms over her chest, and hiked a brow at Ava.

"Dumb as ever," Ava offered, feigning confidence she severely lacked. She sat ramrod straight, but her hands twisted in her lap almost uncontrollably. Ava Shepherd needed a power pose more than a lawyer. It didn't matter if he believed in her innocence until proven guilty, if she didn't believe in it.

She placed both hands on her hips and shifted forward. Gray's steady gaze ticked off the movement.

"There you go." Abbott lifted her palms up in a sorry-I'm-not-sorry pose.

"Ava." Mason Beaumont, the lawyer her father had sent to represent her, met her gaze. "You know—"

Abbott slammed the door in his face. "You know he objects. You've heard the speech too many times already." She crooked her hand and pointed all her fingers at herself. "Well, I have for sure. What I would like to hear about is your Friday."

"You haven't heard that too many times already?" Ava asked.

"Whoo." Abbott fanned herself and tilted her head toward Gray. "That little power pose she adopted seems to have worked miracles. But that's okay, I like my perps sassy."

"You haven't indicted me," Ava shot back.

"Not yet." Abbott grinned. "So how about that Friday?"

"As I told you before, I woke at four-thirty a.m. and went for a run."

"You didn't press snooze?" Abbott asked in her usual indelicate manner.

"I don't snooze. Why snooze when you could sleep soundly the nine or twenty-seven minutes you spend hitting a snooze?"

"Why indeed?"

"I ran the usual five miles. My route is highlighted on the map in front of you. After my run I showered, dressed, and then ate."

"Why dress before you eat? Why not eat while wrapped in your towel? Or better yet, why not eat in the nude?"

Ava's face probably matched the red line drawn on the map of down town DC. The heat of her anger evaporated her earlier sweat. "When people said you were a bitch before I thought they said it because you were a woman in a power position. Now I know you're just a bitch."

"Whatever it takes to catch my man or, in this case, woman."

"I had an egg, dry wheat toast, a glass of water and one of orange juice. In case you were wondering. I read over my notes for the breakout sessions I hosted on crime analysis at the law enforcement convention held at Hilton Mark Center in Alexandria."

"Dry." Abbott tapped her chin. "I'm not surprised."

Ava was surprised she didn't start screaming at the top of her lungs and continue on for the rest of her insufferable life.

"I left my house at eight and arrived at the Hilton Mark Center around eight forty."

"You don't know the exact time?" Abbott raised a brow.

"You can check the stub in my car. Better yet, check the security cameras in the parking garage."

Abbott chuckled. "Are you trying to do my job for me, Ava? After all, you would know exactly how to steer this investigation to make certain we don't find the truth."

"I would know how to commit a murder so that I'd never be questioned for it. You might want to keep that in mind, Abbott."

"Oh, I'm shaking in my stilettos."

After a stare off, Ava continued. "Traffic was heavy that morning. I parked in the garage in the rear and made it into the morning's general session with a few minutes to spare. I hosted four break-out sessions. The schedule for which is also in front of you and can be verified by the people listed on the sheet."

Abbott pulled her chair out from under the table. Its legs screeched against the floor. She plopped down, spread her legs, and rested her palms on her thighs. "What about breaks? Lunch?"

"During breaks I was in the conference center lobby and I had lunch at the hotel with the people also listed on the paper in front of you."

Which I told you four times already, bitch.

"Tell me about after the sessions."

"At the close of the last session at four-fifty I collected my material and headed straight to my car."

"The conference director, Mr. Geno Aconi, reported that you did not return your badge, which means you didn't sign out. Why not? In a hurry to get someplace?"

"First, it was a plastic sleeve with a paper printout of my name and rank, and the only reason they wanted it turned in was for a drawing they had for the workshop hosts. Second, I had no use for a massive large screen TV."

"Man," Gray groaned. "That part gets me every time. Everybody can use a big flatscreen."

"Not the homeless," Ava pointed out.

"You're not homeless," he countered.

"No, but I don't watch TV." She shook her head.

Gray clutched his chest, added a grimace, and then pointed a weak finger at Abbott to carry on.

Ava's arms burned. Power poses were for people who lifted weights. Ava placed her hands on the table in front of her to keep from wringing them again.

Neither commented further. So Ava took a deep breath and got on with it. "Third, yes, I was in a hurry to get to Dulles for a seven forty-five flight to Miami."

"Where'd you stop off on the way?"

"Nowhere. I arrived at the airport around five forty-five and rushed through security. I didn't even stop to gas up or pee."

"Needed every extra minute in between, huh?" Abbott needled.

"I have cooperated with you and Agent Gray. I haven't asked for a lawyer. I denied the one my dad sent, who'll probably charge my dad for the hours he's spent out there pacing the hallway." Ava flatted her palms on the cold table. "I want some questions answered. You keep saying, the victim. Who is the victim?"

"I'm going to hold that information for a little longer."

She snorted a laugh. "You're not going to tell me who I supposedly killed." Ava nodded at the absurdity of that. "Fine. How was the victim killed?"

Abbott looked to Gray. They exchanged some super-secret message with only slight variations of their brows. Then Abbott turned a cutting gaze to Ava. The sinister nature of it sent Ava's heart in search of a hiding spot.

"I have this sick feeling in my gut telling me you already know." Abbott stood half way, reached between her legs, and yanked her chair closer to the table. Ava fought the urge to retreat. She needed to know what the woman had to say. The sadist paused for a merciless minute before relenting. "The victim was rendered unconscious by a blow to the head."

A sheen of sweat broke on Ava's body. Her heart's search for a dark, secluded corner grew more frantic. She wanted to retract the question or smash her hands over her ears, but she held perfectly still. Her lungs burned with the stalled breath.

"The victim was positioned on the bed face down and the carotid artery was severed by a small dagger," Abbott said.

The words seemed to come through ripples of water, under a vast sea that weighed more than she could shoulder. Ava breathed. She didn't want to. But sickening clarity settled over her. "A copycat."

"Brilliant," Abbott sneered. "I assume you know the rest then."

"If I killed whoever it is you think I killed, then I wouldn't have needed you to tell me this to begin with," Ava explained.

Her ticker no longer wanted to hide. It beat strongly and steadily for the first time since she'd been ushered from her apartment. Ava had always feared a copycat killer. If Jack the Ripper, the Zodiac Killer, and films like Scream and the Taxi Driver inspired copycats, of course the most notorious killer of all would. It had only been a matter of time. She'd prepared for the eventuality. She could handle this.

"Why me? Why am I your number one suspect? Is it based solely on the fact that I'm the Blood Red Killer's daughter or do you actually have some kind of evidence against me?"

"We have your hair at the crime scene. The locket of red hair left at the scene. We ran it. It matches yours."

"What?" Ava squeaked the word.

"You see," Abbott grinned, "the Bureau kept that tidbit out of the media. They never disclosed that Blood Red Hardy left a locket of his red hair at the crime scene. It was before DNA testing became reliable. The investigators kept the information back as an interrogation tool."

Ava knew about the hair at the scene because she'd studied her father's digression from every angle.

Abbott slapped the table, calling Ava's gaze. "Gotcha."

"No. If you had me, you'd wouldn't need this dog and pony show. What you have is circumstantial at best." Ava grabbed the end of her ponytail out for Abbott. "This has grown my entire life. It's been cut hundreds of times. Anyone could have followed me and swiped some discarded strands." She released her hair. "Only the original killer, someone with access to the original files, or someone close to him, would know about the hair left at the scene. It's not a large pool of people, but it's more than just me."

Ava offered her wrists. "If you're going to indict me, do it. Otherwise, get me my lawyer."

Chapter Six

A burly night guard scanned Keen's badge even though he'd already used it to access the parking garage and unlock the back doors. The sentinel's lanky cohort studied him up one side and down the other. His dark brows wobbled. He probably wasn't used to seeing special agents in knock-around clothes, and had likely only seen deck shoes on TV.

Keen braced himself for a fight. Two and a half hours confined in the belly of a commercial jet had primed him for one. Add to it that the Bureau was grilling his one-time best friend for a murder she couldn't have committed and the tiniest spark would ignite his temper.

"Very good, Special Agent Hunt." The guard handed over his access card.

He grabbed the card, nodded, and bolted for the stairs, thankful he'd worked at the FBI's DC field office for a year before transferring to Miami. Keen poured some of his anger onto the stairs, pounding up them three at a time. On the fifth floor he barreled through the metal stairwell entrance. The door slammed against the wall, and then closed with a bang. His frown turned into a scowl. A pretty boy in a grey suit that cost more than his rent turned on Keen as though Keen were the first horsemen of the apocalypse. The man's grimace matched his own, or at least it tried.

"You're the lawyer?" Keen barked.

"Mason Beaumont. You must be the knight in shining armor Preston told me about."

"If you're the undefeated, killer defense attorney Preston told me about, why—for fuck's sake—aren't you in the room with Ava?"

"Well hello, Keen." His glare turned to a sour smile. "My, it's nice to meet you."

"Cut the bullshit, Beaumont. This is serious."

Beaumont spread his arms. "Why the hell do you think I'm out here? Because I love to pace empty hallways while my client speaks freely to the Feds? No." His left arm fell to his side, while the right jabbed toward a windowless door. "You know Preston Shepard's daughter. She's independent to a fault, and refused to let me in the room."

"I didn't think the famous Mason Beaumont would let a pint-size woman push him around."

The lawyer stepped forward. His dress shoes landed inches from Keen's worn topsiders, putting them eye to eye.

Keen held himself perfectly still.

"From what I hear," Beaumont whispered, "I'm not the only guy she's pushed around or away. So, back off, Hunt. Besides, I don't think she'll be any more excited to see you than she was to see me."

The muscles in Keen's hands contracted into two perfect fists, but something held him back. Maybe he didn't particularly feel like getting sued. Knocking a lawyer's teeth into the back of his throat would most certainly accomplish that feat. Maybe it was his throbbing shoulder. If it was, he'd never admit it. Maybe it was the odd familiarity in the man's features. And maybe that's why Keen had gotten so riled from the man's inconsequential jab. In those brown, condescending eyes, and aristocratic nose he saw his father. In the strong jaw and concealed rage he saw himself.

"Get in there and throw around whatever legal bullshit you have to. She's leaving now," Keen ordered.

The man's shoulders shook. "Ha, the day I take orders from a grease monkey is also the day hell frosts over."

Keen's fist sank into the man's belly, hard and fast.

Beaumont gasped and doubled over. One hand clutched his gut. The other braced against his knee.

Keen rubbed his shoulder. "It just got pretty chilly."

Beaumont growled. Head down, he ran at Keen. His shoulder became a battering ram. Keen tighten his core, but the man dozed through him, knocking the breath and his legs out from under him.

The wall kept them from hitting Linoleum. Keen's back met it with a resounding thud. Impact shocked his lungs into function. He inhaled a shallow breath, wrapped his arms around the lawyer's neck and his opposite armpit, and then squeezed. They stayed locked for several bucks of Keen's heart.

"Give up, pretty boy."

The ground dropped from beneath Keen's feet. More accurately, his feet left the ground. Keen's hold strained on the man's neck. He doubled down, but cursed his shot shoulder. His grip slipped fractions at a time.

Beaumont's arms locked around his middle. The world tilted.

Keen ground his teeth in preparation to meet the floor head first.

"What the fuck?" A gruff and quite distinct feminine voice hollered.

A groan slipped from Keen's grimace.

Why today, of all days? Wasn't it cocked up enough without throwing Lara into the mix?

The lawyer practically threw Keen off his shoulder, and amazingly, onto his feet. Both their chests rose and fell in rapid succession. The knot of Beaumont's tie twisted to the right, wrinkling the once sharply-pointed collar. His shirt tails puffed out in several spots.

"That's a good look on you," Keen jabbed.

Muscles and veins stretched the skin on Beaumont's neck and the color returned to his cheeks.

"Don't you boys know the rules? No fighting in the building unless I'm involved," Lara said.

Their gazes shifted to the tall woman with her hands crossed at her small, perky breasts. Keen kept the lawyer in his periphery. Just in case.

"I don't hit women," Beaumont argued.

"Looks like you don't hit men either." She pointed at Keen. "Actually, I'm inclined to let you two off the hook. That wasn't even a real fight. More like two men hugging it out." She pointed to the interrogation room. "I can leave and let you guys finish."

"I want to see Ava," Keen demanded, ignoring her snide remarks and Beaumont's apparent willingness—given his clenched fists—to prove her wrong.

"I bet you do." Lara smiled. "But she finally grew some brain cells and requested her attorney, not her hand-holding ex-boyfriend."

She made his relationship with Ava sound meaningless and immature. For a split second he wondered if that had come from Ava, then he remembered his history with Lara. He knew the comment came from a place of jealousy and hurt, though she'd used him every bit as much as he'd used her.

Lara opened the door. "Any day now, Beaumont."

Beaumont stuffed his shirt into his pants, yanked his tie in the general area of straight, and headed for the interrogation room. At the threshold he snatched his briefcase from the ground next to the door.

Keen followed closely behind. Lara's arm shot across the entrance.

"Come on, Lara. Let me in. You're done here anyway." Keen begged.

She met him with a stony expression.

"For old time's sake?" Keen gave his tried and true panty melting smolder.

She laughed, actually laughed. "I've classed it up a little since I let you bow me over the trunk of your sexy car in the Hogan's Alley parking lot. You haven't. Still pining away I see." Her gaze shifted to Ava.

Oh, fuck!

Crickets chirped in the room, which he had barely a toe inside. He looked past Lara into the small gray room to Ava. She sat across from Winslow.

Lara Abbott may as well have kicked him in the nuts. Hell, from the slacked jaw on Ava's chalky white face, she may as well have hacked one off.

Their gazes connected. For a split second time and trouble suspended. Then the second vanished.

Ava clamped her mouth shut. Determination hardened her sweet lips and rigid spine. "If you two are finished stumbling through the past, I'd like to get out of here before dawn."

The screech of metal on metal pulled Keen's gaze away. Beaumont dragged a chair from the table next to Ava. His dark eye shot daggers at Keen and studied Lara a little too long for casual curiosity.

Winslow cleared his throat and sat forward. "Best idea I've heard all night."

The thick metal door closed slowly. Keen stepped back until his shoulders hit the far wall. Ava's mother had sent him here to help. So far he'd gotten into an elementary grade tussle and been proverbially bitch-slapped by an old lover. He plowed a hand through his hair. A long groan escaped.

He needed inside that room. If he didn't have information no way would he do her any good. Ava was in the middle of a shit storm and it wouldn't do to wait around until it piled on top of her. Keen had far too long to plot and plan on the plane to DC. Things weren't working out how he'd planned.

Go figure.

After five minutes of staring at the door willing it to open, he grabbed the cell from his pocket and scrolled through the contacts until he found the person he wanted. He hit send and waited.

The thick Boston accent came through the phone in a sleepy grumble. "Ah, screw you, guy. I thought I told your ass last time not to call at such an hour. I'm an old fuck and I need my beauty rest, especially with these temperatures. You know, sometimes I wonder if you did me a favor at all getting me this job. I swear my organs baked inside my body yesterday. And if I hear, 'Oh, it ain't even hot yet,' from another swamp baked, gator loving son of a Southerner, I'm gonna scream."

"Aw, Smokey, you sweet talker."

"Get to it, Hunt."

"I'm calling in my favor."

"You in some trouble? We need to bash some heads?"

"No, a friend. I need you to get copies of a file to me as soon as you can."

"You know I can't." Smokey sighed.

"I know you can."

"If they pick me, I'll go down. All the way, Hunt."

"I wouldn't ask unless it was important. I don't have a file number or vic's name, but it's Gray and Abbott's newest case." Keen stalled for a second before he could form the words. "Ava Shepherd is the suspect."

"Oh faaahuck," he said in exaggerated disgust.

"Can you do it?"

"For anybody but the piece of shit who saved my sorry life, no."

"Thanks."

"Ah, don't fuckin' mention it. Really don't. Besides, I like you best when we're even."

The door to the interrogation room opened and Ava stepped out of the room and headed away from him. She wore sandals, frayed shorts, and a flowing green top he could see through. Even though the only thing he could see was a white camisole underneath, Keen's throat tightened.

"Me too, Smokes," he croaked into the phone.

Behind Ava, Beaumont stepped out of the room, but turned to say something to the agents. Keen shoved the phone into his pocket and hurried to catch the long red ponytail that swung back and forth in a rapid tempo.

"Ava?" Keen whispered.

Her pace increased.

"Ava?" He tried again, along with doubling his pace. He caught her at the dull metal doors of the elevator.

She jabbed the down button. "Please, I just want to go home."

"Your mom sent me to—"

"To what?" Her head snapped around and she stabbed him with those jade eyes. "To what, pat my shoulder while the world crumbles around me?"

"She sent me to help..."

How? He hadn't a fucking clue.

"If you truly want to help *me*, let me go home. I'm...I'm..." She huffed a breath. "I'm pissed. I'm confused. I'm...I don't know what I am right now, but I know I'm not a killer."

"I know you're not. You know that. No one thinks you hurt anybody."

"No one?" Her brows shot to the cosmos. She tilted her head to look down the hallway. "The two agents glaring me to death sure think I did."

"They're just doing their job. If they really thought you killed someone they'd indict you. Anyway, I was talking about your family, your friends. No one who really knows you believes you could hurt a fish, much less a human being."

He saw it, then. A tiny softening of her mouth. A flash of widening eyes. She understood the reference. She remembered. He remembered too.

It was the summer of his freshman year of college. Nathan invited him to stay a week in Georgia at his uncle and aunt's house on St. Simons Sound. He'd heard tales of a meek red-headed cousin and seen plenty of pictures, but in all the fishing trips they'd stolen away to take during that first year at Florida State and in all the family visits, he'd never met her.

All the boys had come in off the water, cleaned the boat and the cobia and few snapper they'd caught, filled their bellies with lunch Mrs. Shepherd had made, and passed out on the overstuffed furniture in the den. All except Keen. When they'd gotten back from fishing he'd noticed one of the jet skis was missing and had seen her car in the drive.

Keen sat on the dock for hours sketching, since he only did it when no one else was looking. He mapped the sky, the birds, the boat, and the marsh across the way. Ava zipped through his scene as the sun hedged toward the horizon. Her hair lay wet and matted to her head. The bridge of her nose and tops of her shoulders shone as vibrantly as her hair from the time in the sun.

Ava whipped the jet ski into its place at the dock, climbed the ladder, and stretched onto her tip toes with her arms out wide. His body stirred. When her arms fell to her sides so did her gaze and along with it her smile. She hurried to the bait bucket at the side of the boat. Her slender form hunched over the container and a small cry carried across the yards of deck to Keen's ears. He hadn't known what in the world caused her such distress until she gasped, scooped a cigar minnow into her hand, and then rushed to the water.

They had forgotten to throw the bait they hadn't used back into the water and almost all of them had died. But Ava spent ten minutes scooping out the live ones and placing them in the water.

A ding from the elevator yanked him, and maybe her, back to reality. Ava practically leaped into the car. Keen stepped inside and turned to press the button for the lobby. The scuff of sandals on grimy floor told him she retreated to the back corner. He ignored the pang in his chest proximity to her always incited and the beating his ego took from her withdrawal.

The doors slid together, but at the last moment a hand shot through the opening. It stalled the doors. They opened wide in protest.

"We need to talk." Beaumont swaggered onto the elevator and jabbed a finger at Ava.

Keen shoved the button for the lobby, when he really wanted to shove the arrogant prick off the car and onto his ass. "Going down?"

Beaumont rolled his brown eyes over his shoulder at Keen and turned back to Ava. Her eyes were clenched shut and she gulped long breaths.

"Hey," Beaumont snapped his fingers a few inches from Ava's face. "You've been questioned by the FBI in a murder. This isn't just going to go away. We need to determine a defense."

"Who is it I supposedly killed?" Ava screamed. Her eyes shot wide. Red splotches dotted her sclera.

"What? You don't know who the victim is?" Beaumont echoed Keen's thought.

"No! They wouldn't tell me." Her hands shot up and flailed about.

Beaumont's fingers tightened on the handle of his briefcase. "Why would they do that?"

"They wanted her to slip, give something away." The lawyer turned and leveled his familiar gaze on Keen. "It's a common tactic, but the identity of the victim usually comes out before the suspect leaves the room. It's possible they haven't identified the victim yet."

"Then how would they know to question Ava?" Beaumont shook his head in that slight, condescending way rich people seem to know from birth.

"Evidence at the scene must have pointed them in her direction," Keen answered.

"Hair," Ava's voice cracked on the word.

Keen and Beaumont turned to her. A sheen of moisture coated her eyes, but her stubborn mouth refused to crack. Her lips scrunched in a fierce grimace. As though Ava were going to attack them with tears, their hands shot up, palms out, and their pitches simultaneously raised an octave. "We'll figure this out," Keen said, while Beaumont went with, "I've gotten people off with more against them than that."

Ava averted her gaze to the numbers above the door, and then centered it on Beaumont. "Did you ever stop to think that maybe you shouldn't clear murderers?"

"Oh right." Beaumont nodded. "I forgot I was standing in an elevator with people who only see in black and white. Well, Ava, you're about to learn that in the real world there are a kaleidoscope of colors, and most of them are very ugly."

"What do you know about the real world, pretty boy?" Keen bet the man had never set foot in a low rent housing district much less a war zone.

The elevator chimed its arrival. The doors opened. A smile curved the lawyer's mouth. "You've got it all figured out, don't you, soldier."

Keen wanted to know how the hell the guy knew he'd been in the military, but before he could ask Beaumont stepped to the side and tilted his head for them to go first. Keen let Ava lead the way. They hurried through the lobby in silence except for the echo of their shoes.

Instead of banking left Ava headed for the front door. Keen hitched a finger toward the left. "I'm parked in the garage."

"Then, thanks for coming, and I'll see you around." Ava waved and continued walking.

The last knot on the end of his nerves frayed. "I'm driving you home, Ava, either hog tied in the trunk or buckled in the passenger seat. Your choice."

She stopped dead and pivoted on him, every hint of sadness replaced with spitfire rage. He liked the glint in her eyes better than the sorrow, even if it meant he treaded in shark infested waters. "You wouldn't dare."

"You said that at the wedding." He grinned. "And you know me well enough to know I would."

Beaumont stepped around Keen. "He won't have the chance. I'm driving you home. You need to bring me up to speed tonight."

"Ha!" Ava's green eyes swelled. "Why don't you two beat your chests with your fists and I'll go with the one who makes the most noise? Better yet," she jabbed the air with her index finger, "why don't you just whack me over the head, each grab an arm, and play tug of war?"

"I'll take her right arm." Keen smacked Beaumont's shoulder and stepped forward. "You can take the left, and I'll club her, since you don't hit women."

The lawyer lumbered forward. "Sounds like a plan."

Ava planted her hands on her hips. "It's like dealing with children."

Beaumont cocked his head to the side and found Keen's gaze. "She's a bit dramatic, huh?"

"Dramatic?" Ava scoffed. "I was just questioned by the FBI in a murder."

"Thanks for making our point," Beaumont said.

"It may not look like it, but we're all on the same team here. So, while I think I can help you more than this pretty boy, if you don't want to ride with me, let him bring you home and you can talk on the ride." Keen shrugged.

Her delicate hands slipped down her sides, forming the shirt to her curves. She let them drop and hang limply. "I know you're trying to help, both of you, but I need some time...alone...to process what I've heard. Why don't you guys come over in the morning, and bring breakfast with you. I don't have any food."

Keen tried one more step in her direction. "How are you going to get home? Your car isn't here."

"I'll manage. I have for almost the last fifteen years." Ava quirked a flat smile, turned, walked through the turnstiles, and out the front door.

Both men shuffled slowly to the window. Ava hailed a cab, 2W69, license plate 7800247, and climbed inside.

Beaumont plowed a hand through his tidy hair. "What is it with these hard ass Bureau chicks?

"I'll let you figure out Lara. If you can, you'd be the first. I don't think she's figured herself out yet." Keen rubbed his aching shoulder. "Ava's as tender-hearted as they come. She's just scared and would sooner die than let anyone know it."

Chapter Seven

"I said I was good for it. Just wait right here." Ava tugged on the cab's handle and climbed out the back seat.

"Look, lady—"

She slammed the door, venting just a minute fraction of her irritation on the creaky car.

The front passenger window lowered and the paunchy driver leaned over so far she wondered if he'd be able to sit up. "Look, lady," he continued, "I been burned before. Don't make me call the cops."

The cops. That was all she needed.

"See that car?" She pointed to the unimpressive sedan twenty feet away. "That's my car. Unless someone broke into it, my purse is in the front seat."

"Why the hell would you leave your purse on the front seat of your car in this city?"

Ava buried her face in her hand. All this over eighteen bucks. She didn't have to explain herself, but she wanted to shut him up. Her hand dropped to her side and she cinched her features into a mask of detachment. "Because the FBI agents who took me in for questioning in a murder wouldn't let me bring it in the backseat of their car."

The cabbie's eyes bulged. His cloudy blue gaze studied her. He used the steering wheel and dragged himself upright. "I'll just wait here."

Yeah.

She jogged to her car, punched in the access code, and slung herself inside to retrieve her purse. Only the fingers she clamped over her mouth kept the scream from echoing into the unusually still DC night.

An old newspaper lay over her small handbag. The letters of the headline dripped with wet blood, "Life for the Blood Red Killer."

Ava jumped out of the car. Her gaze shot left, and then hooked right. She searched the street, the illuminated spots on the sidewalk, and the dark shadows of shrubs and small trees. No one jumped out of the bushes. No one ran away. But the tingle racing down her spine told her someone was hiding. Someone was watching the fruits of their handiwork.

Why else would they stage the treat?

To scare the shit out of you.

But if they didn't get to see her reaction it wouldn't be as sweet.

"Hey!"

Every muscle in Ava's body tensed at the cabbie's shout. She exhaled and glanced at the yellow car. "Yep, I'm coming."

She sank back into the car and took several fortifying breaths. The extra napkins in the glovebox came in handy for spills and the handling of evidence. She used the starched paper, gingerly grabbed the edge of the newspaper in her left hand, and shrugged her purse strap onto her right shoulder.

Careful to keep the blood from the cab driver's line of sight, Ava fished a twenty out of her bag. She tossed it through the window and then sprinted to her building. Every corner of the lobby had eyes as she rushed through to the stairwell. In front of the familiar door she jerked to a stop.

Ava slipped her hand into her purse. The need to arm herself pulsed in her veins stronger than the need she'd felt to seek comfort in Keen's arms...before she'd seen the graphic image Lara's words had burned onto her brain. Her fingers probed, but only found her cellphone, wallet, three pens, and a tampon. Too late she remembered the damn thing was still in her trunk...unless the bastard who'd broken into her car had taken it.

A hand wrapped around Ava's right bicep.

In an instant, she balled her fist, pivoted, and thrust the backside of her knuckles at her assailant's nose.

The cabbie? Why would he attack her? Before her sailing fist made contact with the stunned man's already crooked nose it hit something more substantial, jarring her arm.

"Whoa there, slugger." Keen caught her punishing blow in his palm.

Just beyond his hand the cabbie's mouth gaped. His gaze jumped from her fist, inches from his face, to her gaze.

"You never put your hands on someone." Keen's sharp blue eyes aimed at the driver. "Especially when you sneak up on them. And *especially* if it's a woman."

The pot-bellied man thrust his chin at Keen. "She owes me eight bucks. I'll grab anyone who tries to gyp me."

"I gave you a twenty," Ava objected. She also folded the newspaper in half, bloody side down, and stuffed it under her arm.

"You gave me a ten." The cab driver shoved a ten in her face and waved it around.

Keen's head shook. "I should have let her bust your nose."

His thumb rubbed the peaks and valleys of her knuckles before lowering her hand to her side. The path he'd traced tingled long after his touch ceased. Ava longed to rub the sensation away, but didn't dare give any hint that he affected her so blatantly.

He plucked a small leather wallet from his back pocket, and then smacked a ten from it onto the cabbie's chest. "Keep the change."

"Screw you, asshole." The driver crumpled the bill in a plump fist. He snarled at Keen while simultaneously back-pedaling.

"You have a great night." Keen grinned. His gaze slid to Ava's. Her breath caught.

"Ah, everything okay over there?" The smack of Ava's fist and raised voices must have snagged the night watchman's attention. He strode around the corner, using his arms to increase his pace.

"We're fine," Keen said without taking his gaze off her.

"Miss Shepherd?" The watchman peered around Keen's shoulder.

Ava swallowed her fright and the bite of lust that swelled in her throat. "We're fine, thank you." She didn't know his name. She should. He'd been working in the building for the last six months, but she'd never stopped to say hello.

After she gave a reassuring nod the man retreated with extra measured steps.

"Still taking the stairs, I see." Keen said.

"I...yes, if I have a choice." She shrugged. "I see you're still making friends everywhere you go."

"It is a gift." His gaze slipped from hers and traveled to the newspaper wedged under her arm.

"What are you doing here?" She tried to railroad questions about the yellowed and bloody paper. Though, he couldn't see the crimson. Thank goodness for tiny favors.

"I know you've taken care of yourself for a long time. I also know you've had plenty of shitty nights, but you've never had a night quite like this. I wanted to make sure you got home all right."

He knew more than most about her shitty nights, but he didn't know that—up until now—he was responsible for one of the worst nights of her life. Well, in all honestly, she was responsible, but he'd been the reason behind it.

"How'd you know where I live?"

"Your mom."

Of course her over protective mother had blabbed. "Well, thank you. I'm okay and I'm home." She turned and grabbed the knob to the stairwell.

His arm shot out over her head. The spread of his palm curled around the slightly open door, but he didn't pull it wide. He held it, pinning her between the unyielding metal and his unforgiving torso.

"Ava, I'm not your enemy. I'm the farthest thing from it. I'm trying to respect your request here—"

"Is that why I haven't seen you in more than ten years?" The words had no place in this predicament, and yet they tumbled out her lips with ease.

Keen's head bent and his long low exhale heated the back of her neck. "You said it would be easier if we didn't see each other at Shepherd or Brewer family functions."   Though she remained perfectly still her hair shifted under his touch. Ava closed her eyes to hold back tears.

"You were right," he whispered. The barest hint of his hot lips hit the shell of her ear, sending a rush of long dormant need through her. "It was easier not seeing you, smelling you, touching you, but you need someone in your corner. So until your family shows, you're stuck with me."

He stepped back and opened the door. It took her several seconds to remember how to move her feet. So long that his hand cupped the small of her back and ushered her forward. It took a year to climb that flight of stairs. When they finally reached her floor she stopped in the doorway.

What if another newspaper awaited her? If Keen saw it, if he knew someone threatened her, he wouldn't leave no matter how hard she pushed. She couldn't deal with him, maybe ever, but certainly not right now when she needed all her wits about her to figure out who framed her for murder.

"I've got it from here." Ava turned toward his broad chest and stayed him with a hand. The moment her fingers touched the worn shirt and the tautness of the muscles underneath she knew she'd made a fatal mistake. She jerked her hand away as though he were fire.

"Thank you," she choked.

"You've been away from home for a few days. I'm not leaving until I check the inside."

"I'm not a helpless little woman."

"That's right. You have help right here." He hiked a thumb at his sternum.

"Lord, save me from ego inflated men."

"You know, you're really cute when you roll your eyes."

"Just hush. I don't need a knight in shining armor to storm my castle. Okay?"

His brows wrinkled and a smile curved one corner of his mouth. "I thought storming the castle was a euphemism for something else."

Ava's cheeks heated. Her chest flushed. "Look, I'm going into my apartment. You're not. End of this convoluted discussion." She pivoted on the balls of her feet and stormed the ten feet to her door.

"Clear your home. Check under your bed, the shower, closets, and your window locks too, and then blow me a kiss goodnight, and I'll leave."

"Fine." Anything to get him out of her hair.

She retrieved her keys, unlocked the door, and braced to find at least another newspaper inside her threshold and at worst a dead body on her bed. The most sinister thing in the place was the scatter of magazines Annelise had left jumbled on the sofa the other day that Ava hadn't had the time to straighten before she'd left the next morning.

Room by room, Ava cleared her apartment with a strategic sweep, but nothing was amiss. On her way from the bathroom and closet she even opened the side table drawer to make certain all the newspapers were where she'd left them. They were.

When Ava opened the door Keen closed the distance. Her hand tightened on the door knob.

"Don't worry. I'm not storming your castle. At least, not tonight. But you better get some sleep because tomorrow we're going to get to the heart of this thing."

Did he mean them? No.

"The who, the what, the how." He ticked each of them off on his fingers.

"Oh," she mumbled like an idiot. Ava clamped her mouth shut to keep from telling him she already knew the how. Those were issues for tomorrow. The who of the victim would be nice, but tonight she intended to figure out the other who— as in who the hell was doing this to her. "Okay."

His gaze studied her. "You're not going to get any sleep, are you?"

"Goodnight, Keen."

"See you in the morning."

Ava closed the door, locked it, and then quietly placed her eye against the peep hole. She watched him go and she wished she could say it was for the privacy she needed to do what she was about to do, but she watched him because she couldn't rip her gaze away from his prowling shoulders and tight ass.

She flattened her cheek against the cool door and rested there until reality crashed against the front of her skull on a monumental wave. Copycat. Blood Red Killer. Her. Framed.

Her sandals slapped against the hardwood as she dashed through the apartment to the back corner of her closet. She pulled a black case from the top shelf and prayed the damn thing still worked and that she remembered how to use it. Ava grabbed a beach towel from the bathroom, and then skidded to a stop next to her bed.

The headlines peeked out from the drawer. Ava's heart dropped a level in her chest. Each one hit a different nerve, all of them raw. Blood Red Killer Suburban Father, Bloody Red Hardy Confesses, More Victims Come to Light, Bloody Red's Reckoning.

Ava spread the towel onto the floor, set the case next to it, flipped the latches, and flung it open. The musk of years and disuse permeated the lavender scented room. The tips of the puffy white zephyr brush were stained gray from the hundred or more times she'd practiced lifting prints for her forensic science class. Fingerprinting technology had come a long way since she'd been in school, but she didn't trust anyone else to search these papers.

At the moment she had trouble even trusting Keen. Once upon a time, she'd trusted him most of all, but she'd wrecked that.

She opened the jar of aluminum powder. Only a thin layer of the dust coated the glass bottom. Hopefully it would be enough. Ava wrestled on two latex gloves. She grabbed a large plastic bag from the kit, dropped the newest blood coated paper inside, and then sealed the bag. Her tiny apartment didn't have DNA testing capabilities, but she didn't need it tested to know it would match the victim's blood.

Carefully she removed the drawer from the stand and set it on the bed. One at a time she liberated each newspaper and laid them face up on the towel. Despite the rapid tremors of her heart her hands remained steady.

The intercom buzzed.

Ava covered her heart with her hand and swore she caught the thing on its way across the Potomac. Her sternum thumped under her gloved hand for several beats before she grabbed the side of the bed for leverage. She climbed to her feet, stepped around the papers, and hurried to the speaker by the front door.

"Yes?" Her voice quaked.

"Miss Shepherd, it's Tim from the front desk. I'm sorry to call so late, but I have a Miss Braden to see you."

"Oh, thank you, Tim." Ava nearly sagged with relief. She hadn't known who or what to expect. With all the horrors her mind conjured in the scant second since the buzzer rang a visit from her friend hadn't made that grim list. "Please, send her up."

"Yes, ma'am."

She unlocked the deadbolt and knob. Apprehension parched Ava's lips. Annelise knew about her father, but how would she feel about Ava being questioned in a murder so similar to those her father carried out? Annie would probably be pissed that Ava would want to talk about that instead of her potential sexcapades on the trip. At least she hoped her friend would.

Latex squeaked and popped under Ava's wringing hands. The longer it took her friend to make it to the door the more frantic the fidget became. She growled at herself, ripped the things off, and then crumpled them into a ball. There were plenty more in the kit. Before Ava realized her feet created a pacing path from one side of the room to the other.

What the hell took the elevator so long at... What the hell time was it? On her next lap Ava veered into the kitchen and stared at the little green numbers on her microwave. One thirty-three a.m.

A gasp from the other room almost made Ava swallow her tongue.

Shit, when would she stop being so jumpy?

She tossed the gloves onto the counter and walked into the living area.

Annelise stood hunched over the towel of newspapers. Her blonde hair swung back and forth over her shoulders in an eerie cadence. Of course, her friend stared at a display of headlines about her father that she had laid out on her bedroom floor, which warranted an odd shake of the head.

"I'm sorry you had to see those," Ava whispered, surprising herself with the hoarseness of her voice.

Her friend jumped and swiveled. Annie's long fingers spread wide over her mouth, a mouth that gaped.

"I didn't mean to..." Ava couldn't finish the words. Annelise's swollen red eyes stopped her. Shakes vibrated her friend's shoulders and the tips of her hair. "Annie, what's—"

A scream crossbred with a cry and a growl crawled up Annelise's throat and procreated before Ava's eyes. Ava stepped forward and opened her arms.

"Don't you come any closer." Her friend backed into the footboard of the bed. She recoiled at the touch and shrank into herself, becoming as small as Ava had ever seen her.

An unsolicited tear slipped down Ava's cheek. "Annie?"

"Shut up! Shut up! You don't get to say a word," her friend cried.

Ava opened her mouth to speak, but no words came out, as though her body followed Annelise's orders instead of her own. She closed her mouth, banking an unexpected sob.

"How could you?" Annie's fists balled into white-knuckled rage. It righted her posture and seemed to give her strength while it stole the little bit Ava clung to. "I was your best friend. Your only friend."

"I didn't," Ava cried. She didn't know what Annie thought she'd done, but she'd never do anything to hurt her friend. Annie couldn't know about her being questioned in the murder, and if she did, she wouldn't believe it.

Would she?

"You stole my only family." Annelise lurched forward. "You took the only other person who gave a shit about me."

"I don't—"

"No!" Snot slipped out of Annie's nose with the force of her shaking head. "Josie can't talk anymore. You can't talk. You can't say a thing that will make this okay." She slipped at the clear mess with the back of her wet sleeve. "Trent wanted to come and slit your throat. I convinced him that Finn needed him more than he needed revenge because I didn't believe you'd murdered my sister, but now..." Annie's gaze slid to the newspapers in a neat row on the floor. "I should have let him."

"Annie, no! I didn't kill anyone." Ava slapped at the tears streaming her face. "You know me. You know—"

"I know your dad fucked you up. I know my friendship with you killed my sister, and I have to live with that for the rest of my life." Annelise walked backward toward the door as though she feared turning her back.

A sob wracked Ava's torso. "Josie? No, please —"

"Don't you dare say her name." Annie averted her gaze, but kept Ava in her periphery. "I've had days' worth of hours to ask myself why. Why would you take my sister from me?" She braced her hands on either side of the painted wood frame. "Tell me, Ava. At least give me that much."

Ava wiped the tears from her lips. Fresh ones replaced them in seconds. "If I could have taken her place, Annie, I would."

"But then you wouldn't have been able to carry on daddy's twisted legacy." She turned to leave, but stopped. "Oh, you don't have to worry about killing Fiona. Saturday when I found out about Josie, I went to the hospital because I couldn't get ahold of her and I caught her cheating on me with some bimbo nurse. So, I officially have no one left for you to take."

The fissures in Ava's heart split in a fiery burst. "Annelise?"

Her friend closed the door so quietly she didn't even hear the click of the knob and yet it brought Ava to her knees. She collapsed forward with her head in her hands. Tears dripped like a tiny leak in a damn. Pressure built inside, threatening to obliterate her brain. But the damn thing refused to leave her in peace. Questions and utter despair swirled in dizzying loops for too long.

If Annie thought she killed her sister, the only way to make her believe otherwise was to prove someone else killed Josie.

Ava scrambled on slick hands and knees from her puddle to the row of newspapers. Print type swam in her watery gaze. She used the backs of her hands to collect her tears, and then wiped them on the sides of her shorts. Her hands quaked on their way to the canister of metallic powder. The metal lid scraped against the glass. Ava covered her teeth with her lips and shuddered through another wave of anguish.

The soft bristles danced on the end of the zephyr brush between her fingers. She dragged in a deep breath and slowly released it, much like she did before shooting at the range. After two more breaths the tremors eased enough that she eased the wand inside the jar and collected the silver dust.

She knocked off the excess powder, and then started at the top left of the first aged paper. The fibers swiveled across the page in even rows.

When a bit of the aluminum collected at the bottom edge of her brush Ava quit breathing. She longed to skip to the spot, but she maintained the straight, uniformed pattern. Her lungs burned with the need to breath, but she didn't dare. On the next line the closer the bristles came to the simmering mark the more she leaned toward the paper.

"What?"

The dust collected in a wide line, not a nice round print. It could be a smudge, but the even lines were too deliberate.

Ava swiveled and circled her brush to the next line. Then the next. An identical line revealed itself parallel to the first. Fast and faster she moved. The sixth line exposed a wide arch.

Sweat gather on Ava's upper lip. Agitation boiled her patience to steam. This wasn't a fingerprint. Already halfway done with the page and she hadn't found one. She broke and swiped the powder diagonally down the center of the page.

"No!" Ava pinned her gaze to the ceiling and willed the smeared word to disappear. "No! No! No!" Her gaze plummeted to the page, but the letters b, l, o, o, d, y remained.

"Bloody." She choked on the word.

Ava reloaded her brush and repeated the pattern on the second page. "Red." And the third. "Hardy."

Tears dripped off Ava's nose. Small letters swam in inky pools. It didn't much matter. Whoever left these for her to find had planned her downfall with elaborate and intricate detail.

She sucked a shaky breath and dusted the fourth page.

Her finger wrapped around the glass container of aluminum dust. She hefted the jar and hummed it across the room.

The bottom edge formed a chalky white dent in the sheet rock. Metal powder scattered across the floor while some of it exploded into a cloud gloomy enough to match her mood and her future.

"Bloody Red Hardy Lives."

Chapter Eight

Fog finally glazed the last section of the windshield. Keen tossed himself into the seat and looked around. Visual clarity of zero left him damn near as vulnerable as open windows. He leaned over and yanked the latch of the rental's glove box, and then slammed it shut. He'd already tried the center console. Not a napkin in the joint.

Sweat suctioned his boys to the side of his leg and broke the stalemate. He placed his foot on the brake, rolled down all four windows with the touch of a button, and sneered at technology. Computers had no place in automobiles. It stole the mechanical artistry from history and replaced it with sensors and microprocessors.

Keen unlatched his seatbelt and scrubbed his hands through his hair. He'd staked out about a thousand different places and people in his day. So why the hell was he fidgeting like a toddler on a sugar high? Probably because the word stalker scrolled across his brain like a news alert ticker. He wasn't pulling a paycheck off the job, but he'd been commissioned to "be there" for Ava all the same. Too bad four stories, some brick, distance, and metal was as close as she'd let him get.

The haze cleared on a hot breeze. So far he'd cataloged a homeless man shuffling his way down the street, a group of guys who stumbled their way into the building, and a hot blonde with soaked cheeks and sad eyes. Since the blonde left nearly an hour ago no one had moved a muscle except him. If New York was the city that never slept, DC was the city that liked its eight hours. Keen liked his sleep too. Somehow it never seemed to like him back.

He scooted the seat back as far as it would go, and then worked on the recline, not too much, just enough that his breaths didn't fog the glass again. His shorts defied gravity, riding high enough to classify as the boy shorts only girls wore. He wrestled the ends down, huffed, and then leaned forward to glare at Ava's window. If she'd just let him in...

Ava's windows had morphed into ominous black panes.

Maybe she'd gone to bed, but Keen couldn't imagine the suspicious woman he'd once known snuggled in bed while her life took a nose-dive into the shitter.

Instinct—also known as the nauseous feeling in his gut—forced him out of the car. He retrieved his sidearm from the door pocket and stuffed it at the small of his back. Quick and quiet, his steps lead him toward the front door.

Halfway to the awning Winslow Gray stepped out of the front door and held it open.

How the fuck had he missed Winslow? Damn humidity and fogged glass.

Ava walked out of the door backward. Her finger jabbed at Lara Abbott's face and her head bobbed. One more step onto the street and Keen heard every salty word that flew out of his fiery red head's mouth.

"Hell no. I cooperated last time and you didn't even have the decency to tell me who it was I supposedly killed. You couldn't say, 'Hey, your best friend's sister was murdered. Oh, and she thinks you did it because that's what we told her.' So," Ava added a bob of her head, "your resting bitch-face self and your mute-as-shit partner can go fuck yourselves. And—"

"What the hell are you two doing now?" Keen sprinted the distance between them before Lara knocked her into yesterday.

Winslow grabbed Ava's wrists and wrenched them behind her. She snarled, but didn't cry out. But one close up look at her swollen, bloodshot eyes told him she'd been crying all right.

"We're taking her in." The big guy jutted his chin and puffed his chest.

"Weren't y'all just there?" Keen hitched a brow.

"This isn't your concern, Hunt," Lara added.

He chuckled, but soon it turned into an all-out laugh.

All three of them looked at him with slacked faces and high brows.

"What?" Abbott sneered.

"You know, Hunt and cunt rhyme?" He put a hand over his aching abs and giggled some more.

"Put her in the car," Abbott ordered.

"Why are they taking you in?" he asked Ava.

"They have another victim," she grimaced. "Can you find out who it is? I can't handle another surprise like that." Winslow wrestled her into the back of their SUV, but she ducked her head around him. "Call Beaumont to meet me at headquarters. I want a lawyer."

He shifted to get closer to the 4Runner parked on the opposite side of the door from him, but Lara stepped in his path. "I'll do it," he hollered.

"You're such a loyal dog, to her at least." Lara grinned.

"I never slept with that girl," Keen whispered. "I didn't even feel her up. I just needed you to see me with someone, so you'd be pissed enough to leave me alone. Our situation needed to end for both our sakes, but you wouldn't listen. I am sorry if I hurt you."

"Ever heard the expression too little, too late?" she whispered back.

"It's all I have to offer." His lips compressed and he shrugged.

Lara shook her head. "You're offering it for her benefit."

"I'm offering it because I was immature and... I don't know..."

"Damaged goods?" she supplied.

"Yeah," Keen agreed.

"We both were. Damaged and immature." Lara didn't apologize, but he figured it was the closest thing to it he'd ever get from her. She averted her gaze. "But it doesn't mean I'm going to let you in on our investigation."

"It's a witch hunt."

"We have her hair."

"Do you have anything else?"

"We don't need anything else."

The SUV's engine roared to life. Lara ran to the car without another word. The black beast lit off the curve with enough extra juice it revved Keen's competitive side. He ran to the open door of the rental and dove inside. One rolled-through stop sign and several miles over the speed limit later he caught sight of them a block ahead.

Her best friend's sister. They could have told her. They should've told her. Whoever killed these people and framed Ava wasn't doing it because of some legacy. They did it to shatter her.

Keen grabbed his phone and called the number Mrs. Shepherd used when they spoke earlier.

Preston Shepherd answered after the first ring. "Is Ava okay?"

"She just told the investigators to go fuck themselves. So, I'd say she's holding up." He left out the bit about the tears and her bestie's sister being the victim.

"I'd say. She sounds like her mother talking to the ticket lady at the airline. We're stuck here for a day longer, at least. Maybe forever the way Sarah cut into that woman."

"Preston, I need you to have Beaumont meet Ava back at headquarters immediately."

"He told me earlier that they finished questioning her."

"They're bringing her back in for more."

"Why?"

"There's another body."

"Jesus Christ," Preston yelled.

"I don't really think this is his territory."

"I'll call him right now," Preston said before ending the call.

Keen caught a light at the next intersection. Had the patrol cop not been rolling past a pair of teenagers who had no business being out so late he'd have blown through it without blinking. Ten minutes later he pulled into the deserted parking garage and eased through until he found the black 4Runner with the sticker on the back window of a screaming gorilla pressing a bar stacked with plates. Like people couldn't look at Winslow and tell he had a close personal relationship with his gym.

"Right."

He pulled in next to the mute gym rat's car, grabbed his phone, and opened the door. Headlights crossed Keen's field of vision momentarily blinding him.

A sleek 1967 Corvette Coupe rumbled to a stop two spaces away. The shiny black paint, chrome trim and wheels gleamed in the florescent light. Its driver cut the engine and stepped out.

Keen stood and locked his rental. "How'd you get here so fast?"

"I was at the office two blocks away."

"Next question. How in the hell does a defense lawyer have such amazing taste in cars?"

Beaumont adjusted the same tie he'd had on earlier, secured his car, and then matched his steady steps heading for the elevator. "I had a thing for putting together model cars as a kid. When I got old enough I wanted a real one."

"Do you work on it?"

"No, but one day I'd like to learn."

"All you need is a service manual and a garage full of tools."

"I'd be afraid to mess her up."

"You will, but you two will eventually come to an understanding."

"I may have called you a grease monkey because I'm a little envious."

"Or you may have called me a grease monkey because I was acting like an asshole."

"There's that too." He pressed the down button on the elevator. "Any idea who the newest victim is?"

"No, I'm working on it."

"You have contacts on the inside—"

"Which I won't talk about to you or anyone else."

"I don't want you to rat them out. I just want to know you're willing to go the extra mile to help."

"There's not much I wouldn't do to help her."

"Good."

"I just need to break into an office and commandeer a computer."

"Try the second floor..." Beaumont squinted. "First door on the left. Name plate Rachel Canna. Access code 1980." When Keen raised both brows he added, "We shared lunch a few times."

"In her office?"

"With the blinds closed. Don't ask."

Keen offered his palms. "I was just admiring the security of our fine headquarters."

"You were going to break in."

"True." They stepped onto the elevator and Keen pressed the button for the lobby. "She doesn't want to answer any questions and she requested her attorney."

"Ava Shepherd?"

"She's pissed. When she gets pissed all bets are off. The first victim is her best friend's sister and they didn't tell her. They're not giving. Make sure she doesn't give. And don't leave without me."

"We won't. After we left I did some research on you. I think you're what Ava needs to get out from under this thing."

They hit the lobby at a brisk pace and made it through security with minimal hassle. Keen headed for the stairs while Beaumont veered toward the building's main elevators.

"If you get her out before I'm done, meet me at your old stomping ground. If I get done first, I'll see you outside interrogation."

Beaumont nodded. "Good luck."

"To us all."

***

"I'm driving her home and you're not going to argue with me on this." Keen said after Ava disappeared behind the bathroom door in the lobby of FBI headquarters.

"I'm not?" Beaumont frowned.

"No."

"It's what people pay me to do, especially at..." He paused to look at his Rolex. "Especially at three o'clock in the morning. So, why am I not going to argue?"

"I need more time to read the original Hardy file, but I think I know how to get her out of this."

"Just like that?" Beaumont leaned his shoulders against the wall.

"It's a hunch, but after three bullet holes I've learned not to question my gut."

"Maybe your gut needs to speed its alert process." He twirled his fingers around in a circle, and then tugged on the knot of his tie.

"It told me in plenty of time. I just didn't listen."

"So what in those files is going to get her out of this?"

"You don't want to know." Keen switched the thick stack of papers into his right hand.

"Wouldn't have asked if I didn't." Beaumont snapped the end of the tie through his collar and stuffed it into his pocket.

"The clues are in these files, but I'll have to dig *elsewhere* for the answers."

The man's strong jaw waggled back and forth. "You're right. I don't want to know. I would like to know about your and Ava's history together."

"Tough shit."

The bathroom door opened. Both men straightened and turned to Ava.

"Okay then." Beaumont shifted his briefcase. "Ava, I think you should let Special Agent Hunt drive you home."

"All right." Her head shook so emphatically it looked more like a tremor. "Let's go." She swiveled and marched toward the exit.

"That was way too easy," Keen said.

The first hint of a laugh rumbled from Beaumont. "I figured you were going to have to follow through on that hog tying threat."

"Ya'll are hilarious. Now come on." Ava coaxed them with a hand.

"I'm going to go back upstairs and pester Lara, try and stall that warrant." Beaumont walked backward in the general direction of the elevators. "As it is they probably won't be able to get it until lunch or later tomorrow, but every bit helps."

"Thank you," the befuddling red head called out over her shoulder and kept walking.

Keen touched his brow with two fingers and took out after Ava.

"Keep me informed, Hunt." Beaumont's words echoed through the open space.

"But not too informed," Keen said.

That earned him a curious look from Ava, but she didn't break pace. After seeing him on the move she actually picked it up several beats.

"Will you slow down?"

"Will you come on." She blew through the turnstiles and then out the front door only slowing when she slammed the call button for the elevator. "I thought field agents had to pass a more strenuous test than us desk jockeys?"

"Extended time in a hospital bed puts a hurting on stamina. Not to mention all the blood loss."

Ava really looked at him for the first time. The elevator arrived and they stepped in together. "I'm sorry. I didn't even think..."

"I'm not an invalid. I just pushed a little too hard yesterday." He pressed the button that would bring them to his rental.

"You would."

Keen grabbed the back of his neck and squeezed. Of all the times for her to bring up old stuff, this was the worst.

"I didn't mean it like that," she whispered. "I just meant you don't take it easy on yourself. You hold yourself to a higher standard than anyone else would hold you to. Darndest thing is you usually hit your mark and make the rest of us look like slackers."

"Says the woman who's put away over forty serial sons of bitches."

"Who's now in a class among them." As soon as the doors opened she rushed out. "What are you driving?"

"That white piece of crap." He pointed to the sedan.

"It's a brand new car."

"Yep." Keen unlocked the car. They got in and buckled up. "Look at this thing. It doesn't even have a key."

"It's called technology."

"Or an abomination." Keen shoved the files between his seat and the door.

"What are those?"

The sedan whined as he backed it out of the space and headed down the ramp. "The Blood Red Copycat file."

"What?" she gasped. "Why didn't you tell me?"

"I just did."

"Earlier."

"I got them while you were in interrogation."

"How?"

"I can't tell you," he said simply.

"I want to see them."

"I want you to tell me why you're in such a hurry to get to your apartment."

She hesitated. "If you'd just been questioned by the Bureau, wouldn't you be in a hurry to leave if they let you?"

"Nice deflection." Keen flipped the turn signal and wheeled onto the main thoroughfare.

"You deflected first." Ava grabbed a ponytail holder from somewhere, fought her hair into a pile on the top of her head, and secured it.

"Where'd you find that holder?"

"On the floor."

"Are you worried about cooties?"

"Bigger problems here." She rolled her beautiful eyes and sighed. "I want to see the file."

"And you can. Just not tonight."

"Why the hell not?"

"Because you're holding on by a thread and I'm not ready for your free fall, and neither are you."

"I'm fine."

"Look at your hands."

Slowly she lowered her head. Her hands vibrated like an eight-point earthquake rocked the ground. Ava balled them into fists, and then straightened her fingers. The quiver remained. She stuffed them under her legs. "Shit."

Her shredded voice cut right through him.

He needed to get her talking. "Did they tell you the name of the second victim?"

She didn't respond for several seconds. When seconds stretched into a minute Keen shifted his gaze. Ava stared at her quaking hands without seeing them.

"Ava?"

"What?" Her gaze lifted to his.

"Did they tell you the name of the second victim?"

"No."

"Not even with all your swearing?"

She half scoffed, half laughed. He considered it a major win.

"I've never talked to anyone like that. Never screamed like that either. I couldn't stop myself."

"It was bound to happen. You can't keep everything so bottled up. Eventually the top pops off and wham."

"Oh, God!"

Keen's gaze whipped left to right, and then back to front. He didn't see an impending collision. "What is it?"

"What if I snapped, had a mental break, and went on a killing spree?"

"That is the stupidest thing I've heard all day, and I've heard things that topped crazy today. The first of them being that you murdered someone. Why would you say that?"

"Just forget it."

"Not likely."

"Take this right. It'll cut out three minutes. Maybe five with no traffic."

"That ready to get away, huh?"

When she didn't speak he decided to keep his mouth shut. She had plenty to deal with and didn't need his shit added to it. He veered right like she suggested. Three minutes later they pulled into the spot where Lara and Winslow had parked to take her away.

"I appreciate what you've done for me. I'm sorry my mom made you come all this way. I'd hoped she wouldn't bother you, but I should've known better than to waste my breath with her."

"She's worried about you."

"She has a lot of guilt from before, but it wasn't her fault."

"It wasn't yours either. It isn't now."

"Huh."

Ava's finger wrapped around the handle and pulled. They didn't shake as much as they had, but she still wouldn't want to apply makeup. Not that she needed any. He climbed out of the car with the file in tow and met her at the front door.

"You don't have to walk me in."

"I'm not."

"Oh." Her shoulders relaxed and she nearly smiled. "Then goodnight."

He grinned, opened the door, and walked in ahead of her.

"You said you weren't walking me in," she whispered as loudly as her regular talking voice.

They looked to see if they'd drawn an audience, but no one lingered in the entry. The night watchman had deserted his post.

Keen continued walking. "I'm not. I'm coming up."

"No, you're not." Her hips waggled with her rushed steps, trying to keep up with him for a change.

The stairwell door creaked under his hand. When he pulled it wide she dipped around him, much like she'd done to Winslow, and barricaded the walkway with her body.

His gaze sank into hers. At this distance the broken blood vessels in her eyes looked like tiny bomb blasts. More disheartening, the fractures of brown that defined her green eyes pulled him under like they used to. "If you think I flew hundreds of miles to drive you from an interrogation room to your condo, you really aren't as smart as I've given you credit for being. For starters, we need to talk about the case they have against you."

A huge sigh escaped her lips. It tickled and warmed his neck.

"I'm exhausted. I'm in shock. I can't even function. I..."

"Then we'll talk in the morning," he agreed.

She perked up a little with a stern gesture toward the open door. "Then I'll see you in the morning."

He ducked under her arm and started up the stairs. "That's for sure."

When he reached the main door of her apartment she freaked. Her hands and voice trilled. "You can't stay here! I don't have a guest room. I..."

Keen cupped the tops of her shoulders.

Her gasp quieted her argument.

"I'm not trying to get in your pants, Ava. I'll sleep on the couch. Just go into your room, close and lock the door, if it makes you feel better. You need some sleep."

"I don't have a bedroom door. The bedroom and living area are one and the same."

"Do you have a bathroom?"

Her chin bobbed.

"Then change in it, and if you sleep in the nude I promise not to peek for more than ten seconds." He turned her toward the door and gave her a little shove.

"Just come back in a few hours."

"Fine, but you won't get to see the files."

Her mouth gaped, and then snapped shut. "You weren't going to let me see them tonight anyway."

"Right, but I was going to let you see them eventually."

Ava stood rigid for a second, and then her forehead bumped into the door with a thud. "I'm not getting rid of you, am I?"

"Not until we get this mess figured out."

The thought of leaving her hurt already and he'd only been in her presence for the sum of an hour. And most of that time she'd spent trying to get rid of him. He needed to slam his head in the door.

"Fine." She took a key from her pocket and slid it into the door. "Just don't freak out."

That peaked his interest. "I promise not to freak out for more than ten seconds."

Ava threaded her fingers through several loose strands at the back of her neck and shoved them through a stranger's ponytail holder. After she dragged in a long breath she unlocked the door, swung it wide, and stepped back for him to enter. "Just remember you promised."

He stepped into Ava's home and indexed several things at once. It smelled like her, soft and sweet with a mysterious edge. The colors on the walls surprised him. Before everything she'd owned was white. Aluminum powder and glass littered the floor. A nice dent concaved the sharp paint job.

Judging by the scatter and indention she'd thrown it from the other side of her bed. He moved farther into the room and stopped cold.

The headlines were as familiar as the Pledge of Allegiance. The messages uncovered on them, not so much.

"Where'd you find them?" he asked in an amazingly even tone, considering the frenzy blistering just under his skin.

"Under the edge of my door."

"Did you test to make certain they can fit under your door when it's closed? Whoever left you these could make it look like they dropped it off under the door, when they were actually inside your apartment."

"I didn't think about that." She rushed around him and to the paper farthest from him.

"Don't use the paper."

"Grab about three of those magazines and try. Did they come all together?"

"One at a time."

Her answer ramped his irritation. "When did it start?"

"Two months ago."

"Did you tell anyone about them? The police? A coworker? Your family?"

"No." Ava grabbed the magazines and scurried toward the door.

"Fucking hell, Ava!" Keen stepped into her path.

"You promised not to freak." She pointed at him with the rolled tips of the magazines.

"For more than ten seconds. I still have two seconds." He stepped forward, pushing her a bit with his chest. "How could you not tell anyone about this?"

"I didn't know the messages were there."

"The headline and dated papers weren't enough of a message for you?"

"Time's up." She ducked around him and dropped to her knees in front of the door.

He tried really hard not to think about Ava on her knees in front of him, but fuck.

"And no, it wasn't enough for me to tell anyone. If I told someone about every ugly note, prank call, or heckler who passed my way, I'd never get any work done." She shoved the stacked Cosmo, Elle, and Marie Claire under the threshold.

"It's still that bad?"

"Sometimes." With a wiggle and some oomph they cleared the door. "It goes in waves." She turned her head and met his gaze. "I didn't think this time was any different."

Chapter Nine

He stood in the center of her apartment with an angry twitch in his jaw and sad eyes. Maybe she liked the freakout better than the sympathy. His sympathy weakened her defenses.

"I have to get rid of them tonight. Abbott and Gray could be here with that warrant any minute. If I get caught with these... Well, it'll make a terrible situation look that much worse."

"Depends on how you're looking at the picture. Somebody's threatening you, setting you up for murder."

"And if you look at it from the other side?" She didn't give him a second to answer. "I can't prove it. There aren't any fingerprints on these. With the exception of mine. They could look at these as keepsakes or threats I made to send to someone." She pulled the band from her hair, situated the strands, and then tied it up into a fresh knot. "Annelise, that's my best friend, my best friend for more than two years. She sure thought these convicted me."

"She saw them?"

"Yeah."

"Give me one of those Dexter-sized Ziplocks from your kit. I'll put them in my trunk and grab my bag."

"No." She used the handle and pulled herself off the floor. Apparently murder accusations zapped the tendons in your knees and made collapse a real possibility. "If I go down for this, it'll make you an accessory."

"You're not going down."

"Innocent people go to prison every day."

"Not every day." His gaze tightened on her. "You've been spending too much time with Beaumont."

He'd yet to notice the fifth paper—

"Tell me about the already bagged newspaper," he requested without shifting his gaze from hers. "What makes it different?"

So much for small favors.

"I found it in my car after Abbott and Gray questioned me the first time."

Keen's nose and upper lip crinkled.

"No, I didn't tell you. I still hadn't found the messages."

His head tilted ever so slightly. "So why didn't you dust it for prints?"

"Its headline…" He ushered her on with a hand. "It's covered in blood. The victim's, I assume."

"Fu…" His mouth clamped shut. Ever the stickler for a promise. "You didn't want to contaminate it." He stared at the ground and bobbed his head as though working things out in his head. "But we really need to know if there's another clue."

He rubbed a hand over his mouth. The blond whiskers on his chin scraped like sandpaper. For a second Ava forgot about everything and wondered what those little hairs would feel like rubbing across her skin.

"Do you have plastic wrap?"

She heard his question, but couldn't quite get her mouth to cooperate with an answer. A nod worked all the same. It was cruel really, how the brain could compartmentalize the most horrific things. One second she contemplated the palatability of jail food, the next her mouth watered over the assured deliciousness of her ex.

Keen took off into the kitchen. Cabinets squeaked. Drawers zoomed on their rollers, and then smacked back into the counter.

"The drawer by the refrigerator," Ava hollered.

Yellow box in hand he rushed through her apartment. It thudded onto the ground by the newspapers. He bent next to her kit and carefully deposited each paper into its own bag, before setting it to the side.

"See if you can salvage any of that powder." Keen eyed the mess on her floor.

"It's probably contaminated."

"Desperate times." He winked, and then dismissed her, reaching for the bloody paper on her bed.

Ava shoved at the wild flyaways tickling her forehead and made her way to the wreckage that perfectly represented her life. Small shards littered pretty piles of the metallic powder. It coated tiny dust bunnies she hadn't known existed around her baseboards. She honed in on the largest chunk of glass, but only a small dime sized pile of aluminum sat in the awkward bowl it made. With no better options she retrieved the jagged hunk of glass and carried it to the make-shift work area.

Keen's large hands delicately folded the plastic around the back of the newspaper, covering the bloody top section. She knelt next to him and set the glass and powder on top of the towel.

He flipped it over in front of her. "Do your thing."

The bold crimson print smacked her square in the face. Each breath burned. Small fissures of light darted through her field of vision like the opening of *Star Wars* only not near as cool.

Warmth encompassed Ava's wrist. She blinked, still saw the shooting stars, but sifted her gaze to the left.

"Breathe."

Air mixed with the scent of a dangerous man filled her lungs. Keen posed almost as much a threat as this maniac killing people and framing her, because he owned her heart. She'd do well to remember that.

"Again," he ordered.

Her gaze shifted to his. She swallowed and breathed him in once more. The fine lines that had bracketed his eyes the last time she'd let her eyes wander with him this close had deepened. The innocent eyes she'd drowned in too many times to count possessed a sexy and heartbreaking worldliness.

"It's just a piece of paper with some blood on it." Keen lifted her hand from the top of her thigh, his fingers grazing her bare skin. He slipped the zephyr brush between her fingers. "Let's get to work."

"Okay." Ava reclaimed her hand and her composure. She loaded the brush, carefully tapped off the excess, and dusted the lower half of the page in concentric circles.

The tips of a U appeared first. Then the arch of an O. A few passes later the word you and the arch of a lowercase n collected the powder.

"You never..." Keen whispered.

Ava continued dusting.

Something hit the apartment door.

She dropped the brush and clamped her lips together to keep from screaming as the thump reverberated through her.

Keen's muscled calves leaped over the towel and blurred past her. "Where's your gun?"

"Closet."

He deftly drew a pistol from the small of his back. His right palm held the grip at the center of his chest while his left braced the weapon. At the door his steps slowed. His ear cocked toward the door.

She heard it too. Retreating footfalls.

"Get it and stay here." The door yawned under Keen's demands.

"I'm not a child," she hollered, but he probably didn't hear. His feet thundered down the corridor in pursuit. Ava glanced at herself, sitting on the floor with shaky hands—yet again. "You look like a child."

She leapt up and bound to the closet. The matte black S & W smiled up at her from the top drawer. It weighted her hand perfectly. Some women like diamonds. Ava liked guns. She stuffed an extra magazine in her back pocket and sprinted for the front door.

Before sailing out the door, she grabbed her keys off the bed, and then locked the knob. Ava's first foot out of the apartment landed on a raised surface and rolled off the edge of her dainty sandals.

Her left hand and hip landed hard on the gritty corridor. Keys skid across the slick floor. She maintained the grip on her gun. Dull pain throbbed, but she didn't give it her attention.

Ava's gaze locked on the thick paper folded in half in the middle of the hallway. Red stained the center edges.

Had the killer left this? Had Keen caught him?

The smooth bottom of her shoes slipped on the floor. She powered through it and jumped to her feet. Using the tip of her shoe, she shoved the paper inside, and then closed the door.

Whether out of instinct or habit her legs carried her to the stairwell. On the second story her grip on the rail tightened, but a buoyancy she hadn't experienced in years lifted her heart out of her toes. Keen pinned a man by the neck to the floor. Grungy pants covered flailing legs.

"Oh, thank God," she sighed.

The man's hands wrestled with the deck shoe compressing his esophagus.

"I thought we moved past this already." Keen's leg muscles flexed. "Stop fighting. Answer my questions and I'll let you go."

"Let him go?" Ava gasped.

"Open your eyes, Ava. He's not our guy."

Sweat stains marbled his white T-shirt. Gnarly red dots tracked his arms. The man's grease slicked hair revealed dilated pupils. His grimace flashed the black edges of rotted teeth.

No.

Hope seeped through the ventricles of her heart like helium out of a balloon. Only her grip on the railing kept her upright, but the quiver in her knees made that tenuous at best.

"Who gave you the paper?" Keen asked.

The junkie gurgled.

"Oh, you're going to cooperate?"

Another gurgle.

"If you try to get up or spit on me, you'll regret it," Keen warned.

Gurgles.

"If you insist." Keen's knee bent slightly.

The guy heaved breaths, his chest rising and falling in rapid succession. Dirty fingers tried to slip underneath the sole of the shoe, keeping him from air. Keen gave him just enough room. The man cocooned his throat.

"The paper," Keen reminded. "Who gave it to you?"

Ava leaned forward, but couldn't understand the man's gruff whisper.

"Louder." Keen demanded. His palm came up to keep her back.

The wide spread and calluses didn't work. She descended the next three steps on rubber legs, desperate to hear the man's cracked words.

The addict moved so fast Ava choked on a yelp. His left hand shot out. Cold, moist fingers locked around her ankle and pulled hard. Her slick bottomed sandal glided off the step. As she fell her gaze fixed on the man's dark, uneven fingernails millimeters from her pale skin.

Her grip doubled on the railing. A chip of gray paint flecked off and hit her eye lid. In a furious blink Ava became the rope in her own horror show tug of war. She kicked blindly with her other leg, but connected with air.

A deep thud echoed off the stairwell. The pressure around her ankle grew lax. Another thud and the man's grip released.

She clambered up to the landing and leaned against the cool wall. Her legs automatically drew to her chest. The man huddled in the fetal position, clutching his side.

Keen stood over him. A detached reserve relaxed his shoulders, but a dark glint framed his eyes. "Who gave you the paper?"

"A little guy," the man groaned. "A little guy."

"A kid or a Little Person?" Keen whispered. The drop in his voice sent a chill up Ava's spine. This guy wondered dangerously close to a chasm with a spiny bottom.

"Kid." Beads of sweat rolled off the junkie's forehead and puddled on the floor.

"How old?" He asked.

"I don't know. Ten. Too young to be out so late." The guy flopped onto his back. "He gave me the address and instructions, the newspaper, and a hundred bucks to deliver it."

Keen stepped back, his muscles loose and ready for anything. "What was to stop you from taking the money and splitting."

A tear seeped from the prone man's eye. "The kid gave me something else."

"What?"

The tear grew to a sob. "No please."

"What?" Keen ordered.

The junkie opened his hands wide in defense. "It's in my pocket."

"Get it. Slowly."

As ordered he eased an envelope from his grimy pants and handed it to Keen.

Keen opened the flap and pulled out a square of paper or maybe a picture. "Get lost."

"No," Ava hollered.

The man rolled onto all fours, and then sprinted out of sight before Ava climbed to her feet.

"Why'd you let him go? We could have used him as a witness."

"We have all we're going to get from him." Keen held the edge of the envelope in one hand and an almost square piece of paper in the other.

"What is it?" Ava's feet carried her down the steps.

"The writing at the bottom matches your newspapers, and I guarantee only the kid's and junkie's prints are all over this stuff. The instruction sheet with your address on it is in here too."

Keen stuffed the paper that wasn't a paper at all, but two Polaroids, back into the envelope.

"What are they pictures of?"

Keen's gaze met hers. "His first two victims."

She staggered. "After..."

"Yes. And there's a message split between them. On the first, 'Cross me.' On the second, 'And This is You.'"

Ava sank to the step and lowered her head between her knees. Her breaths came in heavy panted waves.

"I told you to stay in the apartment." He reached for her gun in the death grip of her right hand.

She jerked defensively. Her gaze landed on her finger resting against the trigger guard, flew to the barrel, and then to Keen's chest only inches from the circular chamber. "Shit. I..." Her hand released its titanium grip. She offered it hammer first.

Deft fingers collected it from her hand. "When was the last time you slept?"

She shrugged.

His hand wrapped around her upper arm and lifted. "Come on. Go shower, wash off the day. Or try, at least. I'll take care of this."

Her chest squeezed. He remembered. Any time she had a shitty day, she'd scrub it off and wash it down the drain. It'd take a hell of a lot of scrubbing and an extra-large drain to make today disappear.

One step at a time, she ascended the stairs with Keen by her side, someplace she hadn't expected him to be again. Not after what she'd done.

Like a gentleman he didn't say anything when he plucked her keys off the floor, and then opened her apartment. Ava groaned. His hand at her shoulder steered her inside. The bloody newspaper lay in the middle of her floor like a gator in wait. He maneuvered her around it.

"Go shower. If you still take an hour, this'll all be gone when you get out."

Her gaze honed on the closet door. "Thank you."

"Anytime."

Ava took one step and another until the scent of clothes and soap enveloped her. She closed the door, locked it, took one more step, and caught movement in her periphery. Her feet left the carpet, but she managed to clamp her scream off before it split her closet in two.

For the second time in the very long day she'd jumped at her own reflection. She very well should. The woman staring back had wild eyes, hair as greasy as the junkie's, and skin with the consistency and color of chalk. One touch and she might crumble.

She inhaled, closed the bathroom door, and glared at herself. It wasn't any easier than it had been just a few days ago when Annelise had wanted her to, but the distance between her and her father vanished in the matter of seconds. It had been a bubble, clear and fragile, but she'd clung to it all the same. A bubble in the tornado of her life. No surprise it hadn't lasted long.

Her hands bracketed her face and hovered there for a minute or more. Her breaths heated her

palms, lifted and sank her shoulders. The tips of
her fingers quivered. A handful of minutes later she
worked up enough courage to trace the bridge of
her nose, the sunken hollows of her eyes, the line of
her cheeks, the curve of her jaw.

Before she'd enrolled in college she'd
convinced her mom to take her to a specialist. The
doctor had asked why she'd want to change such a
perfectly symmetrical face.

People pay me to give them this gentle slope.

He'd touched the tip of her nose.

"I don't want perfection. I want different." She
breathed her answer to herself. Too bad a different
nose hadn't made her see her father in her
reflection any less.

The door to the apartment opened, and then
closed.

Her fingers traveled down her neck to the
hem of her shirt and camisole. Ava pulled it over
her head and tossed it onto the floor, three feet
from her dirty clothes basket. She stared at the
small breasts most girls would've gone ahead and
plus sized while they were at it. The clasp of her bra
popped easily under her hand. It fell into the
growing pile.

When her gaze hit the button on her shorts
panic compressed her throat. Tears slid down her
cheek. They dripped onto her breasts and rolled
down her belly. Shame was harder to face than the
past, but she refused to let her mistakes rule her
any longer.

Ava's grip slipped on the wet button. Once.
Twice. Three times. She set her quaking jaw and
ripped the thing open with a grunt. The tears
continued, soaking the edge of her waistband,
turning the fabric to a deep khaki. The cloth shorts
crumpled in her fists.

The burn of emotion and alarm stung her lungs. She sucked one more breath, held it, and yanked the shorts off her hips. A bubbled tip of scar tissue peeked from the lace of her panties. Her hands and jaw clamped shut. Her soul, if she—the devil's spawn—had one, shrieked.

She toed off her sandals and kicked them and her shorts to the side. Changing her face hadn't worked.

Cutting herself had ebbed the pain. Traded it really. Emotional pain for physical.   Who wouldn't exchange the two? She didn't know many who wouldn't. Neither did her shrink. If only Ava had sought help before, before she'd changed her face, before she'd scarred her body, before she'd pushed Keen away.

Ava pulled the triangle of lace and silk down her legs. She stepped out of them ritually, one foot at a time, and then threw them to the side. When she stood her gaze found the ceiling. If Annie knew why she found it so hard to look at herself in the mirror, she'd flip her shit—or she would have— before.

That fucking word pushed her over the edge. How much longer would she let a man she hadn't seen in almost thirty goddamned years rule her life?

Her eye found the series of puckered scars that fit neatly inside her bikini line. If they'd just fit as neatly into the ordered life she'd created for herself after ten years of therapy.

She hadn't lied to Annelise when she'd said she masturbated, but Annie probably would have said in bed under the covers with clothes on and the lights off didn't count. And maybe it didn't. Ava had yet to be intimate with a man. First and second bases didn't count to junior high-schoolers these days.

After her first cut she'd opted to have her pubic hair lasered off, so it wouldn't interrupt the healing process. Now she had to look at the marks of her instability every day or ignore them. The ugly lines drew attention from her bare pink lips like a flashing neon light that read, 'I'm fucked up.' She put on a good show, but that's all it was.

"I'm so fucked up," the maimed girl in the mirror told her.

Ava's grip slipped off the edge of composure. She released the lie of fortitude and her fingers clamped around the ballerina figurine her mother had given her their first Christmas with Preston Shepherd. Ava launched it at her reflection. She launched it at her past. She launched it at her cursed future.

The mirror shattered and rained onto the floor.

She shoved the jewelry box and picture frames off the top of her shelves. Next she yanked at the prim outfits lining her closet. They fell off the hangers with little fight. Her foot reared and sank into the side of her wicker clothes basket. Breaths heaved in and out of her lips.

An arm clamped around her waist. She kicked and swung with no discipline. Rage fueled her fit. Rage fueled her life.

"Stop before you slice your foot open." Keen shook her with one jarring whip of his body.

In the panic there was no room for modesty. No room to worry about the flimsy lock on her closet door. No room for lust or need. No room for the past or the future. There was only the fall. Wide and deep. Dark and consuming.

Muscles she didn't realize she had knotted in her legs and middle. She hunched in defeat as her mind swam through the pools of hell. The closet changed to her bathroom. His arms guided her to the cool tile floor. Her body convulsed and crumpled into a pitiful heap.

She was vaguely aware of his presence. A penlight in the blackness. He didn't scoop her to his chest, didn't hold her hand or caress her back in comfort. He draped a towel over her bare skin, cocooning her in misery, and sat next to her on the floor, his presence a quiet, solid comfort.

When her sobs dissolved into the air his presence did as well. For that she was grateful. She lacked the energy for explanations. With physical strain she heaved herself off the floor and trudged to the shower with one goal. Wash away the filth.

She turned the water to scalding and stepped under the spray. Frantically, she lathered and scrubbed. Fresh tears sprang forth. With gritted teeth she muffled the sobs that accompanied her anguish. She scrubbed until her skin was red and burning. Her hands fell to her sides as she stood under the sterilizing water and tried to wash away the hurt, the anger, the fear.

Chapter Ten

Imagine slowly starving to death.

Imagine the pain an unfed hunger brings. The thirst so fierce it constricts a throat and drives a man insane. The want for moisture so strong a man would drink his own piss just to wet his cracked lips and parched tongue. The need for nourishment so great a man would begin eating his own flesh to stave the emptiness.

Now, imagine a deterioration that never ended. A starvation that wouldn't bring death, only a life filled with pain and want. James Red Hardy lived thirst and hunger every day for the last twenty-nine years of his life. While others at Angola found Jesus, Hardy wouldn't repent something that once fed him like no meal he consumed ever could or ever would. God could feed some, but only the kill, only the blood could feed him.

"Hardy."

The guard's bark demanded he stop whatever it was he was doing. He'd been daydreaming, his body spread out on the small cot which served as his bed. Hardy stood and slowly approached the door of meshed metal and brick. Four walls of it snuggled him in its embrace. When the guard stopped in front of the door Hardy met him there and poked his hands through the opening in the middle.

Gone were the days of provoking the guards. Taunting them had served to entertain him for a time. In those long-forgotten days he could taunt a guard into a good fight, which typically left him broken and bleeding. A hell of a bit of entertainment in a place where the nothingness bore holes into a man's brain. Now, taunting them only served to get him thrown in the hole. While it hosted a change of scenery, the view hardly entertained.

The only guard from the old days Hardy never taunted, Henry, retired nearly a year ago. Too bad he couldn't have gone with him. He always liked Henry because, forgoing protocol, he constantly blabbed about this and that. It should've been annoying, but to a man in solitary, it was music. It made the time go by just a little faster. This guard, a serious down-to-business type with hulking arms and a mean disposition, refused to fraternize.

Henry, despite his blabbing, had been serious. Hardy found out when he tried to escape ten years into his sentence. Everyone wore false fronts. James Hardy's had been a dashing rescuer to women in need.

Let me hold that door for you, miss. Is this your puppy I found wandering in the road? My that looks heavy! I don't mind lending a hand.

Henry's false front had been the hillbilly-slow, good ole' boy cadence of his stories.

Hardy had silently planned his escape for three years. His plan included a nurse he had wooed to do his bidding, a guard's uniform, and an unconscious or perhaps dead Henry and his set of keys. Only Henry refused to die. The slow good ole' boy was a damn ninja wonder who evaded injury and subdued Hardy before his plan got good and started.

Damn the olden days.

At sixty-six Hardy still exercised regularly and longed for the day he could take another life. As he walked back and forth over the length of the exercise yard, a place he only saw three times a week, he smiled. The bodies and the blood made him smile.   Finally he killed again. Through the years of sitting inside a solitary cell on death row he'd played the many killings over and again in his mind. Now he had a new death on his mind. He walked with his face turned toward the sun. He swung his arms as the humidity moistened his skin, bringing forth beads of sweat. He smiled and thought about the fresh blood.

Chapter Eleven

Ava opened her eyes with as much caution as she would the door to a crack-house. He hadn't crawled into her bed during the too-short night. Bottom lip between teeth and a crease in her brow, she inched the covers back without a sound. When enough room allowed it, she eased her head from the pillow and peered into the living room. The room was vacant save for her small collection of antique furniture and a decidedly uncomfortable modern couch. She eased to the edge of the bed and reached one foot onto the floor. Her tired muscles strained, but she leaned out, scanning the open closet and bathroom doors. Empty.

When she'd finally left the bathroom only a handful of hours ago the mess from her tantrum had been cleaned. Keen hadn't been in the apartment. She'd taken the opportunity to hide under the covers, and amazingly it hadn't taken long for the day to catch up to her.

Once both feet were on the floor, she leaned forward to peek inside her closet. The ballerina rose on point minus one arm and a foot, which lay beside her base. A warm, gooey emotion threatened to transform her into a weepy heap. She turned away.

Just when she'd begun to breathe steadily in her home again, thankful that Keen had taken the hint and vacated the night before, she saw his broad back. He stood in front of her dining room window. He didn't have much of a view, she knew. The stone buildings across the road. Traffic on the street, auto and pedestrian alike. A few scattered trees and birds, and a hint of the blue sky on the breaking day.

She, however, had a devastating view. The edges of his blond hair darkened with moisture. The grey shirt he wore clung to his wet body in a provocative V, showing the contours of his muscled back. His arms jutted out from short sleeves in corded lines. Sweatpants never looked so good as they did molded to his firm tush.

Ava hated herself for staring, but she figured it would only hurt her since he was oblivious to her presence. He'd obviously been for a run or morning workout already. She swallowed hard and struggled to look away.

Movement stopped her. His hand extended a steaming mug toward her. Damn. How long had he known she was there? His body functioned like a fine-tuned radar to his surroundings. He'd probably heard her eyelashes flutter open.

She shuffled into the kitchen, took the cup from him without a word, and sat at the small table. He stayed at the window, looking out while she slowly drank. It soothed her raw throat and bolstered her shaky nerves. When she swallowed the last of it Keen moved through the kitchen. He refilled her cup with the remainder of golden-black liquid in her French press. Next he pulled a muffin from a white bag that read The Bakery, set it on a plate, and slid it in front of her.

Their gazes connected. Her heartbeat skipped. Ava schooled her expression. She looked away first, using the pastry as her excuse. The sugared top and golden crust flipped her stomach.

She grimaced and offered Keen an expression that said, 'Thanks, but I don't feel like eating.'

He nodded toward the muffin. His stern jaw said, 'Eat the damn muffin.'

Ava slowly picked off pieces and shoved them into her mouth. Keen leaned back on the counter and watched her. She tried to ignore his study. But her mind ran a checklist anyway. Her hair hung loose, parts framing her face and others falling long down her back. It curled in some spots and flattened in others from sleep. Her face probably sported two dark circles under red puffy eyes.

She'd donned a worn T-shirt and a pair of cotton shorts. The smile that normally graced her face was so absent it may have never existed—like a unicorn or something—and wasn't that a shame. Her entire frame caved a little from the impact of yesterday's accusation. Zero for five on appeal. Add that to the list of shitty.

After she finished her muffin she dared a look at him. His arms crossed over his chest in a relaxed stance that told her he'd stay there forever if he had to. He cocked his head to the side in gesture and she knew exactly what he wanted. Her vacant dejection slowly turned to anger. Her jaw grew taut and she stared at him with new life.

He waited. No words. No gestures. He simply waited for the inevitable. How she hated that he knew her so well. Unable to take his scrutiny any longer she exploded with words.

"All my life I've been running from him. In my dreams at night and in the reality of the day. I've tried everything to distance myself..." She broke off as his gaze narrowed on her. Yes, she had done many things to distance herself. None of which needed ruminating. Determined, she started again, "...to protect myself from him and the horrors of what he did. And every time he hurts me! In my life and in my nightmares. Just when I think, now, I've run far enough, pushed hard enough, sacrificed enough."

She stopped, lost in her words, lost in the nightmare for a moment. "Yet, every time I relax for a mere moment, he's back."

Finally she continued, "Twelve years. For twelve years I've waged war with him hanging over me in the Bureau, working harder and longer than anyone just to make it, to be recognized as something other than the single scion of Satan."

Ava wrapped her arms around herself. "I have scars inside and out and the fight has cost me more than I can bear." The words nearly caught in her throat. But she shoved them out. The truth. Ava looked at Keen for a long, silent moment, wondering what he would say or do, wondering if he understood their meaning.

He didn't move. He didn't rush to her to give comfort. His head simply shook. "You won't give up now and have those scars mean nothing."

She didn't recoil from his harsh tone, only straightened in her chair and listened. He continued in a voice slightly gentler, but no less earnest.

"You know, I've kept up with you in the Bureau. Shouldn't, but I have," he added with a wistful laugh. "And I always hear the same things. Shepherd's a bulldog trapped in the body of an angel. Hardest worker and brightest mind in the bunch. Woman's got a mind like a steel trap."

His knuckles whitened. "And yeah, everyone knows your father is Bloody Red Hardy and they think it's fucking amazing you succeeded when normal people fail. In spite of who your father is, and maybe because of who your father is, you succeeded."

He moved forward, hooked his foot on the leg of her chair, and turned her to face him. Bending over her, until they were eye to eye, his large frame dwarfed her. Frustration radiated from him and seeped into his words.

"See Ava, as horrible as it may seem, you are who you are, a doggedly focused crime fighting machine, because of him."

He straightened and nodded toward her bedroom. "So, collect all that fierce determination of yours and an overnight bag because we have places to go."

She stared at him. Her head moving back and forth in confusion.

With another nod toward her room he added, "And hurry, it's going to take a while to get there."

Ava stood and folded her arms across her chest, as much in defiance as modesty for her braless chest. "Where am I going that's going to take a long time to get there? I can't leave town."

"Says who?'

"Abbott? Gray? My lawyer? The Bureau?"

"Do you always follow the rules?"

"Yes." She nearly yelled the answer.

"I know." His smile broke wide. "But I don't."

Keen rinsed their dishes, set them in the dishwasher, and then headed toward the living area. He continued into the bathroom and closed the door behind him.

Ava sat, arms and legs crossed, brooding at the edge of her bed. She listened to the shower come to life and its curtain sliding opened and closed. She let out a huff and stared at the bathroom door. As much as she hated herself for doing it, she pictured water sluicing off the contours of his chest, the carved muscle of his abdomen, the bulk of his legs, the length of his... Her cheeks warmed immediately, flushing her cheeks as red as her hair.

What a pain in the ass. He had always been strong-willed, but now he proved to be downright hard-headed. Why, of all the people to come to her aid, did it have to be him? He didn't fix anything, only added complications. When the shower quieted she rolled her eyes for her own benefit. At least now he was showered and he could go, without her. It didn't matter where he went, as long as it was away.

She ran through her argument for his leaving again in her head. It was short, but concise, and the best she could do under such constraints. The man showered and dressed in six minutes flat. She straightened her posture to rigid in preparation for the confrontation ahead.

He opened the door and tossed his bag on the ground next to him. It landed with a thunk. She inhaled a deep breath to begin, but he stopped her with a raised hand. Her eyes narrowed and she ground her teeth. He raised the other hand, palms out, in a gesture of peace.

"Ava, I'm not going to fight with you."

"Well, that's good to hear, and not at all what I expected." She sighed and loosened her arms to her lap.

"I'm not going to fight you. I'm just going to ask you one question."

"Okay."

"Easy or hard?"

"What?"

"We're going to do what needs to be done to clear your name. We. You and me and whomever else we need to get the job done. The only question is, are we going to do this the easy way or the hard way?"

"We're not doing anything together." Ava stood and jutted her chin. "I really appreciate what you did for me last night. I wasn't myself."

"You were the most raw and vulnerable side of yourself."

"Then it's a side I don't want to see again."

"There's something beautiful about losing the part of yourself you cling to most."

"You try losing it, and then get back to me."

"I already have." His arms folded into a protective shield. "It hurt more than any bullet hole and I lived to tell the tale." He sighed deeply and his hands dropped to his side. "And you will too."

Keen strode into her closet. She dogged his heels. Abruptly he stopped and barred the door with his body. "You can't come in here without shoes. I probably didn't get all the glass."

"Well, my shoes are in there."

His big lips pursed and he made an awe shucks sound. "Looks like you're going to have to stay out here then." He turned his back to her, moved farther into the closet, and snatched her gym bag from the bottom shelf. A long sliver of glass fell off the top. He pinched it between his fingers and presented it to her. "See."

He tossed it into the bathroom garbage, and then proceeded to toss clothes into her bag with the hangers still on them.

"That's not even my travel bag. It's still in the car. Half my essentials are in it."

"It's amazing how little a person can get by with." He winked.

"That bag smells like feet."

"Then you'll want to pack some perfume."

"I can't get to the bathroom," she hollered.

He smiled and shook his index finger. "That's right. I'll get it for you."

Ava rushed to her bed, dropped to all fours, and fished her winter slippers from the depths. Dust wafted in an airy pool. She almost snorted a dust bunny, but successfully evicted the thin-soled shoes from a neat freak's version of hell and wedged them onto her feet.

"Ha," she burst into the closet and smacked into Keen's chest. Her shout of triumph morphed to a grunt.

"Stubborn woman." Wide fingers threaded under her arms and wrapped the sensitive spot on her back. Though really, what spot wasn't sensitive to his touch? "I could have trampled you."

Breath struggled to find its way into her lungs. "You didn't?" she wheezed.

His blue gaze hit her mouth, and then the hidden swell of her breasts with the same impact. Cliché as it was, her knees buckled.

"Whoa there." He lifted her like a child and stood her in the closet doorway. "You had your chance to pack your own stuff. Now, if you want to help, stay out of the way. The faster we go the faster we'll get back."

"I'm not helping."

"If we hurry we'll be back before anyone knows you're gone."

She screamed her response, "Just stop! I can't go. I won't go!" Her voice grew shriller by the word.

Keen didn't acknowledge her fit. Only continued throwing things into her bag.

From his periphery he must have seen her hand slicing toward his head. With lightning speed his hand cinched her wrist. He stepped out of the closet, backing her up, and then twisted her arm behind her back.

Ava sank an elbow into his ribs, but it only agitated him. He manacled that arm as well and pressed her onto the bed. His weight pinned her there.

They lay in total silence for several seconds. Neither dared breathe with their faces so close together. Slowly, Keen lifted his weight off of her. As soon as he was out of the way she sprang to her feet with both fists clenched.

With unnerving calm Keen spread his palms wide. "It's far past time to face the dragon and slay the beast, as they say. You've hardly spoken of him since the incident and I know you haven't seen him."

"For a reason!" Her voice trilled.

"Why?"

The question was so simple as was the answer, but she would never let it pass her lips. Silent anger spewed from her ears.

"Well," Keen said as he disappeared into the closet, "you might want to grab the iron on the way out because this stuff is going to be pretty wrinkled by the time we get to Louisiana."

"I'm not going," she gritted between clamped teeth.

"Yes, you are." The zipper of her bag whined from inside. He strode toward her, tossing the bag on the bed on the way.

"No. Please stop this." In desperation her anger subsided. She pled. "I can't see him, please, Keen."

Their gazes met and held. There, standing toe to toe, her head tilted up and her sad eyes begged him to stop.

"Why?" he breathed.

"I'm terrified."

All the fight and all the strength left her at once. She collapsed, her sobs dragging her toward the floor. Keen's arms caught her on the way down. He pulled her into his protective embrace, something he hadn't dared the night before, something she wouldn't have allowed the night before. Self-preservation be damned. She all but disappeared in his arms. Her body rocked with emotion. Her hands shielded her face while she crumpled into him and wailed.

He held her as sobs turned to hiccups, then slowly became small staggered drawls of breath. Gradually, they slowed and steadied. His chin rested atop her hair and his hands somewhere along the way had taken to stroking her. Over her back and arms he soothed her with firm yet gentle movements. When she shifted in his arms he raised her chin up to look at him.

For a while they simply studied each other. Occasionally, his thumbs stroked the length of her jaw. He took in a long deep breath and let loose a sigh.

"Now, grab that iron and get dressed. We're leaving in ten minutes."

Chapter Twelve

When they crossed the Alabama state line Keen notched fifteen miles per hour out of his speed. From experience, he knew all the state troopers from Alabama to Louisiana didn't play around. The last thing they needed was to suspend progress for an hour getting a ticket or getting hauled to jail for the creepy contents of his trunk. The hysterical woman next to him wouldn't help either. Though she'd downgraded to overly dramatic with moments of frenzy, his eardrums still rang from the five and a half hours it had taken to get out of Virginia. Yep, he'd driven that fast.

The roar of the wind whipping past the glass turned to a constant whisper. The scream of the engine turned to a low whine. The tension in the small car crackled.

"What, did the hounds of hell suddenly stop chasing us?"

"Nope. They just fell back in preparation for the kill," he shot back in a saccharine sweet tone.

"Now who's being dramatic?"

"You've tried yelling, pleading, and bitching. Want to give the silent treatment a whirl?"

Her eyes launched grenades at him. He didn't look, but he felt their weighty impact.

"Will it make you turn around and take me back?"

"No."

"Then I'll try something else. Thank you."

"Like what, hanging your head out the window, flailing your arms, and screaming, 'Help me'?"

"I'd have tried it already, if you didn't have the child safety locks on the windows and doors."

"I know."

He merged into the right lane in preparation for twenty miles of road work. "Damn."

A sinister giggle bubbled up from Ava's side of the car.

"If you bang on the windows and act like I've kidnapped you, I'll be forced to put you out of my misery and into yours."

"What's that supposed to mean?"

Keen slid his gaze to hers. "It means we'll talk about the scars on your lower abdomen."

Her mouth opened, gaped for a beat, and then closed without a sound. The silence held through the hills of northern Alabama and into the flat pines of middle Mississippi. Typically, when people rode in a car for a long period of time their shifting and fidgeting took on a beat all its own. Tapping of fingernails. Strumming of restless fingers. Time keeping of a foot. Shifting of legs. Stretching of a muscle here and there. Hums of entertainment. Huffs of boredom. Pulsating music.

Inside the stifled car there was no beat. Neither occupant moved more than what was necessary to breathe.

Hattiesburg, Mississippi, the hub city. Keen had traveled to it and through it a great deal when he was in law school in Oxford. He and his buddies would head down to New Orleans for the weekend to gamble and drink the nights away. But a time or two they got distracted in Hattiesburg on the way to

the big easy by the local Southern beauties and a
particularly chill bar known as Mahogany.

After Keen whipped the car into a parking
space outside The Hog, as it was also known, he let
out a sigh. It was still here, still open for business.
Considering the food and drink they served he
wasn't surprised, but it was a prayer answered.
What he needed now was a good drink in a laid-
back atmosphere. He needed to decompress and
see if he could get Ava to do the same. Their life
and mission would go much more smoothly if she
would.

"I'm not hungry." She knotted her arms just a
bit tighter over her breasts.

"You don't have to eat, but if I lock you in the
hot car, someone will call the police." Keen shoved
the door open. The brutal humidity pummeled the
collective hours of cooling in seconds. He stood,
smoothing the front of his rumpled shorts.

"Let them." Ava rolled her eyes.

The wrinkling of her freckled skin and the
way it hiked her lip hit him square in the jaw. He
shoved a hand in his pocket to hide his burgeoning
erection.

"You'll pass out before they get here, Yankee."
Already she used the back of her hand to blot at the
top of her lip. "But suit yourself." He closed the
door, walked to the front of the car, folded his arms,
and waited.

Good thing she couldn't hot-wire a car. She'd
mow him over, if the look on her red face was any
indication. A bead of sweat rolled across the edge of
Keen's forehead.

"Fine. Open the door," she mouthed and
smacked the glass.

Keen rushed to open her door and held out
his hand. He tried not to smile, but shit it was

hard. When she was mad at him she was so cute. And her flushed skin was a whole lot sexy.

She batted his hand away and shot to her feet. "You're enjoying this too much."

"Oh come on, you're enjoying it a little."

Her mouth formed a hard line with several cracks. A smile fought to get through. "Well, are we going to eat already or just melt in the parking lot?" She pushed passed him, but he caught her hand and ushered her into the restaurant's brick courtyard.

He settled them at a wrought iron table for two and ordered two blackened grouper sandwiches and two Bailey's and coffees. Ava spent the first half of the meal staring daggers into him and the second half devouring her food and drink, despite herself. It was that good.

Keen took it all in for a few moments of nostalgia. Nothing had changed in the place and he liked it that way. Too much had changed in his life over the years. Ivy and other lush foliage traversed the aged brick on one side of the patio while water consistently ran from the concrete fountain in the court's middle. Patrons of all ages flowed in and out at a consistent pace. And yes, the Southern girls were still beautiful.

When no more than crumbs littered his plate Keen stretched his legs out and reclined in the stiff chair.

"Now what?" Ava blotted her pink mouth and laid her napkin on the table. "Handcuffs? Rope? Duct tape?"

"If you're into that sort of thing, I'm happy to oblige." He pitched the last of his drink down his throat.

Snickers wafted from the table behind him where three girls, in sorority shirts large and long enough it obscured their shorts, sat.

Well, he'd never seen her cheeks outshine her hair. Ava jumped to her feet and rushed for the gate. Keen dropped several bills on the table and hurried after her. To his utter surprise she waited by the car.

Once inside he pulled onto Hardy Street, hit a U turn, and headed toward a clump of hotels. "Super 8 or Hilton Garden?"

That earned him an eye roll.

In short order he parked in front of a reputable establishment, neither the eight or garden variety, and retrieved their bags from the back. He heaved one over his good shoulder and grabbed the other in his hand. The scar tissue had seized on the long drive making his entire limb stiff and nearly useless. He pushed through it and through the main door, which thankfully opened on automatic sensors.

She stepped into his path to the front desk with both hands on her hips. "We need two rooms."

"We'll get two beds." He gave her a token smile, hooked his arm around her waist, and steered her forward. "Would you look at us compromising?"

A glint flickered in Ava's leprechaun eyes. Keen eased the other bag in front of his goods.

"You've learned a thing or two over the years."

"Yeah, that you'll strike hard and fast and when I least expect it. And it'll hurt like a son of a —"

One elegant finger pressed against his lips. Her eyes darted to the right. "Kids," she whispered.

If a mild curse word around kids would get her to touch him, he might just develop a sailor's tongue. Too soon her soft skin lifted, but his gaze didn't leave hers. And hers stayed locked on his. Her lashes drifted low and raised once, and then again. Was that desire he saw in the flutter of her lashes?

"Ah, can I help you?"

Ava jerked out of his arms and swiveled. "Yes. Thank you. We need a room please."

"No kidding," the woman behind the counter muttered.

"First floor, please." Keen stepped to the high desk and blocked Ava from the woman's scrutiny.

After he paid, the woman handed him a key. He grabbed Ava's hand and headed for the room before the woman could say anything about not disturbing their neighbors. His...friend? She wasn't his girlfriend, had never been his lover. So, he guessed she was his friend. His friend balked at the hotel room door.

"I need to get some fresh air."

"Okay. Let me stow these bags and we'll take a walk."

"No. I need space."

"I thought you needed air."

"I need both." She jerked her bag from his hand. "And I can carry my own bag. Especially when it's hurting your shoulder."

"It's not hurting my shoulder."

"Now who's not facing their demons?"

Keen pressed her against the door with his chest. "Fine. My shoulder is killing me, but not because of your bag. I didn't do my exercises last night...or this morning."

"Oh."

He swiped the key and opened the door.

Ava retreated on her own, chunked her bag on the nearest bed, and turned on him. "Just let me go for a walk."

"If you think I'm letting you out of my sight, you've lost it." He flipped the bolt and safety lock on the door and then pitched his bag to the other bed. "A cab isn't going to take you to DC from here, and you're sure as hell not taking a bus back."

"I wouldn't," she insisted.

"Besides, it's late and we need sleep. We're heading out before the sun."

Silent treatment ensued. It was different than the last time. More sad than sulking. It weighed a thousand pounds and weakened his resolve to fight her all the way to Angola. Who was he to say when she was ready to face her father. If the situation were reversed, could he do it? Shit, he could hardly face his father and he'd only killed a boy's dreams, not innocent people.

In near unison they dropped onto their respective beds. The springs under him groaned. Keen continued back until the mattress supported his mangled shoulder and back. Minutes passed. The burden doubled, but he was nothing if not persistent. He'd learned the painful way how to be dogged and determined where Ava was concerned.

Keen broke the silence. "You can shower. I'll get one after my run in the morning."

"Before I'm awake?"

"Maybe."

"You don't trust me?"

He had trusted her, trusted her with his heart.

Before he detangled the words Ava sat and unzipped her bag. She rummaged through the things he'd gracelessly packed, plucked shirts from chaotic heaps, and hung them in the closet. A tennis shoe came next. Had he put the mate in the bag?

Ava clutched a wad of lace and silk. Her gaze hopped from the panties, to him, and back in steady strokes. "Oh my gosh." The gosh turned into a roar.

He almost said, 'Hey, I gave you a chance to pack your own stuff,' but thought better of it and buttoned his lips.

"Seriously?" Thin silken straps looped around her index finger. When she lifted her arm two lace nighties sprouted from the duffle.

He smirked. Served her right for being so stubborn.

"One pair of jeans. Too many wadded cotton tops. No dress clothes. Athletic shorts. Panties and two teddies. What am I supposed to do with this stuff?"

"You could go naked. I'm all for women's rights."

"If I hadn't grabbed a suit on our way out, you'd have had me looking like a clown waltzing through the cell blocks of Angola, asking to be assaulted."

"I won't let anyone hurt you."

"So you can control a mob of inmates?"

"We're not going into the general population."

Ava gathered her hairbrush, toothbrush, toothpaste, and deodorant he'd stuffed into a small inside pocket, and then placed them on the counter inside the bathroom. Light streamed from the doorway. The hum of a heater or vent revved to life. She closed the door and marched over to the side of Keen's bed.

"Keen," Her voice was calm and sad. "I don't want to see my father. I don't want to dredge up things better left buried. I don't want to feel anything for him other than the hate I've nurtured for nearly thirty years. I am afraid I'll feel things that I..." She sighed. "I don't want to pity him. I don't want to miss him. I don't want to love him."

He didn't want to love her, but...

Keen pulled himself off the hideous floral bed spread, braced his hands on his knees, and cocked his head, feeling every bit of his thirty-one years and then some. His gaze fell to the junction of her hips. To the scars.

"Running hasn't worked."

He stood and found her bright green gaze.

"You have to face him or be destroyed by him. But...it is ultimately your choice."

"I've been waiting all day to hear you say that. The second part. Then you had to go and use that brain of yours." She swiped at tears clinging to her lower lashes. Emotions juggled her brows. Ava walked to the bathroom, but paused with her fingers on the handle. Her somber gaze found him.

"I hate you...because you're right."

He let out a sarcastic grunt.

"And I love you. We all have our crosses to bear."

Chapter Thirteen

Ava looked past the car's window at the faint grey morning. Misty fog dissipated in the early morning light. Old farm houses and the occasional batch of horses and cows rolled by in the distance. With little sleep to speak of, coffee and the sheer will of the man driving bolstered her resolve.

"What did the other paper say?" Ava whispered the first words of the morning, but they shattered the unspoken truce they made the night before, where she didn't acknowledge what he'd said and he didn't say any more about it.

One problem at at time.

"Deserved him."

"Excuse me?"

"The first paper said, 'You never...' The second said, 'deserved him.'"

"I never deserved who?" She turned in the seat and eyed Keen. Most certainly she'd never deserved him, but why would her tormenter hone in on him?

Because you love him, idiot.

Ava rubbed the center of her chest. "You need to go back to Miami. He can't hurt you."

Keen's hand shot up to catch the coffee that slipped from the top of his cup. A garbled curse slipped his closed mouth. His tongue sneaked out and collected the excess liquid that stained the lip. He coughed. The cup sank inside a holder.

"I don't think he was talking about me."

"You don't?"

"You do?" If his brow furled any higher the thing would create drag and slow their progress.

"I just thought... Well, you're the only him that's ever been in my life."

"The only one?"

Yep, the needle on the speedometer descended. Two cars flew past them.

"I pushed you away and I trusted you more than I trusted myself. If it didn't work with you, how would it work with anyone else?"

"Ava."

She waved him off with a hand. "Who do you think he was talking about?"

"Your father."

"Preston," she gasped. "I need to call my parents—"

"Not your dad. Your biological father."

"Oh." She flopped against the seat. "And I'm the big shot profiler."

"You've never been this close to a case."

Ava prodded the taut muscles at the back of her neck. She let his words marinate. Once again, he was right.

"Okay. If I wasn't so close to this I could wrap my head around it. But I am too close. I can't grab hold of anything right now. Why are we going to talk to my father? I know I have to and I'm working on accepting that. But why?"

Keen battled with the rolled sleeves of his dress shirt. His gaze hit the centerline, the rows and rows of needly trees, and then the car about a mile in front of them.

"Just spill it. I won't shatter. My behavior over the last twenty-four hours hasn't suggested it, but—"

"Are you still cutting yourself?" His gaze bounced to her and held for four dangerous seconds.

Perhaps she would split into a million little pieces.

"You are the strongest person I know, Ava, but I think that strength has cost you. I'm not judging...not you anyway."

"Who are you judging?"

Whiskers scraped under the rough stroke of his hand. "Me," he bit. "God dammit! Some of those were old scars—"

"They all were. I'm not cutting myself. I haven't in a long time."

"But you did while we were together and..." Something caught in his throat. Ava tried to redirect the conversation, to let him know he shouldn't judge himself for any of her horrible mistakes, but her throat thickened at the sight of tears gathering in Keen's narrowed eyes. "And I didn't know." The steering wheel squeaked under his punishing grip.

"I loved you, but I was a horny bastard, too worried about how to get into your panties to worry about why you wouldn't let me."

"You never pushed me."

"But I—"

"Look." Her voice and resolve strengthened. "You didn't know because I didn't want you to know. I didn't do it for sympathy or attention. I did it to forget for a while that I was the daughter of Bloody Red Hardy. I did it because it hurt less than the emotional pain I let him and other people cause. But you? You were the reason I stopped."

Ava folded a leg into her seat and turned toward Keen. "I used you."

"What?" he scoffed.

"I used you to numb the pain. Your devotion damn near eradicated it until our relationship grew too charged, too real. Until I fell in love with you." She drew a wobbly breath. "I was terrified that you would see my scars and try to fix me...because I needed fixing."

"We all do," he growled.

"After I sabotaged us, I found a psychiatrist. She helped me work through things enough to fool the rest of the world into believing I was balanced, normal, but I never believed it. Not until I let someone into my life."

Keen's jaw clenched, but he didn't say anything.

"My best friend, Annelise. She helped me in ways I can't even articulate..."

"And someone took her away from you in the cruelest possible way. Killing her would have hurt, but not as much as seeing her, knowing she's alive and well and..."

"And never going to forgive you for taking her sister away from her," Ava supplied.

"Something like that."

"No. To answer your question, I'm not cutting myself and I won't, not ever again."

His gaze found hers. "If you ever feel like you want to, tell me?"

She nodded.

"Back to your question. I read the reports from the original Blood Red Murders on the plane to DC. I'd read them before, quite a lot after we split." He gestured to a file shoved into the console between them. "After reading this report on the open investigation, I knew we had to see your father."

Keen checked the mirrors, and then changed lanes to pass the car they'd caught. "The copycat's scene was a perfect recreation of Hardy's very first murder. The one in Lafayette. The body was in the same position, head and arms hanging off the foot of the bed, throat and wrists sliced open. There was no blood on the bedding or floor. A lock of red hair had been laid on the spine just below the shoulder blades. And there was no blood on the wall."

"That's right." Ava's world tilted once again. She gripped the center console in a pitiful attempt to steady herself.

"The first two murders were different than all his others. The bodies were drained, but he didn't start painting the wall until the third one. Only people close to the investigation know that."

Ava loosened her hold and latched onto the details of the case. "They kept the story under wraps for the first year, while agencies tried to catch him. By the time the story broke he was known for painting the wall."

"Yep," he agreed. "The fact that he hadn't painted the first two was never released."

"The media loved the dramatics too much. They made it seem like he lined out the edges and painstakingly brushed the victim's blood over each inch of the wall. Let's face it, he was no Hieronymus Bosch."

"What?"

"Who. He was a famous painter. He depicted horrific images of hell. Real gory stuff. Hardy's work was as gruesome just not as precise. No way to paint an entire wall with a few pints of blood." Ava picked up the file, the one Keen had gotten from... she didn't know where. "How'd you get this?"

"You don't want to know." His gaze sliced her way in warning.

"You know I do."

"My tech guy in the Miami office. He could lose his job for giving you that information."

"More than that. He could go to jail for it."

"What? How?"

Again with the eyes. Ava cocked one of her own and waited.

"Smokey has restricted access due to a less than stellar background."

"Why would the Bureau hire him?"

"Maybe because I tampered with his record and then recommended him." Keen's proud shoulders bounced. "Then again, they could have just seen the potential in his abilities."

"Why the hell would you do that?" she shrieked, but tossed up a hand. "Wait, you're right. I don't want to know." A cockeyed smirk curved the edge of Keen's mouth. For a while they sat in silence, until desperation for information got the better of her. "Okay, why, why would you risk your job for this man?"

"He got mixed up with some bad people. Started with small favors. When the favors got bigger, the far side of legal, he tried to cut and run. They killed his family. Wife. Son. He helped me and Nathan demolish the organization from the inside. It was our first big case as a team. We got promoted and raises, all that. But after, he had nothing."

"So, you gave him something."

"Yeah, a thankless job with shitty pay and even worse hours."

"You gave him a reason to live. You're good at that, giving people a reason to live."

"You didn't need a reason. You had the reason and the drive."

"But you showed me that I could."

"I just handed you a mirror, Ava."

"It was more than that." Her head shook. "You showed me myself through your eyes." Keen shifted his gaze toward the driver's window, but she didn't stop. "I've never been more beautiful than through your eyes."

His gaze shifted between trees and road. It never quite made it back to her. Maybe she shouldn't have said anything, but if she'd learned anything over the last forty-eight hours and lonely eleven years it was that time was fleeting.

A few miles later she shrugged, thumbed open the report, and read, which she should have done sooner. She should have been thinking about the case instead of the personal aspects of her dilemma. Solving the murder was the only way to get out of this mess.

She steeled her backbone and flipped through the crime scene pictures, pictures of her friend-by-proxy positioned ritualistically across the foot of the bed where she'd lain with her husband so many times before. Ava imagined them whispering in the night about their plans to bring another life into the world, but stopped. It wouldn't help solve the case. Her gaze honed in on the lock of hair. Again, it wouldn't help.

Finally she found the report and read. When she finished the first she smacked the open file onto the console between them. "Okay, you still didn't answer my question. Why Hardy?"

"I believe whomever copied him learned from the source."

She recalled the pictures, the perfectly gruesome way it matched his first murder, right down to hair color and the skin tone of his victim. "It certainly seems that way."

"He knows who did this." Keen stabbed the air with a finger. "It's like his hand and mind stretched beyond the prison walls, like he committed the murder himself. His signature is too much on everything to think he didn't have a hand in it somehow. He's been training a disciple, molding and crafting him for years. We're going to find out who it is and we're going to use the catch to get it out of him."

"The catch?"

"Have you finished the Ackerman report?"

"Yeah."

"Turn the page."

Ava held at his steady gaze with her own before letting it slip to the file. Her stiff fingers slipped off the edge of the paper. She flexed them and tried again. The leaf turned and her eyes nearly fell onto the page.

She snatched the file from the console and held the first picture so close to her face the stench of ink stung her nose.

"Holy shit."

Chapter Fourteen

The rain fell like fat tears on the windshield of the silent car. Well, quiet except for the rumble of huge drops crashing onto the roof. Keen swore a few of those suckers left dents in the metal.

Through the blur of water on glass Ava's wide eyes locked on the brick sign. Louisiana State Penitentiary. Cheerful yellow flowers, out of place among bars and razor-wire, obscured the bottom line: Burl Cain. Warden. To their left and right a massive expanse of land stretched, decorated with steel, concrete, and more flowers and shrubs.

Angola. Just the whisper of its name made hardened convicts weep. Its past lay marred in brutality and blood. Its future was bright, if you asked some. Its days numbered, if you asked others.

Fisted white knuckles rested in Ava's lap. When she started wringing them like soaked rags Keen placed his hand over both of hers. For a long minute he simply studied the scared child trapped inside the strong and hauntingly beautiful woman's body, the FBI agent tackling yet another monstrous case, the lover unable to let herself be loved. He wouldn't patronize with false comforts.

The flecks of steel grey in her green eyes stood bold in the cast of the day and sheen of unshed tears. Her eyes, those innocent eyes, skewered his gut.

"You are feathers and steel, Ava Shepherd. I know you can do this."

"It's been nearly thirty years since I saw him. That's nearly thirty years of running and hiding who I am because of him."

Her eyes lightened. She pushed back the emotions. A cold shield slid into place.

"I'm tired of running. I'm ready to face my father."

***

Shackles bound his feet to the floor. A pair of cuffs secured to a small U-bolt locked his hands to the table. He sat in the small room, stark with the exception of a religious scene hanging on the wall. Daniel in a gloomy den crowded with lions. Rays of light shone behind him, stretching wide. Hope in the darkness.

Keen nodded to the guard and stepped into the doorway. A smug sneer covered the killer's face. Prison had worn the young, handsome man into a leathery, snaggle-toothed facsimile. But the eyes, the ice cubes with pupils, they hadn't changed from the dead gaze he'd studied in pictures.

"The last time they let me out of the box for a surprise visit I was thirty-nine. My lawyer came to tell me we'd lost my final appeal. You aren't an evangelist or a lawyer." Bloody Red Hardy tilted his head sideways and stared. "You're a soldier."

"I'm Special Agent Hunt."

"Nah. You're a soldier, parading as an agent. That's good for you. I have some respect for men in uniform who lay their life on the line for freedom, liberty, and the pursuit of happiness. I can't abide men who dress in fake uniforms and pretend to defend this country by catching those of us just trying to pursue our happiness."

Ava's hand pressed against his shoulder blades urging him forward. Yeah, he dragged his feet, giving her time to adjust to the idea of seeing the deranged man who'd once been her dad. Apparently, she'd leapt the hurdle and embraced the descent. She stepped to his right and Hardy's glass eyes followed the movement.

"What about *women* who dress in fake uniforms and pretend to defend this country by catching those trying to pursue happiness?" Her words were crisp and sure.

Slowly, like permafrost melting in spring, the killer's blank gaze melted away. Hardy blinked for the first time.

They sat across from James Red Hardy. Keen's muscles tensed. He waited for the man to lunge, to beat his hands against the table, to spit his rage. Silence shrouded the room for a long time.

"Ruby?" Red rimmed the man's green eyes. His cheeks and ears blushed. The grit in his jaw slackened. "My Ruby?"

"I quit being your Ruby the day my mother figured out you were a murderer." Ava folded her hands and rested them on the tabletop. This Ava didn't look like she knew how to ring her hands.

"My only regret was not being able to see you grow. And here you are, a woman. And as beautiful as your mother. Just as strong." An honest-to-God tear slipped down the man's lined cheek.

"My mother had to be strong because you were weak." Anger edged her voice.

"You know I would have never hurt you or your mother?" Hardy's head shook. "Not my girls. Never my Ruby."

The man had no idea how he'd hurt his daughter. Keen's hands clenched.

Ava released a muffled snicker, which drew his gaze. "You could have slit my throat and hurt me less than you have."

Hardy lurched in his chair. The metal creaked from his whiplash. His nose wrinkled as though he finally registered the stench coming off his body. He shook his head so vehemently, Keen thought he might be trying to rid himself of the image of his little girl hurt and bloody. "How can you say such a horrible thing?"

"How could you do such horrible things?" Ava yelled.

"I needed their blood, Ruby. It's a sickness, I know, but I never wanted yours."

Keen decided to give Ava some time to deal with the reality of her father. He relaxed against the chair. "So, are you one of the reformed ones, penitent over your crimes?"

As Hardy's gaze slid from his daughter's to Keen's all caring fled. The man's slacked jaw clamped shut. He could practically see the reflection of his knotted tie in the man's glassy eyes. "I'll take that as a no." No surprise there. "Tell me about your involvement with these latest Blood Red killings."

"Whatever are you talking about? Has there been a murder committed in my name?" The glare turned into a delightfully bright smile. Arrogance thickened the man's words. "I'm honored really. Fans! They are wonderful, begging and pleading for tidbits of knowledge. They love to touch the horns of the beast. But a killer doing work in my name is..." He filled his lungs as though the dank air were perfumed with a high Gulf breeze. "...freedom really."

After the things Keen had witnessed he'd thought himself hardened, but the coffee in his stomach fermented or curdled or whatever the hell coffee did when it went bad. He banked the urge to swallow. "Does your really big fan have a name?"

"Oh," his fingers flitted about, "there are so many. Who's to know which one is the actual killer?" He leaned forward, seeming to forget his daughter sat only feet away. "Why don't you tell me a little about his work, his bloody woman? Maybe I can help." One shoulder bobbed.

Keen knew what he was doing, living vicariously through his zealot. He wanted the gory details, a picture of the scene painted in his mind by Keen's words. As much as Keen hated the pleasure his words would give the monster, he'd set the scene. He would set Hardy up to watch him fall because Keen had a hunch he was ready to play.

"The murder took place in a town house in Alexandria, Virginia. The killer did not force entry, but was most likely allowed entrance by the tenant."

Hardy reclined in his chair. His entire body relaxed. He chuckled and said almost to himself, "I'll bet she was pretty."

"The victim was rendered unconscious by a blow to the head. There was no struggle."

"Of course not," Hardy mused. His eyes closed and a smile played across his lips.

"The victim was stripped. No clothes were found at the scene. Then the victim was laid facedown on the neatly made bed with head and arms hanging off the foot of the bed."

"Artful." He chuckled.

"The victim's throat was sliced with one deep lateral cut. There was no blood found at the scene.

No walls were painted. A lock of red hair was found laying at the center of the victim's back."

Hardy's lids popped open. "And the second?"

"The second was much the same," Keen said.

The killer's fingers balled into a fist. His gaze rolled to the tiles as though looking for the strength to bust the bolt and choke Keen to death with the restraints. A sigh humidified the air. "I'll need details, soldier, if I'm to figure out who committed these honor killings. You see, each person adds their own flair to a murder. They can't help but leave their own signature. It's their flawed nature."

"You can't change nature, huh?"

"Not from in here." Hardy rattled his cuffs.

Ava stiffened, but the killer didn't seem to notice. Her father would have. But this man wasn't her relation.

"There were some differences in this second murder," Keen offered. "The victim was found in a hotel room."

The wrinkles in Hardy's face trenched deeper.

He didn't like that. Keen schooled his features, but inside he rejoiced.

Just wait fucker.

"The victim was rendered unconscious by a blow to the head. There were no signs of a struggle."

Hardy's chin eased from his esophagus where he'd stuffed it.

"Like the other one, the victim was stripped," Keen continued. "No clothes were found at the scene. Then the victim was laid face down on the neatly made bed with head and arms hanging off the foot of the bed."

"What about the throat? Tell me about the throat." Desperation frayed Hardy's reserve.

"One lateral cut bisected the neck." Keen used his thumb and mimicked the cut on his own neck. "No blood was found at the scene. No painted walls. A lock of red hair was found laid at the center of the victim's back."

"All her blood, gone? No one cared about the first few, the ones where I didn't slap their blood on the wall. I can understand that. People appreciate the artistic prowess of the other killings." Hardy grinned.

Ava sat forward now. Her posture matched Keen's as she administered the death blow.

"You mean *his* blood."

"Whose blood?" Hardy's bloated eyes shifted back and forth between him and Ava. "What are you talking about?"

"The victim's name was William Boston," Ava said.

Hardy's eyes narrowed. "No. What kind of trick is this?"

"No trick," Ava sing-songed. "That's right, your guided hand has his own big-ass mark to place on the world."

Hardy jerked against the bonds. His jaw clenched and his gaze narrowed to a spot on the wall. He shifted over and over again in his chair, clanking the shackles, making them sing.

The guard opened the door and stepped inside. "Let's go, Hardy."

"I need a minute." Keen held his hands up in surrender.

"Sorry. Orders are orders." The man's big boots clopped a large step into the room. His hand slid from his Glock to his keychain.

"Please," Ava stood. "This man is our only link to a burgeoning serial killer."

"Sorry, ma'am, but like I told him—" The guard pointed to Keen, but Ava cut him off.

"If we don't catch the killer now, he will become more notorious than yours truly." She thrust a finger at her father.

"Hardy, settle down," the guard barked.

"Or what, you'll put me in the box? Oh, wait, I'm already there," Hardy countered.

"You still have an hour a day to lose." The guard's gaze narrowed on Hardy for a heavy second before he nodded at Ava. He reversed to the door and pulled it closed.

"Give us his name," Keen coaxed. "We'll punish him for you."

Silence resounded like a gong. The fragments of emotions he'd seen in the man's eyes when he'd looked at his daughter disappeared behind a glacier.

They sat in silence for five minutes with no change. Keen had expected the meticulous killer in him to win out, but if anything would, just maybe the father would. He slapped his knees, signaling Ava. She shoved her chair back, screeching the legs across the floor. She shot to her feet and headed for the door.

"Wait," Hardy shouted. "Ruby don't go...I—"

"I can't wait, I have to go back and clear my name."

"What do you mean?"

"Your disciple is trying to pin the murder on me. He planted my hair at the scene."

Hardy filled the small room with a bellow.

"That fucking bastard! It was supposed to be my hair, not yours. Never yours." His fists met the table, making it a gong and rattling his chains louder than any ghost Keen had ever heard. Keen stood by Ava's side. Neither feared an attack. Hardy was trapped in the tormented hell of his own making. Angry at himself and the killer, not Ava.

Three guards rushed the room. Hardy was unaware of their presence. He battled something inside himself. Well, himself and now three guards.

Hardy's apprentice had gone off course. They all knew, if unchecked, it wouldn't end well for Ava.

"Into the lobby and wait there," their escort ordered.

"No." Hardy went slack. "Hunt, you have to protect my little girl! Protect my Ruby and Sarah. He'll come for them before he's through. Promise me you'll keep them safe."

Ava and Sarah. A chill ratcheted its way up Keen's spine. "I will."

"Thank you." Hardy's chest sagged into the guards' arms, defeated.

"His name," Keen demanded.

"His name is Rory Coghlan."

Chapter Fifteen

Stan loosened the noose around his neck—
the slow silken death some asshole invented a
thousand years ago—and kicked the door shut with
his foot. The pizza box nearly toppled to the floor
from his shifting weight. It would've been a fitting
end to the pisser of a day he'd endured. Stan saved
the pizza at the last possible instant and grumbled
all the way to the kitchen counter where he plopped
the box. He walked back to the entryway, removed
his badge and gun, and placed them in the entry
table drawer.

At least Ava had gone and flipped off the edge
of psycho like he'd always known she would. That'd
leave the head profiler position—a position he
deserved—open soon. If only every shitty day had a
silver lining as thick.

While lumbering back to his pizza Stan
looked around the supremely unsophisticated
bachelor pad. Most of the walls were blank and the
white they'd been when he'd moved into the place
five years ago. The carpet was worn, as were the
dining table and chairs squatting atop it. An
overstuffed Italian leather sofa and love seat with
the extra-large flat screen and entertainment
console opposing them were the only signs of new
the apartment offered.

The apartment itself was bigger than small and had potential. Two tiny terrace doors looked out over a small park. With a fresh coat of paint the crown molding and intricately designed ceiling could boast history and class. He kept the place picked up, but it could use a deep cleaning. Maybe he'd look into hiring a cleaning service to come in once a week. Better yet, maybe he should find a steady broad. The place could sure use a woman's touch.

He ran through the list of candidates for woman-of-the-house and attacked a slice of pizza. A knock sounded at the door. Perhaps the knock was the answer to his unasked prayers. He and Holly had engaged in sexual marathons over the last few months. It could be more. And if not, he was still interested in what she had to offer this evening. He smiled and hollered through a mouthful of pizza. "Just a minute."

Stan stared at the half-eaten slice and waffled back and forth. Shove it down the hatch while making his way to the door or set it in the box? He tossed it into the open box with a grunt. If their last meeting was any indication, he'd need both hands and his mouth when answering the door.

He grabbed the deadbolt, but habit made him check the peephole first. Habit paid off. It wasn't Holly. He immediately wished he'd brought his slice with him to the door. His stomach whined. His cock did too.

The guy on the other side of the door hunched a bit. A ball cap hid his eyes. He held a pizza box in his left hand. His right was out of sight.

"Wrong place. I didn't order a pizza."

"You sure? I got the address as building four oh six, apartment thirty-one."

"I'm sure."

"Look man, could you help me out? It's my second day on the job. I'll get in deep shit if I bring it back."

"Any other night, but I've got one already."

"Can I use your phone and get this straightened out?"

Instinct kicked in. Stan stepped back into the apartment. Something about this guy wasn't right.

"My battery is dead," Stan lied.

What kind of scam was this, a simple robbery? Open the door and *wham*. Give me all your money. Or was he just one major screw up who couldn't even get a pizza delivery right?

Before he figured out exactly what was wrong the doorframe splintered into a hundred pieces. The door snapped open like the mouth of a lion about to devour him whole.

The man barreled into the apartment with no pizza box in sight. He used his body as a battering ram. Stan lunged for the drawer. The blow caught him in the side. Fighting for air, Stan also fought to right himself. The glint of gun metal set his heart to free fall, but the guy didn't shoot.

Stars, however, shot in all directions. They sparked new stars and pinged into the universe. After what seemed like an eternity Stan gulped in air. With the air came the taste of blood, and outrage.

By God, he was an FBI agent. No way would some punk rob him.

Through the blows Stan aimed one ball-fisted uppercut to the intruder's jaw. A crack split the air. It was so much more comforting than the thuds that had echoed on his skull. The man staggered back. Stan teetered to his feet.

The two men stood eye to eye, evenly matched in girth. Stan was five eleven, well muscled, and trained in hand-to-hand combat. His rage fed his skill.

The haze clouding the man's eyes lifted too quickly. Stan had little time or option. He grabbed the man's gun hand, stepped in close, out of the line of fire, and jerked the man's hand in an unnatural position. Stan tried to grab the gun, but the man's other hand latched onto his neck.

The gun clattered to the floor.

He barred the man's arm, keeping him close. Stan pivoted away from the gun, bent at the waist, and dropped to one knee. The intruder flipped over him onto the floor, and then Stan made a critical error.

Instead of striking his already disoriented opponent, he lunged for the gun.

The intruder's biting grip dug into Stan's legs. Stan crashed to the ground, taking the dining table with him. He tried to stand. Searing pain annihilated all thought. His leg went limp. It refused to obey.

Stan dug his forearms into the dingy carpet and army-crawled. He inched toward the shining metal just inches out of reach.

His whole focus shrank to that gun.

Pain eased from his ankle. Relief pushed him on.

Stan screamed. No amount of reason, no determination would mute the sound. Something sharp split the flesh of his right thigh. He gave up on the gun. He turned over to fight his opponent any way he could.

He kicked out. The connection possessed all the impact of a wet noodle.

Blood streaked across the floor. It pooled around his lower leg. A knife protruded from his leg. The intruder grabbed the handle and pulled, trying to extract it from his thigh.

Stan grabbed the man's lapel with one hand. He rammed the heel of his palm into the man's nose. Crimson exploded. His next blow connected to the man's ear.

The man staggered.

Again Stan turned his body toward the gun. He had to get the gun or die trying.

***

The last gurgles of air left his severed throat. The killer patted him on the shoulder with a blood-covered hand.

"Sorry, Stan. You should have just cooperated. This would have been a lot easier for you."

He straightened and looked around the room. Broken glass littered the floor. Pools, splotches, and smears of red also ruined white carpet and walls. The large flat screen TV slumped over in the corner much the way its owner lumped in the center of the room.

"So much for no blood at the scene." With one hand he smoothed back a tuft of red hair. With the other he grabbed his broken nose and yanked. He walked over to the mirror hung over the couch to appraise the damage. The front of his shirt hung wide, ripped at the buttons. A swollen eye stared back at him.

Stan had been a fighter. Stan had royally messed up the plan. Then again he'd certainly sent a message.

He walked back to Stan and reached over his prone form, fishing in the dead man's back pocket. He extricated the wallet. It was a simple tri-fold and held three-hundred-forty bucks. Rory pocketed the dough. He flipped the identification over and read it for giggles.

"Supervisory Special Agent Stanley Watts, F.B.I." He glanced down at the crumpled heap. "Pretty weak for FBI, if you ask me." He inserted a lock of hair into the wallet, closed it, and set it on the corpse's back. He thought about moving him to the bed. But really, what was the point? The bitch would get the message.

Chapter Sixteen

"You did it." Keen looked at her with wide, reverent eyes.

Like she'd done anything more than hold on while he dragged her into hell and out the other side. She panted from the proverbial sprint. "I can't believe it worked." Her head thudded on the wall outside the door that read Records. The cool surface felt great against her heated face. "Part of me didn't want it to work," she whispered.

Keen paused with the phone halfway to his ear. The man of action already poised to move again. He kept silent, waiting for her to fill it.

"If he didn't tell us, it would mean he didn't care. I could go right on hating him with a clear conscious. Now...it's muddy."

His smile slipped. Something that made her naughty bits tingle moved into its place and held. "A lot of things are muddy right now." A guard churned boots down the corridor passed them. The connection splintered. "But we'll deal with first things first."

He punched in a number, hit the speaker icon, and waited.

She looked a question at him.

"Winslow."

"As in Special Agent Winslow Gray?" she squeaked.

He touched the tip of her nose.

The lead investigator for the case—despite all Lara's posturing—answered on the third ring. "Who is this?"

Keen's smile reappeared. "That's a terrible greeting for the man who's going to solve this case for you."

"Right. And my wife loves me for my money."

"No. She loves you for your cheerful demeanor."

"What the hell do you want, Hunt? I don't have time for bullshit."

"Me neither, so listen up. You need to find out everything you can about a Rory Coghlan."

"Who the hell is that? And what the hell are you up to?"

"I'm finding out more, but I need you to trust me on this."

"The only thing I trust is you'd do anything to get Shepherd out of this mess. Anything."

"You're right. I'd do anything, unless she actually killed Josie Ackerman and William Boston. Ava Shepherd didn't kill them and you know it. That's why you have an uneasy feeling in your gut. Look up the name."

"It's called indigestion. Where are you?"

"Later, Winslow." Keen disconnected the call and then punched more numbers.

"Who are you calling now, WABC News to tell them wanted murder suspect Ava Shepherd skipped town and is currently conspiring with her father on the next string of murders?"

His brows knitted, but his fingers continued dialing. "How can you whisper and scream at the same time?"

"It's a gift." She jabbed him in the stomach with two fingers. They hit immovable abs and she gulped.

"You're so cute when you're dramatic."

Liking their proximity and the tingle in her belly far too much, Ava flatted her palm on his abdomen and pushed.

Keen's hand banded her wrist, pivoted his body so her hand slipped off him, and then pulled. Ava's breasts pressed against the firm, hot muscle her hand had just touched. Her breath caught. Without thought her chin lifted. She met his gaze. Her free arm slipped up his back and clung to him. Emotion clogged her throat, but desire overtook it. His head lowered slowly. A whimper escaped her lips.

She wanted his comfort, but she wanted his taste more. Would he taste different than he had so long ago? Would he move differently than he had? Would she push him away again?

The blond whiskers on his chin pricked her skin. Ava's lungs faltered.

"Hello?" The phone crackled to life inches away from her face.

Their convergence stalled.

"Hello? Can you hear me? What's going on, Keen?" her dad shouted from thousands of miles away.

Keen's gaze dropped to her mouth, lifted to her gaze, and lowered again. Striations in his jaw flexed. He exhaled through his nose. When his gaze met hers she saw it. He'd hidden it so well the past two days, but there it was. Her dad's frantic plea for response didn't hold him back. It made a convenient excuse. Pain arrested him. A pain she'd caused.

Tears that had obeyed her through the most horrifying experience in quite a long time slipped free. Keen caressed her cheek. His head bowed. He braced his forehead to hers for a fleeting second, and then he slid from her grip.

Before she could chastise herself for not holding on to him then and now, he put the phone to his ear. "Yeah, Preston, I'm here."

He didn't go far, either that or her dad talked really loudly. She heard his relief as clearly as she heard her heart crack in two. Her dad rambled. "We're waiting in line to board our flight home now. We'll be in DC late tonight. Tell Ava we're on our way. Tell her—"

"Preston, listen to me very carefully," Keen interrupted. "Don't board that plane. Get out of line. Take Sarah and get lost. Stay on the island or go someplace you've never been, where you don't know anyone."

"Why? And what about Ava? I can't just abandon her with all this going on."

"You have to. We got a name from Hardy. I'm working on getting more information. But what I do know is that this is personal. He's coming after Ava. Hardy believes he'll come after Sarah too."

"Why Sarah? Why Ava? I don't understand."

"I don't know, yet. Take your battery out of your phones. Buy a prepaid one, text me so I'll have the number, then get lost. Don't call anyone else. I'll call you when I know more."

A long minute of silence came through the line. "You'll take care of our girl."

Why had her dad said that? She wasn't Keen's—shit, she wasn't even Preston's—no matter how much she wanted to be. Keen would keep her safe, but those eyes made it pretty clear anything more wasn't an option.

"Yeah, I will." Keen pocketed the phone, but didn't look at her.

They'd been told this structure didn't house prisoners. It was strictly human resources staff. Ava moved to a thick glass window. Prisoners in white or chambray shirts and blue work pants walked in long neat lines over the gravel path from one building to another. In the distance, outside of the main gate, a similar line of prisoners walked down the fence line. Shovels and other yard tools rested on their shoulders. A guard on horseback toted a shotgun in the same fashion.

She wondered how often a man got brave, stupid, or desperate enough to run. Twenty miles from the nearest major city and surrounded by gator and leech infested swamps, the fortification of the prison rivaled that of medieval castles.

"You ready?" Keen asked.

"Are you?" she shot back before she thought better.

He opened the office door. "After you."

She nodded a thank you but, afraid of what she'd see, didn't hold his gaze for long. Through the door a receptionist ticked away on her keyboard. The man clacked long after they stood in front of the desk. Keen smacked his badge onto the counter. "The warden sent us."

A heavy sigh accompanied the man's attention. "What do you want?" He eyed Keen's credentials.

Customer service.

"We need to see records—"

"No kidding?" The guy looked to be in his late thirties, but he'd never develop a pooch. In fact he bordered on the skeletal. He rolled dark eyes. "You're in the records department."

"Look," Ava shouted. "You can shove that attitude up your ass. I've been accused of murder... no, two murders in the last forty-eight hours, faced my father—who is a serial killer—spent too many hours being bossed around by a man I have history with, and I just got a name for the man trying to frame me. I need a list of all the people who've ever visited James Red Hardy during his incarceration now or I might just kill someone."

"All right, miss." A man who probably devoured all the food the other guy didn't stood halfway into the corridor. "I just got off the phone with Warden Cain. Why don't you two come on back before there's bloodshed."

Toothpick's gaze and overly pursed lips followed their progress around the desk and down the hallway.

"Jasper Mills." One of Jasper's hands patted his belly. The other extended.

Ava shook it and tried her best not to flush.

"From what I heard you're the bossy one?" He offered his hand to Keen.

The two men exchanged glances. "That's the word on the street."

"Right in here." He ushered them toward two chairs opposite a tidy desk and sleek computer. The door shut with a quiet click. Jasper's chair creaked under his size. "I apologize for Berry. End of the month reports always put him in a mood." He adjusted his waistband, which—after his hand moved—promptly fell back down his belly. "Let me get Wanda purring and I'll have your info in a jiff."

"Thank you." Ava held herself rigid and stared straight ahead. The last thing she needed right now was Keen's sexy smirk and laughing eyes.

Jasper's fingers glided smoothly over the ergonomic keyboard. No finger pecking here. Was it bad that she'd expected it? Probably.

Two minutes and thirty-six seconds later— where else could she look but at the clock—Jasper grunted and then slapped the screen around to face them.

"This is a list of all the people who've ever visited Hardy. Notice there are two names that repeat over the years. Hester Ludlow is an evangelist who visits several other of our death row inmates. See if any of those names ring your bell and I'll make you hard copies."

Ava touched the screen. One name repeated a lot. One. Two. Three. Twelve. Twenty-four. Forty-eight. Sixty. Sixty visits in the last five years. Nothing before that. "Who is John Hardy?"

Jasper handed Keen the papers, took the screen back, and wiped her fingerprint from the glass with his too short tie. "Let's find out."

Another minute later he slapped the screen around, and then pressed the play icon with his mouse. Before them the screen came to life. James Red Hardy sat on one side of the table in a room that looked much like the one in which they'd just spoken to him. On the other side of the table sat a man the same size as Hardy.

"This is Hardy's last visit," Jasper said.

"One month and two days ago," Keen whispered.

In the soundless video the younger man talked with large gestures and wide eyes to James Red Hardy. Her dad's grin shined brightly through the grainy footage.

"Can we see the first visit?" Ava asked.

Jasper skipped back to the first visit between the two men. Immediately Ava recognized the role reversal. John Hardy sat still. His lips parted in an awed smile as James gestured wildly. They watched several more videos. The visits were all short, ten minutes, but the progression of the relationship between these two men was clear.

"This is the apprentice," Ava said. Keen nodded his agreement. She sat forward. "Do you do background checks for inmates' visitors?"

"Sure do. We house some pretty dangerous men, but ah, you know that." The man's grey beard waggled back and forth.

She cleared the air with a swat of her hand. "Don't worry about it. Just tell me who this man is to James Hardy."

Again he took back the screen. Buttons clacked. "James' younger brother."

Shock punched her in the chest. "That's impossible."

Jasper wiped at an invisible spot on the desk, then waggled his jaw. "He passed a pretty stringent background check. What makes you say that?"

Ava took several breaths before the words formed. "James Hardy was an only child."

Chapter Seventeen

Ava's phone vibrated against her forearm and the car's center console. The racket of metal jumping on plastic shattered the quiet. Her reflexive jump rattled her bones. Over half the trip was spent in silence, both she and Keen deep in thought. The anger that'd consumed her during the ride to Angola had vanished only to be replaced by angst. They'd taken the first steps toward catching this killer, but there was so much more to be done.

She looked at the screen and groaned.

"Abbott?" Keen asked.

"Mm-hmm." The phone shook as though from the woman's anger. She eased it with a press and slide of her thumb. "Hello?"

"I can't believe you left the mother-fucking state," the agent screamed.

"I can't believe you thought I killed someone." The authority and bite of her tone settled her jumbled nerves. Ava grinned, ended the call, stuck the phone inside her purse, and zipped it closed.

"She got our package from Angola?"

"Oh yeah."

"Maybe now she'll do something productive, instead of hounding you."

Ava veered her mind away from Keen and his relationship with Lara Abbott. There were certain things she didn't need to know. When she opened her mouth, though, the question popped out anyway. "Were you and she close?"

He kept quiet so long she didn't expect him to answer. "My and Abbott's exchanges were the polar opposite of ours." He swung his finger between them.

So they fucked like ducks. Great. He might have to pull over so she could vomit. Images of the woman's long lean legs coiled around Keen's lean hips scrambled her brain.

"She never loved me. I never loved her."

Her gaze flitted to his for a second, and then sought refuge in the twinkling stars just beginning to brighten in the bold darkness of night.

"I—"

Keen started to say more, but she cut him off. "It's not my business. I shouldn't have asked."

"Ava," he coaxed.

"Please, just forget about it." Seriously. Why had her mind chosen the most inconsequential thing to fixate upon?

Funny, the fear Ava had of being wrongly accused seemed like it never existed. Even the trauma of facing her father was lost in the buzz of progress. They had to locate Rory Coghlan before he killed again. There were so many miles and unanswered questions between them and this virulent man.

Ava shoved the last bite of her six-inch sub into her mouth and forced herself to chew and not gag when she swallowed. The moon waxed gibbous and lit the car's interior. As much as she'd like to shrink into the seat and have exhaustion take her, Ava needed to capitalize on this small sense of momentum.

She tucked one leg underneath her bottom and shifted toward Keen. His gaze remained on the

yellow and white lines screaming past them. He let
her take the lead, but she wasn't quite ready to
speak. Large steady hands firmly gripped the
steering wheel. The ropes of his muscles were
obvious even through his dress shirt. The tie, so
precisely knotted at the prison, hung loose on
either side of his thick neck. Maturity and raw
masculinity had taken hold where youthful beauty
had left off, chiseling his features to a weep worthy
profile. Faint lines plucked the corners of his eyes.
Smile lines etched around his full lips, the best
kissing lips she had ever met. She sighed lightly. He
hiked a curious brow.

"Thank you," she breathed.

"For?"

"Believing in me."

"Always."

"For coming to my rescue. Making me face
my father. Staying calm in the madness. I let my
emotions cloud my judgement. I should have
known to look to my father for answers, but I was
too afraid."

Her hands twisted in her ritualistic dance of
discomfort. She stilled them. "Until today I couldn't
admit that I love him. It seemed wrong. I still don't
understand it. For so many years I raged against
the feelings, terrified if I loved a monster I would
become one myself. Today, watching him, I realized
he is two people in one body. One I hate. One I
love."

She rubbed the tip of her nose to stall the
tears gathering in her eyes. What do you know, it
worked. "Anyway, I'm clear now. And I have some
insight about the apprentice."

Mirth spread across his face. "Finally. I was
beginning to think you lost your touch. I'd have
hated to call Nathan and your brother and tell them

our crime fighting wonder kid was going to drop out
of the Bureau and become a security guard at the
local mall."

"Wonder kid?"

"Tell me about the apprentice."

"Hardy was a disciplined killer with precision
and grace, if those terms may be applied to killing.
He was meticulous, the most elusive killer ever
hunted. He spent years training his replacement,
carefully molding him to perfection, blinded by his
own need for legacy."

"Blinded?"

"Yes. He never recognized the disdain in
Coghlan's eyes, only the adoration."

"So..."

"He hates him and loves him," she supplied.

Keen gnawed his lower lip. "I need more."

"It's similar to my feelings for James Hardy
only reversed. Coghlan admires Hardy as the
ruthless killer. There is another part he equally
loathes. If we can figure out what that part is we'll
catch our man."

"Keep going." Keen's head bobbed, but he still
chewed the lip.

"Coghlan honored Hardy with his first kill,
but defied him in a big way with the second.
Normally I would say Coghlan wants to make his
own mark on the world, but there's more here. His
focus on me, on destroying me... He holds a grudge
against Hardy."

Ava tucked her other leg under her and
practically bounded on her heels as the words
flowed. "Coghlan could be a relative of one of
Hardy's victims who has gone off the deep end.
There is no better way to ruin a notorious serial
killer than to muddy his legacy. But then there's
the issue with me again, and my mother. It's a

grudge against us. The three of us represented a family, for a time. There's still devotion on my father's part, as confusingly sick as it is."

She scooted a flyaway hair from her eye. "Coghlan is solitary. Once Gray and Abbott find his record it will show that he has never been married. He probably hasn't had a serious relationship. He's held menial jobs. He has little or no family life. He may have been orphaned at an early age and sees Hardy as a father figure."

Ava breathed deep and let it out slowly. Keen pursed his sensuous lips, "You got all that from a few video snippets?"

She smiled. "You going to call me Wonder Woman now?"

"No."

They drove through the night and walked into Ava's apartment as the sun's rays crested the horizon. "I need a shower. You?"

"I'll get one in the morning."

"It is morning." Her head tilted toward the window.

"Please tell me you have blackout shades."

"Like any good agent would."

He clamped a hand on the back of his neck and dropped his bag on the floor next to the coffee table. "I'm about to crash. Whenever we wake we'll check in with Winslow."

"Sounds good." Thinking about Keen sleeping a few feet away, she tightened her grip on her bag. Sure he'd slept in the same room with her the last two nights, but she'd been near comatose the first night and too consumed with fear to register it the second. Tonight was a whole different animal, a horny one at that.

She tried to walk to the bathroom, but her feet stuck to the floor. The nod of his reply slowed, and then stopped. This was her exit. Or was it her entrance? Keen wouldn't kiss her. Okay. This was the freaking twenty-first century. She could kiss him, couldn't she?

The grip on her bag loosened. If she was going to do this, she wanted to use both hands. Before she could drop the damn thing he chucked her on the arm like an old pal and turned to the sofa.

"Goodnight, Ava." His hand balled into the end of the throw and yanked it off.

"Night." Embarrassment propelled her through the open closet door. She managed not to slam it shut behind her, but just barely.

Ava let the monotony of getting ready for bed after one hell of a long day take hold. She stripped, scrubbed, rinsed, brushed her teeth, lotioned, and dried her hair. Then something odd happened. She sat down her blow drier and marveled at herself in the mirror. Gone were the markers of her father. Sure vibrant red hair flowed around her head. Sure freckles dotted her cheeks. Sure near-neon green eyes stared back. But now these were her features, not his.

She held her face. A short laugh stretched her mouth, revealing her white teeth. Her head tilted. Diagonal rows of scarred flesh stared back. With one hand she clutched her hair back. The other slipped down her belly to the puckered skin. Her finger rubbed the storied flesh in gentle even strokes.

"I forgive you," she whispered. Her gaze lifted to the mirror. "I forgive you," she told herself once more. "And," she gulped, "I accept your apology." She nodded and walked into the closet.

Maybe Amadi had a point about that self-love mumbo jumbo. The knot she'd carried in her stomach for the last...well, forever, smoothed itself out. She sighed, reached for an extra-large T-shirt, and pulled it over her head.

When she opened the closet door her gaze hit a wall of blackness. She looked toward the sofa. Not even the outline of Keen's form shown in the dark. Using the light from the closet, she found her way to the bed and pulled back her covers.

Ava sat on the edge and waited for her eyes to adjust to the darkness. Still she couldn't see his outline on the couch. Against her own good judgement Ava eased off the bed and tiptoed across the room.

Definitely a bad idea.

Her heart plummeted at the sight, burning a trail through her on its descent. Keen lay on the living-room floor. The heft of his bare chest rose and fell with easy breaths. One hand stretched over his shoulder and bent at the elbow, cushioning his head. His wounded shoulder and arm stretched out beside him. His scar puckered in a jagged line discolored from the rest of his smooth bronzed skin.

Ava's gaze slid south and reached another discolored scar on the left side of his lower abdomen. This one was older and looked very similar to another scar on his right side just below his ribs.

"Oh God." Instinctively she stepped forward with her hand outstretched. The need to heal and protect his marred body took hold.

In a flash he pulled a gun from beneath the small throw and aimed its barrel at her chest. His eyes opened. Quicker than he'd brandished it, Keen flipped on the safety and set the pistol next to his leg.

He sat. His gaze skittered up her bare legs and she dragged hers from his naked chest. Their eyes met and held. Her pulse raced and her body quickened in preparation for the feast it desired, the pistol forgotten.

"What's wrong?"

"Nothing. I just... I came to see if you needed a pillow or blanket. It didn't occur to me the other night." She lied

"I can sleep anywhere, standing, sitting. I'm good."

She hesitated to leave. Her gaze fell yet again to his chest.

"What?" His was gruff, bordering rude.

"How many times have you been shot?"

"Go to bed, Ava."

"Or what?"

"Or I'll do something we'll both regret."

Lust flash-fried her brain. A sheen of sweat broke over her belly. Her chest rose and fell in erratic pants. "I have my fill of regrets, but this wouldn't be one."

His eyes flashed hot, but cooled before he spoke. "It would be for me. Now, go to bed."

Pain backed her up a step, but she couldn't go back to the numbness of conciliatory living.

"How many times have you been shot?" The steel in her own voice surprised her.

Maybe it surprised him too. "Three."

"My mother called to tell me you were in ICU. I was up to my elbows in techs, agents, and precious evidence of the strangler's next to last murder. For the first time in my life I didn't care about catching the bad guy. When you woke I wanted to be at your bedside. I would have been, if I wasn't two days from civilization in the thick of the Boise National Forrest."

He kept stubbornly silent.

"What else happened, Keen? How'd you get the other two scars?"

"Maybe later, okay?"

"No, it's not okay. You've been shot three times. You nearly died the last time."

"I'm fine, Ava." His arms shot wide, and then his hands scrubbed over his chest. "My body just has character now." He collapsed onto the floor. "It's been a long couple of days and we need to get some sleep." His tone was firm. His words dismissive.

"Fine."

She deserved his brush off. After all, she'd done the same to him. Ava allowed herself one last look before turning back to the bed. She hit the light on the way, plunged the room into faux night, and tossed herself onto the mattress.

The covers irritated her heated skin. They trapped heat and threatened to bake her to death. Not to mention each inhale grazed her nipples against the heavy fabric.

Her fist pounded the pillow. It only created lumps. She flipped onto her stomach. Bad move. The tip of her swollen clit pulsed onto the firm mattress. Her breasts also had full-on contact. A moan bled from her lips. She drowned it into her pillow, flopped onto her back, and tossed the covers off her primed body.

Shit, it wouldn't take much to make her come. One finger. The scent of his skin.

"Go to sleep, Ava."

"I can't."

"You can do anything you put your mind to."

"Even seduce you?"

"No," he barked.

"I can try."

Three days ago she wouldn't have had the guts to say that. Two days ago she would have curled into a ball at the rejection. One day ago— who was she kidding—one hour ago she wouldn't have had the balls to do this.

Ava arched her back off the bed. Her fingers dug into the soft cotton of her shirt and slipped it over her head.

"I may be a virgin, Keen, but that doesn't mean I don't understand desire. It doesn't mean you haven't made me come a thousand different ways, a thousand different times, over the last eleven years."

"Ava," he warned.

Her hands cascaded down her sides, molding to the curve of her back and the swell of her bottom. Up they traveled, teasing the swell of her lips for the briefest of seconds. A moan broke free and she let it seep into the chilled air.

"Fucking hell," Keen growled.

"I need this. I need to have you, if only in my mind. I need to come." Ava tweaked her nipples. Blood rushed to the tender peaks. She pinched again, harder. Her back bowed. She rustled her legs back and forth enjoying the pressure they placed on her swollen sex. "Yes."

"Ava, don't do this." Desperation clung to Keen's voice, a desperation she understood all too well.

"Make me stop," she dared.

A groan, sexy and sweet, rumbled from the other side of the room. "I can't make myself stop. How am I supposed to make you?"

"You're not." Ava bent her knees and spread her legs wide. Cold lapped at her hot flesh like Keen had one time after drinking ice water during their last summer together. The only time she'd ever let his face wander south.

Her father and the boys had taken the boat as usual, but stayed in the bay, catching specks. Ava had felt herself pulling away. In a desperate effort to push past her insecurities and salvage their relationship she'd driven the jet ski to the boat and dared him to come with her. Through cat calls and boos he'd dove into the water and paddled to her. She'd stolen him away to her favorite private marsh. They necked for hours. The sun heated her skin to the point of melting and Keen's practiced hands hadn't helped.

"Do you remember the last time on the marsh?" she asked.

"Panties stay on." His response came in an almost pained cry of ecstasy.

That had been her unbreakable rule. That day he'd nibbled and kissed her clit through the thick layer of her bikini bottoms. She'd been mindless, right at the precipice of orgasm—much like she was now—and he'd side stepped her rule.

His fingers slipped into the edge of her swimsuit, pulled it to the side, and his icy tongue lapped her into his mouth.

"I never wanted you to see my scars, but I've shucked the rule." She slid two fingers over her labia, bottom to top, spreading her slick excitement over the primed nub.

"You're not wearing panties?"

"No. And I'm quite wet."

"Fuck, Ava."

She couldn't hear the lewd smack of his flesh —not like it had been when Annelise had made her watch a porno—but his breaths came faster and there was a rustle of fabric. She knew he touched himself. Her ass cheeks clenched at the image her brain concocted. Keen's powerful body bowed. His fist clasping his girth. The drive of his hips as he pumped his silky length in and out of her.

"I can see you," he moaned. "The light is reflecting off your bathroom mirror onto your bed. I can make out your silhouette. The bend of your knees. The arch of your back. The points at the swells of your breasts."

Instead of making her shrink, the declaration emboldened her. "Good."

"You're not touching yourself enough." A fine strain bordered his words.

"If I do, I'll come, and I don't want this to end. Not yet."

Ava turned onto her knees, straightened, and faced Keen. With the moonlight filtering in through the bathroom mirror she couldn't see him. Though she had told him this was about her, it was about him, about him seeing all of her—even the parts she didn't like.

Her left hand toyed with her nipples, but she let her right hand drop to the junction of her hips. She held his gaze, or at least where she thought his gaze might be, while she ran a finger over each gnarled scar. A tear welled in one eye. Her index finger looped her erect peak and twisted. "Oh, yes."

She pulled again. Her hips bucked. She longed to let her fingers drop to her pulsing clitoris, but she hadn't stroked every puckered line.

"Do it again," Keen breathed.

Her finger switched breasts, coiled, and yanked.

"Shit."

Ava flattened her palm over all her scars. Slowly her fingers lowered, bracketing that raw bundle of nerves. Her hips lunged forward. She pressed down. "Keen."

"I see you. I fucking see you. Damnit, you're so beautiful." The curses made his confession all the more sweet.

"I'm swollen and ready." Ava rode her hand. Her breaths deepened. The sweet edge of oblivion caressed her.

He growled. "You're ready for me." The restraint slipped from his tone.

"Yes. I'm ready for you." Her left hand slid from her breast, over her belly, across her hip, to her bottom. She dug her nails into her cheek and pulled. "I'm so ready. I can't wait."

"Come, Ave. Come for me." He hollered and shouted his own release while she silently arched into her own bittersweet release.

It coursed through her, searing away the past, the pain, and the hurt. It wrung her muscles like wet rags, rubberized her bones. It zapped her angst and fear. Then it was over.

She collapsed onto her heels. Her quivering arms hung by her sides. Her chest heaved with shuddered gasps. His panted breaths rolled across the room, matching her own. Never had it been like this. Not on her own. Not with Keen all those years ago.

Before, she'd been a willing, but reserved, participant in their love play. Tonight she'd given herself over to the experience, to Keen. He hadn't taken her, but neither had he been able to completely deny her offering.

His breathing slowed to near silence. It rippled across the room in a cold wave, severing their connection. Instinct begged her to cover her nakedness. She ignored it. The vulnerability gave her an odd sense of vitality, as though she'd just taken her first real breath in thirty-three years of existing. She lay on her side, stretched out on the soft sheet, propped her head on the pillow, and continued facing Keen though she still couldn't see him.

Her chirping phone broke the silence. She debated declining the call. Gray would just yell some more and ruin her post-orgasmic peace. But she swiped the screen and snapped into the receiver. "What?"

"Get down to headquarters now. You and Hunt," Gray ordered.

"Make me."

She saw him then. Keen's bare chest materialized from the dark. Her eyes cataloged the dips and swells of his physique, the scars, and the throw around his otherwise naked waist.

"What is it?" he asked. Her gaze lifted to his. Regret? Was that regret that clouded his blue eyes, or concern?

In her ear, papers shuffled. She kicked the mouth piece up and whispered, "Gray wants us at HQ."

Keen's gaze narrowed on her breasts for a fraction of a second before flying back to her face.

"What time did you get back from Angola?" Gray asked.

"An hour ago, if that. Why?" Suspicion lined her voice.

"There's been another murder."

Chapter Eighteen

They walked off the elevator and headed toward Winslow and Abbott's office. Keen hadn't said a word since he ordered Ava to come. His inner monologue though, read like a bad episode of Judge Judy. Weak testimony. Even weaker defenses. Lots of self-deprecating. Even more cussing.

What the fuck had he just done? Rules were rules for a goddamned reason. Ava'd had hers. He created his after she knocked his heart out of his chest.

Never take what you can't have.

He couldn't have Ava, not like he wanted or needed to have her. So, why the mother fuck had he let himself succumb to the scent of her arousal, the whimpers and moans of her desire, the hints of desperation in her voice, the shadows of her undulating curves?

Who the hell was he kidding? As much as he hated himself for buckling, he'd do it again if given the chance.

Anger, the ugly emotion he didn't like to admit he sheltered toward Ava was the only thing that kept him from gripping her hips and plunging so deep inside her he'd never find himself. As amazing as the experience would've been, he couldn't lose himself again. It had taken a long time and a lot of bullets to do it in the first place.

He didn't want to hurt her either. Not emotionally. Not physically. Had he gone to her tonight, he wouldn't have been able to control his charged passion. His bruised cock could testify to that.

Ava stopped outside the office door. He drew a lungful of air and waited. She stepped backward.

"Look on the bright side. With the time of death being nine p.m. yesterday, you have an alibi. You're no longer a suspect."

Her tousled mane shook. "Somehow, it's not all that comforting. Someone else is dead."

They walked through the door. Ten or more sets of eyes followed them through the rows of short cubicles to Winslow's door and through the glass of his fish tank office.

"Took you long enough." His voice sounded like sandpaper on rocks. Winslow raked his hands over his face. He dropped the file he'd been reading onto his desk and stretched back in his chair.

"You look like hell," Keen said.

The man's rumpled suit looked much like the one he'd worn three nights ago. The whites of his eyes were no longer blood-shot, but two Easter eggs dyed red and decorated with the pupils.

"If you want to make out later, I'll go brush my teeth." Winslow sneered.

"Tempting," Keen mused.

"Let me get this straight. I tell you to stick around." He sliced a finger at Ava. "I say stay close, and you take off out of the damn state."

Keen drew his attention from Ava. "You told me to stay close? I didn't get that memo, but now that you've hit on me, I'll be sure to." He winked.

"We never said we went out of state," Ava cut in.

"No, you didn't say you went to Louisiana, but that's the only way you'd have gotten all this information." Winslow gestured to the clutter on his desk.

Keen shrugged in answer. He wasn't going to confirm what Winslow knew to be true. From the smile that slowly grew on the man's face, neither was he going to demand an explanation.

Winslow gestured for them to have a seat and they complied. "I have to admit, as much as it pains me, you two are downright saviors." His red gaze shifted to Ava. "I never liked you for this Ava, but damn, with the evidence it was looking real bad. It's still bad. Just not for you."

He rubbed at his monumental shoulder. "I've got two dead lawmen and a killer who's dropped off the grid."

Two dead lawmen. Keen's gut clenched.

"Who's the third victim?" Ava whispered as though any volume would shatter her reprieve.

"I hate to be the one to tell you this." Winslow's gaze bore into Ava's. The rise and fall of her chest stilled. "He killed Stan Watts."

"No." Her hands clamped against her temples.

"Who's Stan Watts?" Keen met Winslow's gaze.

"They worked together," he answered.

"What kind of relationship did you have with Stan?" Winslow asked pointedly.

"A contentious one." Her words were muffled by her wrists. She sat slowly and dropped her hands. "We worked in the same office, saw each other almost daily, but we weren't close. He was good at his job, but never as good as he thought he was. I tried to keep him grounded, focused, and he didn't always appreciate the help."

"Did many people know this?" Winslow jotted notes in the open file.

"Stan could get loud about it at times. Indignant." Her narrow shoulders shrugged. "Most people in the office knew about it. I have no idea how Rory Coghlan would know."

"I think I know." Winslow tossed a file in Ava's direction. "Coghlan's last known address is two blocks down from yours."

"What the fuck?" Keen's fists clench. He jumped from the chair and began pacing.

Ava slammed the file onto the desk. The thud resounded in the small space. She lowered her head to the page.

"Have you talked to the landlord?" Keen barked.

"He's still paying his bill, but the man hasn't seen Coghlan for three months and two days."

"What makes the landlord know the last time he saw Coghlan down to the day?" Ava's head canted.

"Coghlan gave him cash for the next six month's rent. For a man who usually has to chase people down to get his money that's enough easy money to make you mark the day," Winslow said.

"Where'd he get the money?" Ava asked in an amazingly calm voice.

Keen didn't trust himself to say much right now.

"He was working as a janitor for Corcoran Gallery. And get this," Winslow's scowl threatened to break his face. "Corcoran uses the same company for badges and uniforms as your office. Shit, our offices too. I have a feeling he spent time snooping around your workplace, listening to gossip, asking questions."

Ava flipped a page in the file. "Tell me what you know about his younger years."

"It seems he would have rather been a painter with his work displayed at the Corcoran than been a janitor for it. He dropped out of LSU's college of art after six rather successful semesters. He moved to New York after that. Ithaca for a year, then NYC for two. He ended up in DC one year ago. We're working on birth records, but he's had some pretty fancy fakes done. It'll take some time."

"He..." Ava's voice quivered. Her gaze swung to his. Her lower lip quaked. "He was in Ithaca and New York City when I was."

Keen choked his rage down and knelt by Ava. "Think it through. Why?"

Her eyes shifted around the room, not seeing it. "I don't know."

"Talk it out," he urged.

"He's focused on me. He doesn't kill for the pleasure of it, not yet."

She looked at him, pleading, but then her gaze fell to her hands.

"Focus, Ava." Keen held his rage together by the thinnest of strands. The sick fuck had followed her from college to college. He'd stalked her for years. And where had he been? "Tell me about Coghlan."

"He's not like Hardy. Not meticulous. He didn't even check to make sure I was here before taking his next victim. He's focused only on his plan, but he's not cunning. He's letting us see too much. It's not the kill, it's the end game with him, the plan. I just don't have a clue what the plan is."

Chapter Nineteen

"I thought you guys already went through the place, and from the looks of things there wasn't much to see." The landlord leaned heavily on the banister and hoisted himself with such dramatics you'd have thought he ascended Everest.

"We appreciate your help," Keen said without managing to sound too sarcastic. That impressed Ava.

"Yeah, well I'm missing my show." He made base camp two, the second floor landing, and rounded the banister. Ava brought up the back of the line and caught an eyeful of lower belly hair the man's *Battlestar Galactica* T-shirt exposed. Again with the show.

"You pressed pause, which means when you're done here you get to go back and press play, which means you're not missing anything." The maybe forty-year-old stopped with his key in the door and looked at Ava. She probably looked like a crazy person with her hands stretched wide in the air, but so be it. It had taken them fifteen minutes to coax him from his apartment and in that time her Battlestar trivia knowledge had gone from zero to proficient, and she didn't give a shit about how many civilian ships remained in the Colonial fleet because, well, fiction.

"It's my sacred time." The landlord rolled his eyes at Ava, and then looked to Keen. "Lock the door and slide the key under the door when you're done." He walked the opposite way around the landing. Ava hurried to the door behind Keen, afraid the man might pull a laser gun on her or something. The angry stomp of his descent echoed behind them.

"Way to go." Keen turned the key, and then drew his gun.

They cleared the apartment in short time. Then Keen hung back and let her work. Winslow and Abbott had already gone through the place and taken anything they thought was worthy. But Ava knew the essence of people lived in places long after they were gone. Not so much in the spiritual sense, but in the way they lived. She wandered through the rooms touching walls, running her fingers over books, getting a feel for the man who had lived there. She meandered through the kitchen and spent five minutes sitting at the man's desk without touching anything or saying a word.

A single notepad, potato-chip crispy from disuse, and a pencil lay on the corner of the drink-ring stained wood. Ancient flowered paper covered the wall. The white had probably yellowed before she was born. A thin layer of dust plus who knew what clung to the roses and daisies. The paper stopped at dusty book shelves that stretched up to the ceiling. A four by six rectangle in the center of the wallpaper sucked her in like a vortex, and there she went with the Battlestar references.

Its flowers shined bright here. The film of dirt hadn't landed on this space, a space where Coghlan had reverently displayed a picture.

So long ago her father had displayed a picture of her and her mother in much the same style, center of the wall in front of his desk. She stared at the spot for what seemed an eternity, then shot up and moved down the hallway into the bathroom. Keen followed her with a curious expression painted on his face. After closing the lid on the toilet, Ava sat down. She glanced at Keen, who, she suspected, strained to keep his mouth shut on a sarcastic remark. Probably afraid to scare away her flowing juju. But this wasn't juju. This wasn't her training. It was experience from her youth.

When she dropped her head between her knees, her hair dangling on the floor, Keen muffled a "Yuck." Her hoot of triumph stopped any further comment. Ava straightened, sank onto the floor, and crawled beneath the pedestal sink.

"Ha! I've got you, sneaky bastard." A smile cramped her cheeks.

Keen crouched next to her. His wide shoulder bumped her off balance...along with his scent. "Sorry."

She didn't know for what exactly he apologized—bumping into her or jerking off to her ample moans. "It's all right."

Ava fingered a section of disturbed grout. The tile around it leaned slightly askew.

He gave a grunt of confusion. "How did you —"

"My father had the same hiding spot when I was little. When he was away I would snoop. He kept maps and notes inside, but I had no idea what any of it meant. I was so young. But I knew if anyone knew I messed with it I'd get in trouble."

Ava didn't know what she expected to find in the hiding spot, but she wasn't prepared for what she discovered. A cry scaled her throat, tumbled out the cliff of her lips, and ricocheted off the tile walls. She dropped the picture and scrambled back. Her shoulders hit the cast iron tub.

Keen surrendered his hands and shushed her like he'd cornered a wild animal. All the peace she'd gained over the last few hours fell away.

The lone picture occupying the space wasn't of a mutilated body or painted wall. It was not grotesque in any way. It was happy and peaceful. Her stomach churned and her head spun. She clawed at Keen's arms and pulled him close. He wrapped her protectively in his hold. His wide chest supported her shoulder. She leaned into him and stared down at the photo.

The faded hue, the tattered edges did not diminish the beauty of two lovers in an embrace or the setting sun and the unmistakable width of Lake Pontchartrain at their backs.

"This was taken at Fountain Blue State Park, in Mandeville, Louisiana. My mother has an old picture taken when I was three in this very spot. It was my father's favorite vacation spot. My parents were smiling just like..." She broke off, unable to speak with the lump in her throat. Swallowing hard, she continued, "...just like they are, and I was sitting right there."

"Do you know the woman?"

Ava shook her head. The woman in the photo was a stranger, but looked so much like her mother. Long strawberry locks flowed straight down the woman's back. Her skin was smooth ceramic cream with the exception of freckles dotting the bridge of her nose. The major difference was this woman was voluptuous, curving, like a pin-up. Her large breasts were made more so by the swell of her pregnant abdomen. Her red lips were so close to the man's face they drew his attention from the camera. And the man in the photo was all too familiar. It was the face which had haunted her dreams for nearly thirty years.

Her father, James Red Hardy.

***

Keen smacked the black top of Winslow's SUV and turned toward Ava. The car took off like a lightning bolt. Good. They needed to move on this lead and fast. This thing circled too close to Ava for his comfort.

"Winslow will have the photo analyzed and have the woman's face run through the facial recognition database."

Ava drifted down Calvert Street. Keen drifted with her.

She'd known her father was a murderer for a long time. He wouldn't have thought finding out the man had cheated would be such an additional blow. In comparison, the crime was paltry at best. Showed what he knew about the way women think. It appeared Hardy had a triple life. Family man and murderer had not been enough for him. Add duplicitous.

He didn't know how to help, but he knew keeping his distance was becoming harder and harder.

"I was in Afghanistan," Keen said, pulling her gaze back to the present and out of whatever hell she trundled through. She watched him eagerly as they walked, as if thankful for the distraction. He scanned their surroundings as he talked, taking in every detail around them. This guy was close. Too close.

He studied the homeless man on the corner, the hooded jogger headed out of the park, the couple walking past them. "We were hunting an American spy who had infiltrated al-Qaeda ranks then flipped. His knowledge helped a group of insurgents wipe out one of our bases, killing thirty soldiers and destroying key weapons and supplies. It was a massacre." His lungs squeezed.

"We tracked him for weeks in Charikar. Late one evening we raided a house he frequented. It was believed to be the home of a high-ranking member of al-Qaeda. We walked into bedlam. Mothers and children mixed among the terrorists. Still our target was apprehended. We managed to take the house with minimal casualties."

Keen's eyes clamped shut. "We were withdrawing when he shot me."

Ava gasped. Tears twinkled on her lashes.

"He'd been standing in the corner huddled with his mother. No more than ten years old. I can still see his face. He was scared. But there was bravery behind the tears. I hesitated when he lifted his arm. I saw gunmetal black in his small hand, but I didn't want to..."

Ava slapped the tears from her cheek. "Keen." When she said his name like that his heart broke all over again.

"If I hadn't hesitated the soldier to my right would still be alive. I wouldn't have been shot. But he was just a kid, terrified and, as it turned out, trying to protect his father."

Her arm clamped around his bicep. She pulled him to a stop and he let her. Their gazes collided. She grabbed his other arm and turned him to face her.

"I am so sorry for what you had to do."

He nodded his head almost imperceptibly. "Me too."

Cars and trucks whipped past and stirred the air around them. They may as well have been in the center of the sea. Ava focused on him. She wrapped a hand around the back of his neck. With the other on the lapel of his suit she stretched up and pulled him down to meet her lips.

Keen paused just above her mouth and hovered, studying her face. Her breath caught and his followed. Decision time. Kiss her or run like hell in the opposite direction?

He couldn't run. It would be safer for him, but she'd be exposed in more ways than he cared to consider. So much had happened to her in the last few days. So many emotions tormented her. He didn't want to cause her further heartache. But what would this kiss cost him?

Everything.

That didn't matter. The only thing that mattered was the taste of their mouths melding together. With great care he moved his lips over hers. Two tentative strokes. His teeth gently pulled at her bottom lip and her mouth parted in a soft moan. His tongue traced her top lip, then swept her mouth. Her tongue caressed in frantic strokes. He pinned it between his teeth, claiming it completely.

He stepped closer, invading her space. Her hands grasped at his shoulders and back, the invasion terrifyingly welcome. The quiet voice of reason got lost between the pants and whimpers. He stroked her tongue with his own until the taste of her filled his mouth.

When Keen left her mouth to nibble a trail down her jaw she melted, pressing her breasts against his abdomen. She smelled like a woman should, sweaty and sweet and ready to be taken.

The world around them had all but vanished when a car horn blasted.

Keen jerked straight. His gaze scanned the area.

A young guy hung out the passenger window of a coupe.

Keen whipped Ava behind him, but there wasn't a need. The college-aged kid pumped his fist into the air. "Yeah! All the way man!"

What had he been thinking? He'd been thinking about his burning body and her gorgeous one. They were exposed, both physically and emotionally. This wasn't the time to screw around with their lives or their hearts. Well, his heart and her body. She'd yet to say anything about loving him other than with her svelte figure.

He stalked off toward the restaurant in between Rory Coghlan and Ava's apartments. The hand that had clutched his shoulder looped around his arm and her dainty shoes ticked like mad, trying to keep up. "That can't happen again."

Damn her, but she just snickered.

Chapter Twenty

Keen and Winslow fought to keep their amusement silent.

Winslow dipped his head behind Keen's and whispered. "You think we could erect a mat around them and sell tickets without them noticing?"

"No, but go ahead and try. I won't mind a front seat ticket to that show."

At eight-thirty that morning the facial recognition software had turned a match for the woman in the photo Ava found at Rory Coghlan's apartment. For five minutes now Agents Abbot and Shepherd argued over who would question Ms. Bree Coghlan. The two circled each other like rabid dogs, one much larger and more ferocious looking than the other, but both with unwavering tenacity.

"Who the hell do you think you are, trying to take over our investigation," Lara snapped.

"I'm the woman you tried to pin it on." Ava thumped her own chest.

"Hey." Lara planted a hand on her hip. "The apple never falls far from the tree."

Ava's upper lip—the one that tasted like sex —curled on one side. "You wouldn't even have an investigation if it weren't for me."

"How are you going to question her? You're a profiler. You haven't been in the field in what, ten years? And your boyfriend isn't even on duty right now," Lara bit back.

Keen took a step forward. Low blow.

Ava tilted her head and zeroed her gaze on Lara's. "What are we, in high school again? He's not my *boyfriend*." She made the word sound like a disease.

"I believed you better when you told me you didn't kill anyone."

"I don't have to prove anything to you." Ava touched her head, and then lifted it toward the sky. "Oh, except my innocence in the copycat murders."

"Well, if you aren't together it's only because you fucked him up so well the first time." Lara threw the surprise hook with practiced ease.

It landed on Keen's backbone. Lara's too. She shrank back like she'd pulled her weapon and it had misfired. Winslow winced as though his partner had just lopped off a unicorn's horn.

Ava stilled.

Lara and Winslow eyed one another. If they thought they'd won, they didn't know Ava like he did. Keen filled his lungs and waited for the killer blow.

Her porcelain chin lifted. Her gaze leveled on Lara Abbott's. She paused for two long heartbeats. "Who fucked you up?" Ava whispered.

Boom. Nail on head or slap in face, as it were.

Lara recoiled.

"You win. Question her." Lara passed Ava and nearly slung the door off its hinges on her way out.

Ava watched her go, and then swung on them, hands on hips and an exacerbated expression on her face. When she honed in on Keen her voice was calm with only a hint of frustration. "Gee, thanks for the help."

"You didn't need it. Besides, that was too much fun to watch. Until it got ugly," he amended. "I thought she was going to attack. A shame she didn't. Now, that would've been interesting. But I didn't have beer or popcorn, so I guess it's all for the best."

Her laugh filled the room, as unexpected as the flutter of angel wings on a bloody battlefield. It seeped into his brain like a drug, making him light of head and body. *Damn!*

He shook off the effects as best he could. "How are you smiling after that? No, I'm sorry, laughing?"

"I won." She swatted a lock of hair over her shoulder. "It wasn't pretty, but right now I'll take it however I can get it."

No shit.

He'd seen that yesterday. He turned to Winslow. "What the hell's your partner's problem?"

Winslow ruffled his hair. His gruff voice responded, "Ah, she's not used to people getting the best of her. And I think someone has been getting her best, for the last few nights. Or trying to, at least. She likes control and doesn't have any right now. Lara's never been the sweet smiling type, but this case and now this guy, has her in knots."

Keen thought about Lara Abbott in a romantic setting. His mind conjured a cage, a lone tamer with a whip, and a lion. Treacherous for all parties involved and just wrong. Curiosity got the best of him. "Who the hell'd go toe-to-toe with her, besides Ava? Romantically, I mean."

"Beaumont," Winslow said.

Better yet, a grizzly and a lion going head-to-head. Funny stuff when you weren't the one in danger of being torn limb from limb.

***

The surveillance team Winslow and Abbott had ordered camped out in an ugly tan hatchback a half a block down from Bree Coghlan's Fairfax home. Not conspicuous, unless you knew what to look for. Keen pegged them before parking. The agents would alert them if Rory chanced a visit to his mommy's house. The surveillance team, fact that Ava wore a wire, that Ava was a highly skilled NCAVC agent, most knowledgeable on the Blood Red Murders, and unyielding to a fault were the only reasons they were interviewing Bree Coghlan as opposed to Winslow and Abbot. Despite the earlier scene.

He looked at Ava, something he hadn't chanced since the drugging laugh in Winslow's office. She hadn't dismembered him all those years ago, but she'd killed him all the same. She'd done it with lighting speed and the finesse of a ninja. Six feet tall one minute, six feet under the next. This petite woman had leveled him like no other person could.

Keen should open the passenger door, shove her out, and squeal tires all the way to the airport. He should get on a plane and take his happy ass home. He really should. Instead, he cut the engine outside Bree Coghlan's white cottage style home in suburban Virginia, where she'd lived for the last five years.

"Eyes open," he warned.

She nodded. They climbed out and hustled across the street and up the brick steps. Ava pulled back the black screen door. "You've got to be kidding me."

"Apples and trees?" Keen hitched a shoulder, and then knocked on the blood-red front door. His other hand hovered near his gun.

"Sometimes the apple falls far from the tree," she whispered. Her gaze swung back to the door. "But most of the time it doesn't."

They waited. No one came to the door.

He tried again, knocking hard enough that the front of the house shook.

A woman pale enough to make Ava look like she had a tan opened the door. Eyes of Irish green met them with curiosity. Her hair was pinned into a messy bun at the crown of her head with a splintered and stained paintbrush.

"Good day to you." The fragile beauty clenched a paintbrush and an accent between her teeth. The palate pinched with her left thumb was scattered with different tones of the same color.

She wore a bright blue smock with bare feet. Her clothing and hands were both splattered with variations of red paint, some fresh, some cracked and stale. She stepped back, not waiting for introductions, and waved them into her house with a gleeful smile. Ava moved toward the door, but Keen took the lead, stepping inside first.

Keen's heart thumped inside his chest. Dread cinched tight in his chest. He scanned for hidden weapons and hidden assailants of the Coghlan variety.

She guided them through the foyer to the living room and patted the cushions of a prim patterned blue and white couch, circa nineteen sixty.

"We're fine," Ava said.

"Please." She slipped the brush from her teeth and patted the couch again. "I insist. I can't carry on a conversation until you take a seat. You want to talk, don't you?"

They sat. Ava poised on the cushion edge. Keen lounged in a gesture meant to calm.

The woman set her paints and brush on a wicker coffee table. A series of groans whined from the mismatched chair she sat in across from them. Her cheeks balled. Her eyelashes batted, cheerfully expectant. "So?"

Ava gave a small smile and began. "Ms. Coghlan?"

The woman nodded, a big grin spreading her lips. "Aye. Bree Mary Coghlan. And you?"

"I'm Supervisory Special Agent Ava Shepherd. This is Special Agent Kenneth Hunt. We'd like to ask you some question about Rory Coghlan and James Red Hardy."

The woman's head and one hand lifted to the sky. She hit the smile with the other. A throaty hoot soared. "Oh, he's done it."

Bree Mary Coghlan slapped her knees. The sharp crack matched her shrill series of laughs.

Hairs on the backs of Keen's arms stiffened. Those laughs. Fuck, had he ever heard anything more sinister? Just one thing. The little boy's father, after the kid had wiped out his team mate and forced Keen to shoot him. His stomach pitched.

Her laugh dulled to a chuckle. "He said he would, but you know how kids talk. But my boy's really done it."

Ava's rigid posture and stalled breath, the hint of perspiration on the back of her neck and several failed attempts to swallow told Keen Bree'd caught her with an uppercut too. To have her suspicious and worst fears confirmed, was bad enough. But to have them chuckled at...it severed nerves, churned guts.

Ava cleared her throat. He watched her turn the hurt into determination. He watched the heat turn to ice before his eyes.

"You're referring to Rory Coghlan as your son?"

"Yes, dear. He is half my heart."

"To be clear, who is Rory's father?"

"The other half of my heart, of course, James Bloody Red Hardy."

Ava paused. The Bloody added to her father's name had zinged her. It had surprised him, along with the half my heart bull shit. Clearly, this lady was as crazy as the man she'd screwed and the son she'd bore.

"Ms. Coghlan, tell me about your relationship with James Hardy."

The woman clutched a slender hand to her heart. "Oh, hurt me he did, when he got himself caught. I told him to slow down. That sooner or later he'd lead the police to his doorstep. But he couldn't, you know? He couldn't stop killing any more than he could stop breathing. Killing was necessary for him as much as air and art are necessary for life."

Ava scooted so close to the edge of her seat Keen thought she might topple to the ground. "You knew James Hardy was the Blood Red Killer before he was apprehended by the police?"

The woman nodded and grinned. "Aye, dear. There were no secrets between us. Besides, he could hardly hide the fact that he was a killer from me. I was to be his sixth victim."

She sighed like a girl remembering her first kiss. "I was living in New Orleans at the time, working late one night in my studio off the Quarter. I was locking up when this dashing fellow asked to use my telephone. I obliged with a flutter in my tummy."

Her hand touched the back of her bouffant do. "I remember waking on the floor of my studio with pain in my skull and a knot to boot. I looked around confused and found him standing in front of my gallery wall. He was transfixed on one of my paintings. I went to him and he took me there on the floor in front of it, body and soul. It was the greatest experience of my life. The beginning of my life."

Psycho.

In a raw voice Ava asked, "What did the painting look like?"

"Come, I'll show you." Bree stood.

They followed her through a doorway and down a narrow corridor into a large white sunroom. Potted plants sat and hung through space cluttered with easels and tables stacked with paintings. The plants should have given the room a warm homey feel along with the countless rays of sunlight that filtered in through the walls of glass, but no amount of warmth—not a fiery kiln nor molten lava —could counter the effects of the paintings.

They were bowel twisting, stomach-churning horrors.

Every painting was a canvas of red, each with its uniquely grotesque act of violence. Murder. Torture. Rape. Crimson bled off the canvas. The white background contrasted the acts.

Keen instinctively placed his hand over his gun, in reaction to the viciousness before him. He'd worked crime scene homicides, suicides, family slayings. Somehow this shook him more. Perhaps it was the way she had portrayed the act. In progress. The victim's agony etched in each brush stroke. Wide eyes and gritted teeth. Gaping mouths and tear filled eyes. Fisted hands and screams for mercy. It all showed through.

His voice sounded stronger than he felt. "Where is the one that captured Hardy?"

She smiled and pointed to the opposite end of
the room. In the center of the wall the massive
canvas hung. A woman's naked body was bound to
a bed, blood dripping out of slit wrists into a bowl.
The torturer, a shadow of red, painted the white
wall above the headboard red with the victim's
blood.

Keen's voice seeped out between his lips.
"Jesus Christ."

Bree looked on at the painting with near
religious reverence. "Inspiring, isn't it?"

"Tell us about Rory," he demanded.

"He was one year old when James went to
jail. He never had the chance to know his father.
And James wouldn't hear of us coming to jail to
visit him. I would have, but he didn't want Sarah or
you, Ava, to know about us."

Every nerve in Keen's body tingled and he
went on high alert, eyes scanning everything
around them.

Ava only whispered, "What?"

"He was afraid that you and your mother
would hurt us, that you certainly wouldn't
understand us and what we meant to your father.
So, we stayed away. Until a few years ago. Rory
decided one day he would go visit his father. He
said it was the best thing he'd ever done. They have
developed a wonderful relationship. The kind you
had with your father."

Ava's red lips moved. "Resentment. He
resents me and my mother for having the father he
never did and not treasuring him the way you do,
for not accepting him and all his habits."

"Aye, he was an angry child. There were so
many things he couldn't understand. But since he's
gotten to know his father the anger is gone. He's

been light and free. He's even been painting with me."

Ava swept her hand through the air, gesturing at the paintings. "Show me what he's painted."

They moved toward the easel she pointed to. A red cross loomed top center with a canvas-white man hanging from it, not centered like Jesus. The man was upside down, bleeding red from a large gash in his neck. His blood poured over a woman with blood-red hair, and red seeped from the cross carved with slashing brush strokes across her chest. To the right a man flew back through the air, a gun blast exploding red behind him. To the left another woman with lighter red hair matched the man on the right.

Ava's hand shot out to the painting to the name scrawled across the bottom right corner. Her finger came away with a little tack from the paint.

"When did he paint this?"

"Oh, he started it last week, but he finished it yesterday. He told me you might be stopping by and that I should answer all your questions."

"When do you expect him back?" Keen asked, Glock in hand.

"Soon," Bree purred.

Chapter Twenty-one

Ava stared at the pizza they'd picked up on the way to her apartment after their long debriefing with Winslow and Lara.

"The digestive process begins with chewing." Keen shoved the last bit of his third piece into his mouth and wiped his hand with the napkin. He leaned over the table, plucked Ava's piece from her plate, and hefted it to her mouth.

"I can't believe he didn't show."

"He's not going to make it that easy."

"Think about it. He's made everything else pretty easy. Maybe he'll show up tonight."

"And maybe you'll eat tonight." He inched the hot cheese closer to her lips.

"I'm not hungry. I don't know how you can eat after that."

"That was hours ago. I hear men are better at compartmentalizing. There's a book about it, I think." He didn't drop the slice.

Her gaze centered on the gooey cheese before narrowing on Keen. She yanked the pizza from his hand and snapped off a bite.

They were all on high alert after meeting with crazy-ass Bree Coghlan. Viewing the macabre painting of her demented offspring had been a square shot to the heart. The painting threatened

Ava, her mother, Keen, and even her father—Rory's father.

Their father was the upturned body on the cross. Coghlan planned to kill them all to heal the wounds of an orphaned boy who envied a family relationship. The family to deny him that would pay, along with all who got in the way. Namely, Keen with a bullet to the chest as the painting depicted.

She set the piece of pizza on the box.

Keen's phone chirped. Ava felt the bite of cheese and sauce slide down her esophagus.

"Chill. It's your dad. He got a throw-away and is entertaining your mom." His brows waggled.

"That doesn't help the digestive process."

"If you're not going to eat, go grab a shower. There's nothing we can do but wait until someone spots him or the weaselly bastard shows his face."

She rose from the sofa and reached for the pizza box.

"I'll get it." Keen pushed her hand away.

The inconsequential contact thawed the chill that had cloaked her all afternoon. He withdrew his hand as though she'd burned him. They hadn't talked about their shared orgasm. Judging by the way he collected the napkins and box and high-tailed it into the kitchen, they never would.

She slammed the closet door, stripped, and tossed her clothes into the basket. The water helped melt the rest of the ice that clung to her spine—well, the water and deviant thoughts of Keen stroking himself.

Ava turned off the shower. Butterflies replaced the coldness. They coursed ferocious paths down every nerve ending in her body. Her legs shook with excitement. She opened the shower door and stepped onto the plush rug in front of the vanity. Her hands trembled with it as she pulled the towel from its hook and blotted away the gleaming crystal droplets on her skin.

After hand drying her hair for a moment she flipped it to her back. She studied the woman in the mirror. She knew every inch intimately, more so than most women knew their bodies. Such things happened when a woman with a naturally healthy sexual appetite hides herself from the world—from men especially.

She refused to hide any longer. She had known pleasure a thousand times over and in a thousand different ways from her own touch. Now she was determined to know pleasure from Keen's. She craved his touch. She craved his love. She'd craved him nearly her entire life and had denied herself, but no more.

When she stepped out of the bathroom Keen's back was to the door. He held the phone to his ear and faced the window. The street lights front-lit his hair, making it lighter around the temples. No one in their right mind would mistake it for a halo, though that's what it looked like. Did devils have halos?

The veins in the hand clamped to his narrow hip bulged. His suit jacket lay discarded on the couch. The cuffs of his sleeves were rolled up around his thick forearms. His blue tie hung loose around his collar, as it had been at dinner. Though his stance was casual he stood tall, his feet braced apart. He ended the call and turned into the room with it loose in his hand. He stopped dead when his gaze caught her.

Fiery red hair, still damp, clung to her shoulders and the tops of her bare breasts. Her light-pink nipples beaded to small points. Her flat stomach quivered. The swollen lips of her sex throbbed. Ava stood boldly, excited, wanting.

His expression changed in steps. She easily read them all. Stunned fit perfectly to the first. The second was pure animalistic lust. His grip on the phone tightened and his chest began expanding and contracting at an accelerated rate. If that weren't clue enough the bulge in his pants and the look in his eyes were. Slowly the lust turned dark and anger settled. His jaw clenched tight and both his hands turned to fists. His gaze went cold.

"What are you doing?"

Ava stood her ground and maintained her composure, though she'd never felt more vulnerable in her entire life. "I'm through hiding."

"Good for you. Now put some damn clothes on."

"No. I've been running for so long and now it's done. I'm ready now. I'm not scared anymore."

"So what, I'm the lucky recipient because I happened to be here? Am I part of a therapeutic process?" Anger poured off him.

"I'm sure a therapist wouldn't recommend doing what I'm doing," she breathed. "Keen, I want you to touch me. I need *you* to touch me. No one else."

"If I touched you right now, I'd hurt you."

"Then hurt me if you have to. Just touch me."

"No!"

He pocketed the phone and keys off the coffee table and headed for the door. He didn't even look at her as he crossed the room and skirted past.

She grabbed his arm.

His normally steady voice shook when he said, "Let go of me, Ava."   Her hand tightened its grip. His arm straightened with a jerk, breaking her hold. He clamped her shoulders with his large hands. The breadth of his chest backed her against the entrance wall. His face came down inches from hers.

"Please," she begged. Each heaving breath pressed her breasts against his shirt. Only two luscious scrapes of her nipples on the starched fabric and he removed his body.

He stayed her hand. It spread across her sternum, warming her insides to goo. A moan whispered across her lips.

"Ava," he warned.

"Keen."

"Don't," he growled. "Don't ask me to give you something I can't."

"You don't have to give me anything. No strings." She laced her fingers with his on her chest and pressed. Centimeter by centimeter his hand moved under hers. Her head lolled. Her body arched. She pressed her left breast into his hand. "Yes. No expectations. I just want you to take away the—"

He jerked his hand away.

"That's what you always wanted. Me, but not all of me."

He turned away and laced his fingers behind his neck.

"In the beginning you wanted my friendship. Someone who wasn't bound to you by blood or marriage, who didn't judge you by your father's actions. Now you want my cock. Someone to erase the pain of the past few days and right your world."

His paced steps brought him to the door of the apartment. He strangled the knob.

"That's not true. I..." He stalled at her words. She knew what he wanted to hear. She knew how she felt about him. But the words stuck to her tongue.

"I need some air." His words echoed in her ears long after the door closed behind him.

Chapter Twenty-two

Keen needed time and space to calm his rage. He retrieved the phone from his pocket and ordered Winslow to put a car outside Ava's building while he was gone. Fifteen minutes later, the agents showed. He briefed them on the situation, then left.

He walked aimlessly, fists bunched at his sides. Everyone he came across gave him a wide berth. He had no idea where he was going, but he knew away was the only safe place.

Horns blared. Pedestrians shuffled. Cars whizzed. Women of the night waggled brows. He pounded the pavement.

When his fists finally relaxed he shoved into an old Irish pub and took a seat at the bar.

Deep in brooding thought he didn't order, only sat, fists on the bar, lost. After ten minutes the bartender, a seventy-something real McCoy, set a pint down in front of his face. "Beamish Stout," the man said in a thick brogue. "A dark ale for your dark fret." Keen gave a grunt and a sorry excuse for a smile.

He pulled several long drinks off the draft. He didn't survey his surroundings. He didn't move, only sat and wandered through jumbled thoughts.

Ava had hurt him so completely his heart had more scar tissue than his body. To a young man in love, down on one knee with a ring in his hand was the most vulnerable position there was. His hands had shaken and his voice had quivered.

When she'd turned tail and run away she'd yanked half his heart out of his chest and taken it with her. As he replayed the scene in his mind over and over throughout the years he could see his heart, a string tied tight around it binding it to hers, leaving a trail of blood as she ran.

So he'd stitched his heart and closed it off to everyone, especially Ava. It was the only way he could hear her name or see her face without dying. And it was exactly why he had sex with no emotion. Sexual passion numbed his senses. But he would never allow true passion, true connection.

He'd known—until tonight—he could never have her in any sense of the word. The finality had been the only thing holding him together, allowing him sanity. When she—seemingly on a whim— changed her mind and opened the possibility to him she ripped away another quarter of his heart.

She had hurt him so deeply, that in a sick way, though he loved her, he wanted to hurt her. He wanted her to feel the pain, the longing for something she could never have. And if he had gone to her, he would have hurt her, physically and emotionally. His emotions had been so raw in that moment. The thought terrified him, because in hurting her he would have ultimately hurt himself.

He was also terrified because if he went to her, if he took her physically, there would be nothing left of him. She would have his entire heart, his mind, his soul. But she would never give hers to him and he would die when she retreated, like she always did. He would die of nothingness.

Keen put a twenty on the bar and headed back toward the apartment. The bartender shook his head after him. His pace was quicker and more frantic than when he'd left.

Ava was everything to him. She always had been and always would be. There was nothing he could do to change that. It had been fated long ago.

If he could have her—even just once—he didn't need his heart.

Chapter Twenty-three

Ava woke in confusion. Unusually bright morning light seeped in through her puffy lids. *Shit.* She'd just cried herself to sleep and wasn't ready to face the day or Keen, if he'd come back. His dismissal had been complete, and too earned for her conscious mind to handle.

Noise from someone in her room brought her head from beneath her pillow. Peeking out, she swallowed hard. She blinked past the harsh overhead light into Keen's harsher stare.

Keen stood bare-chested beside her bed. His eyes locked intently on hers, his expression schooled. His shirt and shoes lay discarded on the floor. He held her gaze for a long minute, then his hands moved to the belt and button of his pants.

From her lips a soft question touched the air. "What are you doing?"

"You wanted me to touch you. I'm getting ready to touch you." With those raspy words he shoved his pants, boxers and all, to the ground and stood in front of her, naked and beautiful.

"Look at me, Ava. All of me." His voice was hot and demanding.

If she tried she couldn't tear her gaze away from his, but his body... Uncertainty and innocence kept her gaze transfixed on his. His command bolstered her confidence and she shifted her gaze over his body.

Muscles, taut with tension, covered his entire frame. Thick arms and a chest she longed to reach out and touch, skin to skin, taunted her. His abdomen was lean; the rippled V above the arch of his hips pointed her eyes toward his erection, which took over her every thought as she watched it thicken still and rise pulsing at his belly button. Its color darkened with the flow of blood.

Stout legs propelled him forward. He stopped at the edge of the bed, reached down, grabbed a handful of covers, and flung them to the ground. She propped up on one elbow. He pushed her onto her back and slid his fingers into the collar of her pajamas. His finger made the first electric contact with her bare skin. The simple touch was enough.

"Keen."

One by one he unfastened each button in measured pace. She watched in wide eyed wonder.

When all of the buttons were undone he gave a throaty command. "Take it off. All of it."

The sound itself caressed her skin and seeped deep inside, shocking her core. Ava sat and faced him. Boldly, she opened her top and slid it off her arms onto the floor. She shifted to her knees on the bed in front of him and slid her pants off as well. For the second time that day she was naked in front of him, aroused and ready to be taken.

He touched her under the chin and raised her gaze to meet his. "Once I touch you I'm not going to stop."

Her heart soared and her body hummed. She whimpered. "I don't want you to stop."

"You're going to moan and beg and call my name."

"Yes," she agreed breathlessly.

Her chest heaved against his words as they aroused her further. They warmed her skin to a simmering blaze. His words were true. She had already begged him and was willing to beg all the more for his touch, his love.

Her hands hung loose by her side. Keen grabbed them and brought them up, his deep eyes studying their lines and creases before he buried his face in them. He breathed in deeply and raked one palm down the side of his face, nuzzling it as though it were his lifeblood. Her other palm he ran over his thick lips. Each texture was different and exhilarating under her hand. One rough and hard. The other wet and pliant. Both warm man. When he got to her fingertips he bit them, and then licked away the exquisite pain.

He freed her hands and moved his to her flushed face. His thumb traced the arch of her brow, and the bridge of her nose, and the wet pout of her lips. His knuckles brushed her cheeks and the length of her neck.

While she pressed into his touch Ava's hands scoured his body, molding to the topography of his arms, chest, and stomach. When she took the length of him in her hands, her mouth watered.

"You did this last night? Stroked yourself like this?" She fisted his girth and pulled the silky skin to the tip.

A fierce growl broke from his lips. "Not so tight."

Ava repeated the motion once more, but loosened her hold.

In quick motion, one hand tangled into her hair at the base of her neck while his other hand latched hold of her bare ass. He pulled her off the bed to meet him. Her hands instinctively released his cock and wrapped around his body. Her legs twined his hips. He held her so tightly, so possessively, she might meld right to him.

The contact of sex on sex shocked a buck out of her and he groaned deep in his throat. When her mouth fell open from surprise he inhaled her gasp with his mouth.

His hands twisted in her hair. He bombarded her lips, her mouth, her tongue with his. He raked his teeth over her lips, biting and nipping. Over and over their tongues caressed, battled, and mated like he couldn't taste her enough.

Ava's body took control. She began to grind her slick sex against his dick. He abandoned her mouth to lean back and watch her work.

She didn't disappoint. There was nothing timid or shy about the woman she became in his arms. Ava rubbed herself up and down his length, teasing them both at the tip.

He whirled around, took two steps, and plastered her against the wall, his body dominating hers. His hands rubbed over her bottom to the core of her femininity. His touch was gentle and driving. The perfect pressure against her slick folds.

A wave of pleasure, raw and overpowering, threatened to bury her alive. Ava stopped rocking. She pulled close to his face, locking in a gaze so deep and full of meaning she could have drowned in it. She pulled him closer still and feasted on his mouth with the same enthusiasm as he had consumed hers. His hands abandoned her sex and cupped her face. His hardness stood in stark contrast to her supple skin.

He broke the kiss, strode forward, and tossed her onto the bed. Quickly he followed and covered her with his massive body. Her hair splayed out on the sheet and he nuzzled it. "My God, you have the most intoxicating scent."

He burrowed into her neck and repeated the ritual, then kissed his way to the other side. He moved to her breasts for an eternity, tasting and tempting. He moved slowly over her body, reveling in her milky skin. The curves she'd deemed average to boyish now seemed sensuous and alluring under his spell.

Ava's heart jumped at the way he savored her in this moment of abandon, of intimacy.

When he turned her onto her stomach to rove her back, her butt and legs, she panted. "Please, Keen. Now. I can't wait."

He ignored her pleas and continued on, licking and tasting her flesh. The trail his mouth forged stoked the fire inside her to raging.

"Keen, now," she begged again.

Finally, he answered her plea by rolling her to face him again. He spread her knees wide and rested her thighs across his. She was open to him. Vulnerable. Ready.

"Ava, I want you to look. Watch us come together."

She watched as he pulled her up to meet him. The head of his plump cock positioned at her entrance. He prodded her wet opening. He stroked and tantalized her. His fingers grazed her scars with maddening care.

"Keen, please. God, please."

He sank his head in an inch and froze, dead still.

"Ava?"

She didn't answer, except for wiggling her hips trying to fit him into place. But he stilled her advance.

"Ava," he said again more desperately. "Tell me."

She looked at him with love and honesty in her eyes. "I already told you. I've never been with anyone. I've never had sex with anyone."

From the expression of shock and pain on his face her words had nearly knocked him on his ass. Ava hadn't only denied him all those years ago. No, she had been denying herself forever. For all these years she had been hiding, but not from him and not from her father. She had been hiding herself from the world.

"Ava, I can't stop," he gritted.

Tears streamed down her cheeks. "Please don't. You can't. I want this. I want you."

He eased himself in inch by inch while she watched. When he was firmly in her entrance he plunged the last of his sex deep inside her with a quick thrust. She cried out a gasp of pain and awe. He collected her into his arms. Quiet and still, he stayed firmly embedded inside her. He kissed her face and licked away her tears.

Slowly, he withdrew and thrust back inside. Pleasure marbled with pain at the invasion. Over and over she shouted, begging for more. His strokes became longer and deeper. Her cries turned to moans. Her hands on his shoulders anchored her body to his. The pressure of the orgasm building inside her was like none she'd ever experienced before. It was a tangible force looming over her with certainty.

When he lifted her butt to gain better access, the fuller contact bombarded her senses. She was washed over by a climax so ferocious it robbed her of breath. Sounds emanated from her mouth, loud and primal.

Around him, her inner muscles clenched and his control unleashed. Three more solid thrusts and he spilled himself into her.

Satisfaction unlike any she'd ever known made her limp. Keen collapsed on top of her. They lay face to face and drumming heart to drumming heart. He rolled her on top of him and settled her head into the crook of his shoulder, holding her close with one arm and caressing her hair, shoulders, and face with the other.

His soothing touch, the body contact, the post-orgasmic high lulled her lids.

A chirping tone woke them only an hour later. In an attempt to hide from the still-blinding bedroom light Ava nuzzled her face under Keen's neck. The sating scent of male warmth she inhaled sprang forth new ideas. Shifting up, her teeth scraped the sensitive skin of his jaw. Her tongue drew on his lobe and trapped it in between her lips.

His loins stirred and he grew hard inside her. Of all the ways to wake up, this was far and away the best ever.

"Yes."

She rocked on him and worked a deep groan out of his throat. Levering up, she looked into his eyes. A blue so pure it cleansed hurtful memories stared back at her in wonder. The phone's chirping silenced.

His hand cradled the back of her neck as his smiling lips kissed a path from her temple down to her mouth. After feasting there, he pushed her back, his blue eyes challenging her to finish what she'd started.

Her desperate hands ran over his body. A thick neck led to broad shoulders and a hard chest. Her hands dug in there, using his muscles for leverage while she rode him. She moved her hips in rhythm to her own need. His hands slid up her thighs and settled on her hips, helping keep time. When his hands raised to stroke her breasts and pinch her nipples, her pleasure peaked. Head thrown back in abandon she panted, rode out her climax, and worked him through his own.

Hot, wet cum seeped out of her body. Her heart stuttered. *Shit.* Shit. *Double shit.* They hadn't used protection. She wasn't some naive barely-teenager. Condoms. The pill. The shot. An IUD. Birth control. Ava knew about all the options, probably more so than any other woman her age, most of whom were trying to grow their little families.

Odd as it was, but since she'd never used any of them she found them deeply fascinating. But apparently not more fascinating than Keen's naked body.

He pulled out of her for the first time in hours and she was caught by a sense of loss, until he pulled her close and nuzzled his cheek to hers. For Ava, the need to cement things between them was suddenly overwhelming. She couldn't imagine living one day without Keen in her life. He couldn't leave, not without her. Or he could stay with her. But life without him was no longer an option. She just hoped she hadn't put the cart before the horse, as her mother used to say to her, Ford, and Nathan.

His eyes were closed and his jaw was set. The rhythm of his breath steadied. She leaned in and kissed the tip of his nose. The corners of his mouth turned up ever so slightly.

"Keen, I—"

The chirp of the phone cut her off. He shifted to reach the phone. Ava threw her arms around him, trying desperately to keep him anchored to her, to finish the words she'd started to say.

He must have seen the panic in her eyes. His smile doubled. He tossed her onto her back and leaned over. "We'll talk when there aren't any

interruptions. Trust me—I've waited long enough
for you to tell me you love me. I can wait a minute
more."

When he rolled over to grab the boisterous
phone she smacked his bare butt. *Arrogant prick.*

Keen answered the phone with a smirk.

"I'm not on any birth control," she blurted.
And I love you. She kept that part to herself for
now. Why? She had no idea. Maybe she wanted to
see how he'd react to that two-by-four between the
eyes.

He cupped her face and something played in
his clear eyes.

After only a moment the smirk fell away. He
stiffened. A stony expression clouded their joy as he
listened intently to the person on the other end of
the phone. The expression wiped the smile from
Ava's face. He covered the mouthpiece with a hand.

"Go get cleaned up. It's Coghlan. Abbott's
been stabbed."

Chapter Twenty-four

Keen pointed his hand in the direction of downtown. The button-down stretched across his ample chest. "This is going to sound damn heartless, but let's bypass the hospital and go to headquarters."

"What?" Ava leaned forward and swiveled her entire body toward Keen, pressing her seatbelt to its limits.

"We'll only be in the way at the hospital. We can help Lara more by swimming through files until we find the missing piece of the puzzle. Complete the puzzle. Catch Rory Coghlan."

Ava understood the need to take action, to do something, anything, to help. When one of your own was down it hurt. It hurt more when it was someone you knew and respected like hell, in spite of their prickly demeanor.

"Your plan is logical, but we need to go to the hospital. Sure, all the files, timelines, and databases aren't there, but the evidence of his changing patterns is. I need to talk to Winslow."

"You need to assuage your guilt."

"That's only part of it."

She couldn't pinpoint a singular reason, but she felt pulled to the hospital. Maybe the argument she'd had with Abbott earlier in the day spawned the tiny droplets of guilt pooling in the back of her brain. Maybe the fact that their roles could have easily been reversed bridged a connection to the woman whose life hung in the balance. Maybe finely tuned instinct told her there were no answers in files, but in the violence of the man haunting her.

"When I talked to Winslow they were just getting her on the gurney. Text him. See where they're taking her."

Ava dialed.

"Gray." His greeting was reedy, far weaker than the tank of a man he was.

"What hospital?"

"Inova Fairfax."

Ava mouthed the location to Keen. "Bring everything you have on this case inside. We'll be there in twenty."

"Judging by the slug's pace of these EMT's you'll fucking beat us there." A bit of the strength flowed through the phone in impotent frustration.

"They're stabilizing her for transport." Ava balked at her clinical response, and then added, "Abbott's a bruiser. No way will she let a simpering daddy's boy get the best of her. She'll fight."

"Yeah. I just hope it isn't..."

"We'll be there soon," Ava said. Like their arrival would somehow save Lara Abbott's life.

Nope. If anything, Ava's presence would send her into V-tach.

Winslow disconnected.

Keen's hand centered her chest and pushed. "For the love... Would you please sit back? Your seatbelt won't work if you've already got your face in the windshield."

"Yes, sir."

"Hmm, I like the sound of that." Keen removed his hand from her chest, but she swore it left a sizzling burn under her shirt.

Absentmindedly he rubbed his palm on the charcoal-grey leg of his slacks. He concentrated on the road. The buildings shrank then dwindled. Conversely the trees grew then multiplied. Sixteen minutes later they parked outside the emergency room entrance and headed for the door.

Pouty red lips and massive breasts greeted them. If the woman said, "This is a stick up," Ava would raise her hands in the air. Betty Boop's weapons looked that deadly. Instead, she said, "Can I help you, handsome?"

Ava quaffed her surely frizzed hair. "Well, thank you."

Ms. Boop, or Boobs as it were, covered her mouth.

"I'm looking for an FBI agent just brought in or on her way. Lara Abbott," Ava said.

"She came in about ten minutes ago. Critical." Boob's dark gaze slid to Keen. "The others are in a private waiting room on the right just before the double doors of the OR."

Boobs leaned forward, leading with her only assets. "I'm sorry."

Keen ignored the blatant gesture. His fingers wrapped Ava's and he tugged. "Come on. I see the OR."

Despite everything, their past, the killer looming, and the life in question, Ava's heart did a little song and dance in her chest.

That's right lady, back up. He belongs to me, and I finally have the balls to claim him.

A smile bloomed and her cheeks heated with unmeasurable joy. This was love. Ill timed, inappropriate, headless-of-its-surroundings love.

Ava firmed her grip on his hand and pulled him into a small alcove near a little desk with a computer and a phone. She planted her hands on either side of his face and stared into his brilliant eyes. The feelings inside her bubbled out in a near-giddy squeal. She wasn't prone to squeals, giddy or otherwise, but hell if she could control it.

"I know this is the worst time, but I can't wait for a time when we're not being interrupted or chasing a mad man or surrounded by people we don't know. I've waited too long already. I wasted so much precious time running scared. I can't control it any more and I never want to again."

She leaped into his arms and crushed him to her. Their lips collided in a heated tangle. His arms tightened around her, securing her body to his. The zig in her belly zagged to the tips of her extremities.

Ava pulled back for a breath and filled her lungs with him. Warmth cocooned her.

"Keen, I love you."

He smiled his devilish smile and took her mouth. When her hands began to roam he broke the kiss and set her on her feet. He steadied her and blew a breath. "It's about damn time."

After straightening themselves they continued down the hallway and turned quietly into the waiting room where a mixture of lawmen and family paced or sat, their faces trenched with various depth of grief.

The cloud of elation she'd soared upon moments ago dissipated. Life giveth and life taketh away. What if Rory tried to take Keen away?

They shook hands with several agents before they made their way to Winslow, who sat in a far corner with puffy red eyes and a tear soaked face.

Ava tried to politely ignore the quiet sobs of the woman across the room, but when Keen broke away from her and moved toward the woman she stopped to watch. His large frame nearly blocked the woman from her view when he knelt in front of her. A huge fella, who made Keen look small and Winslow look average sized, rubbed a hand up and down the woman's back. Ava stared on as Keen spoke in hushed tones to the couple.

"Lara's mom and dad," a deep voice said in her ear.

Turning to the voice, Ava came face to chest with Mason Beaumont. When she took a half step back and brought her face up to his she could see anguish etching it. "Mason?"

"I'm an interloper. Not family. Not Bureau." He shrugged. "But she matters."

"I'm sorry. Yeah, Gray said you and Lara were...well, you know." How did one say *screwing around* delicately?

"It's not like that." He shoved his hands into his pockets and rocked onto his heels. "We've never even gone out. She won't accept my invitation. I don't mean this as arrogantly as it'll sound, but I know she wants to. I can see it in her eyes." He winced. "Man, that just sounds creepy. Forget it."

"No. Well, maybe," she conceded, "if other people didn't see it too. Gray did. He said you affected her when most men don't."

"In a good or bad way is the question. I never expected a woman like Lara. I never expected her to matter."

Ava smiled. "When she wakes up, ask her."

"Sure."

"She'll be fine, Mason." And though she didn't get along with the woman, she hoped it was the truth.

Keen stepped into their small circle. He shook Mason's hand and patted his shoulder.

The dark version of Keen nodded. "How are her parents holding up?"

"As well as can be. They have each other to hold onto through the storm."

"What'd you say to them?" Curiosity got the better of Ava. It always did.

"I just told them that if a weak ass like me could make it through a tough spot, a fighter like Lara was a sure bet."

She just stared at him in that gooey wonderment of love until Mason shooed them toward Winslow. "Go get the details so y'all can catch this piece of shit." Several nods and here-here's flashed through the room.

They would've huddled in the corner with Winslow, but his guilt ate up the space. Tears trailed the man's cheek. "It's my fault." His head hung as though someone had snapped the vertebrae in his neck.

"That's bullshit and you know it," Ava disagreed. "Rory Coghlan is the one to blame. Not you. Not me. Now, dry it up and tell us what happened."

"Damn, you're bossy." Winslow wiped the moisture from his face.

Keen nodded his agreement.

Winslow drew a ragged breath. "He had to know we were watching the house. That son of a bitch...he baited us like fucking trout. Just before nightfall he moseys up to Bree Coghlan's front door, rings the goddamn door bell, and waits for her to let him in. I got a call from my guys watching as soon as he showed. They wanted to move, but I told them to stay put."

"Abbott and I...we really wanted a piece of him. More than that, we didn't want him to slip through two suits. I instructed Mitch and Dan," he said pointing to two agents sitting near the doorway, "to watch the house, contact us if anything changed, and to follow him if he left."

"We made it to the house in record time, but it was dark by the time we got there. Mitch and Dan took the front. Abbott and I split up."

He let the story hang there while he rubbed his palms into his eyes and took several rattling breaths.

"We were supposed to meet in the back. Lara down one side of the house, me down the other. That sick fuck hid under the house. Took her from behind." A grunting mixture of laughter and disgust escaped his throat. "He didn't expect a fighter. He nicked her throat, but she blocked him from..." His head shook.

"He would've slit her throat. But she stopped him. There was a short struggle. I heard the sound, the unmistakable grunt of effort and satisfaction Lara gives when she really nails somebody. I knew she was fighting Coghlan, but I just jogged toward her. I knew she'd just cocked him a good one and I actually smiled. I knew she had him. Then she screamed."

Gooseflesh rolled in long waves over Ava's arms, across her middle, and down her legs.

"She's never screamed before, not like that. It can't be the last thing I hear from her." Again with the head shake.

"I ran then, all out. When I rounded the house she just lay in a heap. I froze. Worthless. Mitch called for an ambulance. Then he and Dan searched for Coghlan. They called for the dogs."

"I finally went to her. She rasped these shallow, wispy breaths. But she was breathing. I tried to stop the blood. But it just kept coming." Fresh tears dripped off the end of his nose.

"It took the ambulance five minutes to get to her. It seemed like that many hours. The dogs came. Followed a trail back under the house, out the other side, and through back yards two blocks. Then lost him. He probably hopped in his car and drove away clean, like he was never there. But he was. I didn't see him, but he was there."

He dissolved into silent tears.

Ava patted his back and looked desperately at Keen for some guidance. He pinched her chin lightly between his thumb and folded forefinger. "Coffee. We all need some coffee."

"Yeah, coffee would be a good start."

She watched him weave his way out of the crowded waiting room. When his bright blond hair, broad back, and cute butt vanished from view, Ava adjusted in the hard chair and eased back. Taking in the room full of hopeful mourners, Ava began to reason out all the information she had on Rory Coghlan. Her hand stilled on Winslow while her training and instinct went to work.

As she began to calculate all the facts the room around Ava dimmed. Her father, James Red Hardy, had begun killing at an early age. Long before he'd met and married her mother, James had a long-standing love affair with Bree Coghlan. So why had he married Sarah and started a family like he was the perfect business and family man? Because he needed a false front? Because he loved Sarah? Why hadn't he married Bree?

Too many questions she couldn't answer there. On to the next. He continued to kill women, built a family, and maintained an affair. His affair ratcheted up a notch when he knocked up Bree nearly eight years in. Shortly after his son was born, James Hardy got caught. The killing stopped and two families, legal and not, imploded.

It galled Ava, but she was forced to admit both she and her half brother had been wounded in the blast. Over the years, those wounds festered from the infection that was her father. They festered in vastly different directions, but abscessed all the same.

Ava fixated on work, on curing the evil in the world. Rory fixated on hurt and hate. He begrudged her and her mother for having the father and family he never did. The hunger for his father morphed into revolt and he plotted a course for revenge. Long planned and far thought out. Further than she'd ever anticipated.

Needles pricked trails down her sensitive skin. Her, a doe-eyed freshman trying to learn the layout of a massive university. Him, watching and stalking her every move. She'd been naive and blind and he'd been there all along. The quiet in the night. The eyes in the shadow. He'd followed her through the years, learning her—his prey— patiently waiting to mangle her world.

He'd likely played the part of student while he watched her from the next table. And when she'd graduated he'd likely been a face in the crowd. When she changed schools he'd followed. When she'd excelled in the academy and become an FBI agent he'd wormed his way silently into her world, a deadly parasite found too late to stave its havoc.

Why had he never presented himself? It was obvious he wished her harm, but death was too swift for his liking. He wanted to strip her of all she held dear. From watching her he'd learned that little was more important to her than the job, being the hero, and catching the bad guy.

Coghlan had formulated a plan to take it all away from her by framing her for murder.

He'd disguised himself as a janitor, infiltrated enemy lines, and gathered intel he'd later use against her. Her schedule at the conference left just enough time between her final session and flight to kill Josie Ackerman and William Boston. Her contentious relationship with Stan Watts would have sealed the coffin of suspicion over her head, had she stayed in town as ordered. She wondered what else Rory had learned on his mission and what or who else he would try using against her.

How had he known about Keen? Her heart skipped two beats and she bolted upright in her chair. Winslow stopped sniffling and turned toward her.

She and Keen had been in a relationship during college. He had come to her rescue in her time of deepest need.

Ava squinted tight and tried to think like Keen's life, like her life, depended on it.

Gray's words played over and over in her mind. Then she breathed them. "He baited us like fucking trout."

They were here in the hospital because Rory wanted them to be. With all the time and planning he'd put into this, no way would he not know that Lara Abbott could handle herself. He had known if one of her own was hurt Ava would come help. He'd been playing them from the start, moving them around like puppets on a damn string.

Gray's shirt front crumpled in her hand before she could blink. His expression blurred from sorrow to confusion to concern. Straining to keep her volume in check, Ava pulled him in close.

"Lock down the hospital. He's here."

Chapter Twenty-five

Years of training prepared Ava for tense situations. She'd been shot at, punched, and bitten by a serial killer who refused to go quietly. She'd even been in a knife fight and unfortunately stabbed. Through it all, Ava's training kept her alive.

Training taught Ava how to take the body's physical reactions to a volatile situation and use them to her advantage. When panic flared in her chest, threatening to stop her heart. When adrenaline snaked through her veins, making her knees quiver with weakness. When her breath shallowed so drastically it was as if oxygen suddenly ceased to exist. When fear quaked her mind so forcefully she wanted to collapse. Ava stopped.

Three deep breaths filled her lungs by force and concentration. Her shaking hands balled into fists, then released several times. She took the fear, kicked it into the cellar of her mind, and slammed the steel door shut. Ava checked it all. The panic, doubt, and fear. She focused on the task at hand.

Find Keen. Subdue Rory.

A familiar calm settled over Ava. Panic morphed into something else—clarity of mind and a physical alertness. Ava could hear Winslow talking to the hospital director in hushed tones, his free hand cupped around his cell. She ignored the words and checked her weapons.

First, she folded down and released the Glock 26 from her left ankle holster. She kept it low to keep from alarming the stressed crowd of the waiting room. The magazine ejected smoothly into her hand. She checked the load. Full. The chamber slid back like silk bed sheets. She checked it. Empty. Popping the magazine back in place, she advanced one in the chamber and engaged the safety. She repeated the ritual with her side arm. Turned toward the wall, she kept the well-oiled G21 hidden from view.

With guns ready, Ava felt the waist band of her left hip. The cold metal clip of her three-inch pocket knife reassured her. Ready to go, she scanned the room to make certain none of the other agents noticed her commando readying. She had to move quickly and silently. She needed the element of surprise to get any kind of advantage against Rory.

Most eyes honed in on Gray. *Great.* Ava made her way through the crowd, much like Keen had five minutes earlier, and into the hallway.

Ava scanned the corridor—left toward the ER's entrance, then right to a set of double doors with a sign barring all but hospital staff beyond them. The space was deserted, except for an old man being carted by a transport aid down a bisecting hall. Ava went left, the way she'd seen Keen go and her only real option. She scanned the cross hall dotted with nurses, people in ultra-sheer hospital garb, and their loved ones. She pushed on toward the emergency room.

No Keen. No coffee. There were, however, pouty red lips and massive breasts behind the counter. *Why not?*

"Excuse me," Ava said in as pleasant a tone as she could muster.

Long, totally fake, lashes and the eyes hidden underneath them scanned her from head to toe. The sneer said Betty Boobs remembered her. Ava smiled back at the sneer and pressed on.

"The man I came in with, have you seen him?"

Boobs Magee let out a sound akin to a moan. "Oh, yes. He stopped by here just a minute or two ago."

The woman licked her lips and Ava pressed hers together. She drew a lungful of heavy perfume, like whipping cream. "And?"

Bombastic Boob's lips curled. "He was looking for coffee. I was more than happy to help him out."

Ava practically shouted, "Where did he go?"

Boobs hopped back at her tone. They undulated far too long. "Up the hall back the way you came. Turn left. Just past the nurses' station there's a break room on the right. That's were I told him he could get coffee."

Ava didn't look back. She bolted down the hallway and hooked a left at the intersection. The nurses' station was in the middle of the long stretch of white wall and sterile tile. Her petite legs carried her with surprising speed past a quietly grieving family, the station with a single nurse, and into the break room.

The empty break room.

"Shit."

She checked the bathrooms.

Empty.

She checked the storage closet.

Well, she wasn't looking for a five-year supply of Styrofoam cups.

Back in the hallway Ava scanned. Everyone was gone. The nurse. The family. There were no patients being carted. An eerie quiet set in. She scanned again. Nothing to the left. The same to the right.

No, wait. There was something near the end of the hall, near the stairwell. She couldn't make it out at the distance and needed to advance, but her entire body tingled in warning. She had to proceed cautiously in this logistical nightmare. There were, at least, seven doorways lining the corridor on either side. And Rory could wait for her in any one of them. The chances were slim, but a chance was a chance all the same.

She breathed deeply once, hefted her sidearm, and began a wary advance. It took only a moment to clear two rooms. Two more. Behind the next she heard an old couple arguing about a question on Jeopardy. Ava had halved the distance when she looked again at the thing in the hallway.

Ice split her stomach with barbed fractals.

Blood streaked the bright tile where a body had been dragged across it. Next to the blood, a small bag and, presumably, its contents were scattered.

She drew closer.

A hospital ID badge and medical paraphernalia littered the wet floor.

Her mind raced on without her. Rory had disguised himself as a doctor, stalked Keen to the break room, and baited him to the stairwell where he sliced his throat. Tears came without permission, blinding her until they coursed in wide paths down her cheeks.

She raked her forearm over her face. "Get it fucking together."

Ava scanned the hallway again. Nothing. Voices echoed in the distance, but they might as well have been a world away. Here, alone, fear and doubt weighed a ton. Ava swallowed them. A hard lump to dislodge. She squared her shoulders toward the stairwell door and braced for whatever she might find behind it.

Chapter Twenty-six

Ava stepped over the winding roads of crimson, positioned her back at the hinge of the heavy metal door, crouched low, readied her Glock, and placed her hand on the lever. The handle twisted like the hands on a stop watch at the end of a race, one heart-stopping click at a time. The breath in her lungs turned to a solid, weighing her down. It combined with the weight of the door against her shoulder. She pushed.

The door gave way. Ava swung the gun high, scanning high to low. No one there. Committing again, she rushed to the corner of the stairwell and cleared the remaining area that had been blocked by the door.

Empty and quiet.

The trail smeared its way down the stairs into the bowels of the hospital. To the modern-day catacombs.

Thank God for sufficient lighting.

An ear-cracking slam came from her left and Ava's heart lodged into her esophagus. Her skin seemed to stretch off her skin and snap back into place. So much for centered.

The fucking door.

In all the scanning and clearing and blood trailing she'd forgotten to catch the door.

Shit!

If Rory was still down there, that surely alerted him. Though her drumming heartbeat might've given her away had the door not. Every tiny noise reverberated in the concrete cave like a beacon.

One step at a time, Ava followed the trail.

Focus on the present.

Fear batted around in the back of her mind. What if this was Keen's blood? What if this was all a well-baited trap?

One step to go until she reached the next landing. Ava clamped her hand over her mouth to seal in her scream.

Two legs in charcoal dress pants lay prone on the last two steps of the landing below. The scuffed soles of two wingtips stared up at her.

Chapter Twenty-seven

She didn't so much as run as gravity yanked her down the steps. Her hand squeaked on the railing, but she held tight. If she let go, she'd topple over.

Black hair. The man on the steps had black hair.

Air moved again in Ava's lungs. Her Gumby legs toughened to bone. It wasn't Keen. At the same time her throat constricted and tears obscured her vision. Unable to give the relief its proper reverence, Ava sucked it up, literally.

Rory was still out there and a body lay a few feet from her.

Ava rounded the landing. She put the entire next level into her view. Just that quickly she faced the barrel of a gun.

Gun to gun they stood frozen for the slightest of moments.

"Jesus Christ, Ava, I could have shot you," Keen whispered.

She glanced to the blood on the ground between them. "I thought you were dead."

They lowered their weapons. Keen stepped around the body and came toward her. He grabbed her shirt front with his free hand and pulled her close. His head nestled atop hers for a sweet moment. She grabbed him back, buried her face in his chest, and inhaled.

One hit was all she got. He kissed her hair and then unfolded her from his arms.

Ava blinked the tears away. No time for them now. But later, she feared the emotional letdown. She'd thought she'd lost him right after she'd found him, really found him.

Keen cleared his throat. He trapped her chin with his knuckle and thumb and made her look at him. Her heart squeezed. Here in the scary cave of death, Ava smiled.

When he stepped back and the body came into view, her smile faltered. She stepped closer and leaned over the man. With two fingers she checked his pulse, but the skin held no warmth.

"He's not even... He's been dead a while."

"That doesn't make sense."

"I know."

"From the look of things on the ground floor, this guy just happened to be in the wrong place at the wrong time."

He squatted next to her and reached into the man's pants pocket. The edge of a small brown double billfold peeked out. Keen opened it. "Doctor Eric Reiter."

"No." She tried to stand, to get away. She landed on her ass in the trail of blood.

"What is it? Who is it?"

"He was a great guy, a little full of himself, but he saved lives every day. That would heighten anyone's sense of worth, right?"

Keen stuck out his hand. "I'd fall over, just trying to get out of bed or tie my shoes."

Ava grabbed his hand and held on, literally and figuratively.

He hoisted her off the floor. "At least you're wearing black pants."

She knew he was trying to lighten the mood. Her fingers squeezed his extra hard before letting go. "Rory must have seen us together. We went out a few times two years ago."

Keen turned to continue the descent. "Stay behind me."

She clutched his arm. "It's a trap."

Her hand didn't halt his progress or even slow it. The only thing grabbing him did was tip her off balance. She stumbled down the steps and collided against his back. The blood on her pants suctioned them to her bottom.

Keen's gaze remained locked ahead. "I know."

Ava clamped both hands on his arms and dug in her heels.

When he turned toward her, all the warmth that'd been in his eyes when he'd pulled her to him had dissolved. A darkness she'd never seen before clouded them. He pulled her hands off his arm.

"He won't haunt you another hour or kill another person. This ends now."

Damn. Damn. Damn.

He was right and she hated it. Uncharacteristically, she wanted them to fall back into a defensive position. She wanted others to take the lead. Others to be in the killer's sights. She wanted Keen protected above all, even more than she wanted Rory Coghlan's head on a spit.

The only way she could shield him from harm was by moving forward with him. There was no stopping Keen. There was no backing down for him.

She agreed with a nod and they cleared a path one flight at a time until they reached the sub level. They moved as a team through the doorway and into a long corridor that branched at the far end into what seemed a maze of halls.

Gone was the stark white of the hospital. In its place, a forgotten world of grey. Exposed pipes ran overhead with raw concrete under foot. Stale air assaulted her nose. A fine sheen of sweat clung to her skin.

They moved down the main passage in search of the killer. Keen took the most vulnerable position, shoving her a step behind him.

With a nod of his head, Keen pointed out a series of blood droplets. Two were perfectly round spots with a third smudged...by a shoe. A hint of red stamped the floor in stride-length intervals until it faded completely two yards away.

Maybe Rory had gotten socked in the nose. Perhaps Eric had busted the bastard's lip. Maybe he'd left her another body. She strangled the gun in her hand.

Keen signaled and they advanced. The corridor ran the length of the hospital. They moved one step at a time. Several doors lined the sides. Ava tried the first. The latch didn't budge.

The second, third, and fourth were sealed tight. Literally, there was no place to go. If Coghlan decided to pop out of any one of the doors—which seemed more and more likely by the second—they were carnival targets, only easier.

They'd walked right into his hands. Keen knew it too. The gleam in his eye and the set of his jaw said as much.

Ava's mind screamed at them to run. Run back down the corridor and into the stairwell, the only place they weren't open marks.

Before Ava could voice those thoughts Keen snatched her hand and propelled her forward with such speed she could barely keep up. Her heart galloped in her chest. Her legs did the same across the dank floor.

Each door they passed was a kill shot waiting to take them. An opportunity for life's end.

Two-thirds back toward the stairwell door a sinister voice broke the silence. "Uh-uh!"

Keen spun with the agility of an NBA star. His big hand caught her by the shoulder in a smooth motion. Before she could blink she was on the ground. Keen skidded to a knee in front of her.

"It's not your time yet," the sing-song tone mocked.

Two shots that said otherwise zinged above their heads.

Keen fired two shots before the first crack of Rory's bullet smacked into the concrete behind them.

He turned toward her. His expression was tight and calculated. "Get to the door now."

She rose, unwilling to waste a moment arguing. The balls of her shoes dug for traction on the damp concrete floor. Her muscles, honed from years of running, tensed and stretched. She pulled the air and pushed it back.

Another shot split the air. She couldn't see where it came from or where it landed.

"Hurry," Keen yelled.

The reassurance of his voice carried her to the door. Her shoulder jammed into the metal frame, bouncing her into the cover of the stairwell. She dropped to her knees and scrambled to the threshold.

Keen still knelt on one knee, his gun aimed at the last door at the end of the hallway.

In a roar of terror and fury Ava screamed to Keen, "Move!"

He fired off one shot, turned in a crouch, and
ran. He took to the far wall. It left him more
exposed, but it gave Ava the line of sight she
needed to obliterate Coghlan. If only he'd give her
the chance.

Ava's finger itched to pull the trigger. All she
needed was a target.

Come on, move out just a little.

No movement came from the door Coghlan
had shot from. Before she even got a chance at a
target Keen crashed into her.

They sailed back through the door way,
landing with a thud. His hand caught her head,
cushioning its blow against the concrete floor. He
crushed her with his weight and force. Behind him,
the metal door closed with an echoing *gong*. Above
them, furious footfalls reverberated, growing closer
by the second.

Ava lifted her gun.

Again Keen didn't give her a chance to shoot.
He grabbed her shoulders and lifted her off the
ground, and then shoved against the wall. His
broad back steadied her, or rather trapped her,
from moving. Gun at the ready, her guard—Keen—
waited. His breathing steadied and nearly ceased as
the steps grew nearer.

Ava kept her gaze and gun on the door they'd
just flown through. Well, the closer the footsteps
drew the more her gaze bounced back and forth
between the steps and door.

On the landing above, all sound ceased.
They'd reached the body.

A shadow moved cautiously around the
banister and into their line of sight.

"Christ, Beaumont! What the hell are you
doing down here and why the fuck do you have a
gun?" Keen interrogated.

The gun, which had been at the ready, lowered. He eased it to his side, but his gaze fluttered around as though looking for the right explanation, instead of the truth. "I saw Ava sneak out of the waiting room and when she didn't come back I got worried. As for the gun, I usually carry one. After all these murders and Lara's attack, I'll have it close at hand from now on."

Keen maintained his centennial stance from in front of her. He'd caught it too. Mason was hiding something.

"I was in the ER when Winslow talked to the nurse about locking the place down. So, I knew something was up. There were agents outside the OR. I figured Lara was safe enough in there. I also guessed you were up to your ass in it and here you are—a dead body up there and I heard the shots at the top of the stairs."

Finally, Keen eased off Ava and dug his phone out of his pocket and dialed. All the while he kept his gaze on Mason Beaumont. "Winslow, where are you? Is the hospital locked down?"

Apparently satisfied with the answers, Keen switched to demands. "Get plans for this bullshit they call a sub level. We need to find all the entry and exit routes. Get someone with keys to the twenty doors down here. Get a crime scene unit down to the first level of the southwest stair case. And get me lots of men with lots of guns, now. Coghlan was down here, but I have a feeling he's running."

Chapter Twenty-eight

Goddamn son-of-a-bitch!

Keen hated it when he was right. The weaselly bastard had vanished.

I mean, grow a pair. Stay and fight. Be done with it already.

But no, after taking two shots Coghlan had escaped through the guts of the hospital like the cowardly shit he was.

Keen braced his forearms against the frame of Ava's living room window. In brooding thought he stared blankly out the glass at the vibrant moon. Small arms wrapped around him.

Highs and lows.

For so many years he'd been high on her. Then low without her. Now she was his and there was no way he'd let anyone hurt her.

"I won't let him hurt you."

"And I won't let him hurt *you*."

"The illusion of control," he scoffed.

"The illusion of love. It tricks us into believing everything will work out, that everything will be okay because we have love."

He grabbed her hands and brought them to his mouth. They were so little they nearly disappeared in his own. His lips trailed over her sweet palms and he remembered the feel of them on his dick. His shaft grew with the memory. Keen smiled a wicked smile she couldn't see and eased her middle finger in his mouth. Leisurely, he teased it with his tongue, grazing it up one side and down the other. He suckled.

Behind him, Ava shifted from one foot to the other. She tried to pull away, but he clamped her arm under his, barring her escape. He moved to the other hand, doing the same.

Her dance changed from frustrated to seductive. Pointed nipples brushed back and forth below his shoulder blades. Hips ground against him, pushing him forward against the glass.

"Let's embrace the illusions while we can." Her words tickled the back of his neck.

When he dropped her hands they went straight to the fly of his pants. She massaged his rigid shaft. He gave a grunt of appreciation. In reward her hands worked his button, fly, and then boxers, releasing him from the binding cloth.

His pants shucked, Ava turned him around. Half-closed lids and pink cheeks nearly undid him. Her eyes flashed with mischief. Her lips curved on one side in pure devilry. That hot gaze dropped to his dick. He knew what she wanted. His breath hitched, waiting to see if his innocent Ava would take what she desired.

Slowly, she slid the shoulder holster off his broad back and set it aside. As she unfastened each button her mouth kissed a trail over the revealed flesh. And by God, when she got the final button she sank to her knees. Her lips kissed the tip of his throbbing cock.

Sanity gone, he watched as she took her first taste of him. Electricity sizzled all the way to his toes. She savored him, rolling her tongue over his shaft again and again.

She applied suction and took him deeper. Then the tug of war started. One second she pulled him out to the unnerving end. For one heavy second she waited before she plunged him back inside. Keen braced his hands on the window frame. She worked him with skill she had no right to possess, tugging and slurping at just the right times.

His knees bent and his hands plunged into her loose hair. A moan vibrated her sweet throat and nearly kicked his ass off the edge of ecstasy. Keen gritted his teeth. No way would he come in her mouth. Too good at this or not, she'd been a virgin yesterday.

Her nails sank into his cheeks like grappling hooks. She pulled him forward and the tip of his cock nestled down the back of her throat.

"Ava." His chin arched to the sky. His eyes watered from the strain of holding his release.

The tension increased on his shaft. She swallowed him down. Once. Twice. Three times.

"Stop," he pleaded. He couldn't believe the words coming out of his mouth. "I don't want to come yet."

Oh, that was an out-and-out lie.

He wanted to fill her up, but he didn't want to gag her or freak her out. And unloading in his sweet Ava's throat didn't seem like the best way to say *I love you.*

The compression eased. She slid off his tip. He strained his eyes open and looked at her. Her red lips pursed. "You just don't want it to be over yet."

Her words smacked into the tip of his cock. He sighed.

"Just trust me." Ava winked, and then battered his head into the back of her throat.

Mercilessly she used her hands to pull him forward and her mouth to push him back. Forgive him, but he joined in the frenzy, straining his grip on her hair and pumping her on his dick.

Keen groaned and sank deeper into his squat. The pressure of no return squeezed his balls and he let it. A heavy electric current gathered at the base of his spine. Ava's hand wrapped around the base of his cock and constricted. The current zipped along his spine and branched off to every one of the billion nerve endings in his body. The scorched bliss of orgasm hugged him close, but the hot spurts of his ejaculation didn't race to the end of his cock.

Ava eased off the end of his shaft with a toothy grin and tousled hair. "You just didn't want to come in my mouth, hmm?" Her sleek little brow ratcheted.

"Not just yet," he admitted.

"I may have been a virgin until yesterday, but I'm not a prude. Not doing something makes a person that much more curious. I've learned a thing or two through the years."

"Oh." He couldn't keep the disappointment from his tone. The word virgin didn't mean exactly what it used to.

She licked the tip of his still-swollen penis. "Don't look so disappointed. It's not like I blew the entire hockey team. My roommate did. She liked to talk. Really, I think she liked to watch me blush."

"I like to watch you blush too."

He hauled her off the floor. Her puffy red lips drew him in like a bull. He crushed her smug smile under his mouth. The soft peals of her giggle drugged him. So this was what getting high felt like.

Keen wanted more. One by one he unfastened the dainty buttons on her blouse. Like she had, he feasted on each precious inch of skin his fingers revealed. The swells of her small breasts nuzzled his face in heaven's valley. He hovered there, testing the gentle swells at the edge of her lace cups.

For a moment he pulled back and leveled his gaze on hers. She giggled again and he attacked. He caught her bottom lip lightly between his teeth and ground his erection at the juncture of her thighs.

Soon she clutched at the back of his shirt. Her hips undulated. Moans spilled from between their lips. He stripped her one piece of clothing at a time, drawing each article off as though they had all the time in the world. In truth, he had to collect himself or he might beg her never to leave him. She'd said she loved him, but hadn't she loved him before? Hadn't he loved her?

He'd said he could deal with having her just once. He'd lied to himself. He'd told himself what he needed to hear to make taking her okay. He'd taken her all right—and no way could he give her back.

"I'm not blushing yet." Ava spread her arms wide, confident and resplendently naked.

"Huh." Keen spun her around and thrust her toward the table. He shuffled the two feet and planted his hand on the small of her back. "Palms on the top, ass in the air, and don't even think about blushing yet."

He bracketed her hips and tilted her pelvis, revealing the wet pink labia and the pretty pucker of her bottom. His chest brushed against her back. The edge of his mouth
hit the shell of her ear. "I'm just getting started."

His clothes had to go. He toed off his shoes, kicked his pants off the end of his feet, and added his open shirt to the pile. The tie, oh yes, he had plans for it.

Keen held the middle in his hand. The pointed tips dangled. They grazed her arched cheeks. Ava's red head fell between her shoulders. Her sides quivered as he danced the silk up her spine. He let the ends split her neck, and then he released it.

Floorboards creaked under his shifting weight. His knees hit the wood. He found the ends of the tie and grabbed hold. "Spread your legs, Ava."

She shifted her feet wider.

"You're blushing now."

When he traced her lips with his tongue she bucked. He pulled on the ends of the tie. She tipped back into him and he buried his face in her pussy. Ava panted. He tongued her, made out with her intimate flesh, nipping and laving his fill.

Her hips bucked. "Stop, Keen. I don't want to come yet."

Keen popped her engorged clit from between his lips and sat back on his heels. "Trust me, you want to, but you can't. Not just yet." He stood, unlaced the tie from her neck, and secured it around her waist, leaving enough room for his fingers. Part of him needed to control the uncontrollable ascent.

He pushed inside her to the hilt and stilled to keep from coming.

Ava apparently didn't have the same kind of restraint. Her hips rolled frantically, jacking him inside her. "Yes. I want to. I want to."

His grip tightened on the silk around her waist and barred the bulk of her movement. "You will. I just need a second."

"Please, now." Her fingers splayed wide on her white table. Her sides heaved.

"Impatient woman."

"I've been patient too long."

He unsheathed himself. She immediately stood, ready to battle. Keen lifted her by the cheeks and wrapped her legs around him.

Her hands cupped his face and she kissed him full on. He pressed into her body.

He thrust easily at first, but too soon became wild. Keen took her with a ferocity that spoke complete possession and complete loss of self.

Their orgasms came in shouted love words and curses. They clung to one another for a long time, a mass of quivering, clinging muscles.

When he figured he could move without falling Keen carried her to the bed. He collapsed onto his back and expected her to roll off. She doubled her hold, curling around him like a roving vine. Her grasp was so tight he had to shallow his breathing.

Tilting her head to face him, he looked at her questioningly.

"I thought I'd lost you today. I thought it was your blood on the floor. I've never been so terrified in all my life. Not when I found out about the awful things my father had done. Not when I went through the academy. Not when I pushed you away."

She dragged in a choppy breath and continued. "I refused to let you in before because I couldn't stand the thought of losing you. I know I hurt you. I hurt myself, too. And I'm so sorry for us both. Sorry for the time we lost."

Keen wiped a tear from her freckled cheek. His heart revved inside his chest, not knowing where this confession would lead.

Ava swatted away another tear and trudged on. "I don't want to waste any more time worrying about the past or the pain. I want to focus on the future...on a future with you. So," she quickly hastened, holding up a hand to keep him from speaking. She shifted, and on two knees she grabbed his hand. "Kenneth Richmond Hunt, will you marry me?"

One instant his heart was firmly planted in his chest. The next it was lodged in his guts. Of all the things he'd ever expected her to say, a marriage proposal didn't make the list.

Ava sat, breath stalled and eyes wide. The young girl he'd fallen in love with had grown into a woman, the woman he planned to spend the rest of his life learning, pleasing, protecting and, above all, loving.

He bum-rushed her into the mattress before she could speak and smothered her mouth with his own. When his hands began to roam she pushed him hard on the chest. "So? I need to know because I could be pregnant and you know how my mom would flip over an unwed mother."

"Pregnant?"

"Well, I could not be, but we haven't used anything and I don't take anything. Oh God." Her hand shot to her mouth. "You don't like kids? You're not ready?"

He grabbed her hand. "I'll love our kids whenever they come."

Her mouth hung so wide he could see the dangly thing at the back of her throat. A laugh broke deep in his chest and shook the entire bed. She punched him on the shoulder. He laughed harder still.

"Ava Marie Shepherd, I have loved you since the moment I saw you on the dock trying to revive that damn fish. I love you now and I've loved you every moment in between, even when I hated you."

"The day you broke up with me I had a ring to offer you. I still have it, at home, and I still want you to have it. So, Ava, will you marry me?"

"Just remember I asked first."

"Technicality." He kissed the satisfied grin off her face.

Chapter Twenty-nine

A knock grazed Ava's subconscious only enough to cuddle more firmly against Keen's shoulder before settling back into sloppy-drool sleep. If only he'd stayed put. Her pillow disappeared. She free-fell all the way to the sheets, a long way when you're asleep. Her head bounced off the mattress. Her lids blinked the moonlit room into view.

Keen's white cheeks and sculpted legs moved swiftly and silently across the room. His gun hung by his side.

Her eyes bulged. What was going on? What time was it? Where was her gun?

The clock read twelve-forty a.m. Her gun lay nestled under her pillow. As for what was going on... She had no clue.

Three firm knocks sounded on the apartment door.

Keen stopped at the frame and slid her an inquisitive glance. Ava shrugged, and then wiped the drool from her chin. He eased an eye to the peep hole. For whatever reason she thought the whole gun and sneak thing was overkill, but hey, if roles were reversed, she'd probably do the same.

He eased to the peep hole. "Blonde woman. Short. Leather shirt. Tight pants. Nice...ah...face."

"You can say boobs."

"What?" He quirked a look at her.

"I know you were going to say nice boobs."

"No." His hand eased through the air at hip level, and then held up his index finger. "I was going to say nice rack."

"Are they big?"

His hand became a shield. "I'm not—"

"Yep, they're big." Ava jumped off the bed, ran to Keen's pile of clothes, grabbed his boxers, and tossed them over. "Put these on and let her in."

Another series of knocks sounded. "Ava, I need to talk to you," the thin voice called through the door.

"Just a minute." She'd have put her panties on, but they were wet. Her cheeks flushed. Keen's shirt sat on top of the disheveled pile. She snatched it up and fumbled with the buttons.

She heard the flip of the lightswitch a fraction of a second before the beams of artificial light pierced her retinas. Her eyes watered. At least that was what she told herself caused the moisture seeping out of her eyes. But when Keen opened the door and Annelise stood in the corridor hugging herself she knew it was a lie.

"Come in." Ava waved her forward with a floppy sleeve. She hid her hands behind her back and flipped up each cuff.

Annie's hands dropped to her side and she eased into the apartment, her gaze on Ava. The leather halter appeared to be painted on her friend's luscious curves. Her jeans too. She wore black come-lick-me heels and her makeup had never looked better.

But her face...

Sorrow hollowed her eye sockets. It pulled the edges of her pretty mouth into a frown. Its weight dropped her shoulders and hunched her back.

Keen closed the door behind her. Annie jumped and turned toward the noise. The sadness melted away ever so slightly. Her chin lifted. Her rack saluted. The corners of her mouth moved from frown to straight line.

Annie blatantly inspected Keen, starting with his feet and working her way up. Then her scrutiny shifted to the bed, the haphazardly strewn clothes, and then settled on Ava.

Guilt burned a hole in her gut. Her friend was hurting and here she was having the best sex— sure, the only, but she'd been around long enough to know he was better than most—of her life.

"Whoa." Annie's neutral expression shifted to a smirk. "You really need an apartment with a bedroom, now that you're finally getting laid."

"You must be Annelise." Keen switched gun hands, moved it behind his thigh, and offered his right to her friend.

"You must be Keen." Annie tilted her head and inspected his lean abdomen.

He looked from Annie to Ava and back, and then eased around her. "I'll get some clothes on."

"Hey, not on my account." Annelise covered her heart, which also happened to be her exposed cleavage. "Just because I don't bat for your team doesn't mean I don't like to watch the game."

Ava's heart constricted. Her friend was back. Sure they had a long road ahead, but Annie had come to her when she should've gone to Annie.

Keen rubbed Ava's cheek on the way to the bathroom. When the door closed Annie took a step closer. Her gaze hit the floor, bounced off the wall, ricocheted off the bed, and finally settled back on Ava.

"I'm sure you don't want to hear anything I have to say after the way I spoke to you the other night..."

Ava stepped forward. "I love you and I want to hear whatever you have to say."

A tear slipped down Annie's cheek. Somehow Ava managed to choke back her own.

"I know you didn't hurt my sister. I knew you hadn't when I confronted you last week. It was wrong, a real low blow for me to blame you. Especially when I know how much you struggle with being that man's daughter. I was just so mad."

Annie slapped a stream of tears off her cheek.

"I felt guilty for being your friend. If I wasn't your friend he wouldn't have killed Josie. But if I weren't your friend, I wouldn't have had anything all these years."

"That's not true. You're the coolest, most outrageously funny woman I know."

"Do you still feel that way?"

"Hell yes."

"Good. It's been hell losing...but to lose you too? I can't take it."

"I'm not going anywhere." Ava opened her arms, but her gaze snagged on the door opening behind Annie.

"Yes, sister, you are."

Blood drained from Ava's heart and rushed to her extremities so quickly the room paled for a moment. Weakness gripped her limbs and wracked her mind. Cool, calculating thought vanished. In its place came gut-wrenching panic.

The red-headed devil stepped into her apartment. His arm wrapped around Annelise's middle. Silver flashed in his right hand.

"No." Ava shrieked the command, but it flopped across the room like a dying fish.

The blade stopped at the tender flesh of Annie's throat.

"Don't worry. I killed her sister, I think that's quite enough pain for someone who's done me no wrong. Unless you want me to end your misery." His handsome face dropped to Annie's ear. "Huh, cricket, what do you say?"

"Fuck you." Annie jammed her elbow into the man's side.

Rory Coghlan stood a few inches below six feet, but he was built like an Irish ox, complete with horns. A low chuckle rumbled. His chest shook, rocking Annie along with it. "Cute. Do it again and I'll show your nephew exactly how I killed his mommy."

Huge tears ran in torrents down Annie's face. Her makeup went with it, streaking her face in shades of black.

No. This couldn't be happening. Everything was just starting to get on track and now she saw no clean way out of this.

If Keen came out of the bathroom, which he probably would any second, he'd try to shoot Rory. That was great, except the bastard had a knife jammed so close to Annelise's carotid artery his reflexes alone could sever her life. Then there would be nothing Ava could do but watch her friend bleed out.

Ava could get to her gun, but again, Annie.

Plus she didn't want to put Keen in the middle of this.

As though Rory read her mind his gaze shifted to the bathroom. "Where's your lover?"

"In the bathroom." What other choice did she have, but the truth?

"Get him out." His chin jerked toward the door. "And tell him to carry his gun barrel first with two fingers."

Ava's bare feet stuck to the floor. No doubt Keen would try some heroics. She just didn't want Annie to die from them.

"I see you need some incentive." Rory raised the knife into the air.

"No." Ava screamed the command with force this time, but it didn't stop the nightmare.

Rory's hand descended in an angry stroke. He slashed the razor edge across Annie's biceps. The skin flayed wide.

Annie screamed.

He aimed the silver tip at her mouth. "Scream again and I'll cut your tongue out."

Her friend bit her lower lip. Spittle and tears mixed at the sides of her mouth with each labored breath.

"Stop." Ava lifted both hands in the air and walked backward. "I'm going. Stop."

"You stop," Rory ordered.

She did. So did her lungs.

Blood formed a stream from Annie's arm off her elbow to the floor.

"You don't get it, sister. You're no longer in charge. You've pranced around the last five years like you own the fucking world, but you had no idea how close I was, how many times I sniffed your pillow or watched your slut of a roommate go down on me."

Ava's blood froze. She tried to stop her hands from shaking. It didn't work. "I'm sorry—" Her words rattled as much as the rest of her.

"An apology isn't going to help you."

The droplets of Annie's blood formed an expanding circle. Maybe Ava could antagonize him

enough that he'd turn Annie loose and attack her.
At this point it was worth a shot.

"You didn't let me finish." Her gaze found his.
"I'm sorry my father didn't slit your mother's throat
the first time he met her. I'll bet he is too. I mean,
you can't even perform a decent copy-catting, even
with all his training."

Rory stepped forward, throwing Annie off
balance. "I didn't want to take after my old man any
more than you did."

"Yeah, but I catch bad guys and lock them
up. I'm going to lock you up, Rory. And you won't
be known as the great copycat. You'll be known as
the bastard child of Bloody Red Hardy and no
more."

He lunged forward, dragging Annie with him.
Rage etched his features, but then he straightened.
The angry groove of lines softened. "I'll be known as
the man who killed Ruby Red Hardy. Now, you be a
good girl and your friend might live. You and your
lover, you don't have a chance. So don't even try."

Opportunity slipped through her weak hands.
Ava forced her feet forward one stiff step at a time.
The knob jiggled under her hand. She turned it,
and then opened the door.

The white shower curtain hung to one side of
the shower. The toilet seat and windows were both
down. The sink wasn't running. And the bathroom
was empty. She looked behind the door. Nothing.

"Ava," Rory warned.

She turned to the closet, but there was no
place for him to hide. Besides, he wouldn't hide.
Not his style. She didn't have a balcony. The only
thing out the window was four stories of air, and
then concrete. The duct work was too small to
smuggle a cool breeze through, much less a six-
foot-two man.

Ava found Rory's gaze. "He's not in there."

His head tilted to Annie. "I don't guess she values your life very much." He lifted the knife into the air.

Chapter Thirty

The two-inch metal vent protruding from the side of Ava's building continued to bend under Keen's weight. Sweat slipped off the tip of his nose. It fell so fucking far it disappeared from view. A tight row of shrubs cuddled to the side of the building, but he didn't think greenery would make a difference at this height.

Tan brick grated into the open wounds on his fingers. Catching two-hundred-twenty pounds on the unforgiving corners of masonry proved harder than it looked. And he still had one hell of a stretch to reach the living room window.

No time to puss out.

Keen reached his right arm and foot toward the sorriest excuse for a window ledge he'd ever seen. The tiny strip of brick made the tin can crumpling under his acute weight look like a damn helipad in comparison.

The rubber of his top sider wobbled on the ridge. His calf constricted. The shoe steadied. As soon as his raw finger found the side he shoved off the vent.

Metal gave way.

It hit the bushes with a rustle.

One more inch and he'd have been fertilizer.

His cheek scraped the sandpaper surface of fine DC architecture. Keen grabbed the brick side of the window with both hands. One foot braced his weight on the sill. His face steadied his precarious spot on the modern cliff. He had to stay out of sight, without falling. Keen drew a quick breath, and then eased the center of his balance toward the glass.

The point of Rory Coghlan's knife dimpled Annelise's cheek. His other arm locked around the woman's slim middle.

Where was Ava?

The bastard's mad gaze angled toward the closet. Ava. Keen couldn't hear his love's name on Rory's lips for the rapid beat of his heart, but he read it just fine.

Keen doubled his grip with his left hand. He eased his right to the window, hooked the tiny metal ledge with his bloody fingernails, and then pulled, desperate to open the window.

Nothing.

His foot began to quake again.

Annelise's eyes bulged.

Keen followed instinct. He pressed his shoulder into the concrete and reached for the gun in the waist band of his shorts.

Rory arched the knife into the air.

"No." Ava's hoarse roar rattled the window pane.

He didn't have time to do anything but shoot. Twice. The first bullet broke the glass. The second smacked the center of Rory Coghlan's forehead. His neck jerked back. His arms fell slack at his sides. The heft of his body crashed to the ground.

Annelise's cries bled through the shattered fringes of the round hole.

Chapter Thirty-one

Sweet relief buckled Ava's knees. Her grip on the door frame kept her from falling to all fours. The bed blocked Rory's torso, but the lifeless tilt of his shoes and the splatter of blood that painted her wall told her the true spawn of Satan was dead.

Ava followed the line of the shots.

Keen.

Blood smeared the window. A small hole fractured the window where the bullet entered the apartment.

She launched across the room. Her bare feet burned on the wood floor, but she pushed harder.

Annie hugged herself. Heaves wracked her torso.

Ava didn't slow. She cleared the coffee table. Tiny shards of glass sliced into the balls of her feet. She braced her hands on the sill.

"Keen." Her stomach took the four-story drop that Keen could at any second.

He hunched in the window he'd stared out of several times while staying in her place. His back pressed against the small ledge. His right foot anchored him on the opposite side. His other foot wobbled precariously on the bottom ledge. Perspiration dripped from his chin. His bloody hand clasped his pistol, while the other braced the top and kept his weight from tipping toward the ground.

Ava unlatched the lock. Terrified she'd knock him off balance by slamming the window open like she wanted, she eased it open.

"Mind if I come in?" His smile eased the ache in her chest.

When he tumbled on top of her all the fractured pieces of her heart locked into place. She wrapped him in her arms and prepared for the impact of the coffee table. He caught them before the crash.

Keen stood. He hugged her to his chest so completely she thought she might never leave the spot. Their grips shifted time and again, pulling each other closer with desperate grappling.

"I love you," she whispered.

"You are my world, Ava. I wouldn't let him take you away...or your friend." He kissed her forehead and eased back ever so slightly. "Come here, Annelise."

They opened their hug to Annie. Her head lifted, shifting the blonde hair from her splotchy face. One labored step at a time she crossed the distance and then fell into their arms. Her cries crescendoed before subsiding. "Is he dead?"

"The reaper dragged his ass straight to hell," Keen said.

"Good." Annie straightened. Her gaze slid to the man Ava loved enough that somewhere along the way—like Amadi had told her—she'd learned to love herself. She'd finally forgiven herself the hatred and love she harbored for her father. "Thank you."

"My pleasure." Keen's gaze dropped to Annie's arm, then to Ava's feet, and flitted over the mess he'd made of their clothes with his bloody hands.

Ava grabbed his free hand. She turned the sliced flesh this way and that. "Annie, can you get some dish towels from the kitchen."

"I'm fine." Keen confiscated his hand, hooked his arm around her waist, and lifted.

"It'll give her something to do. Besides, I need to get some pressure on her arm."

"What about your feet?" He sat her on the sofa.

"They're still hanging on." The sharp pain had dulled to a throb. "My heart, on the other hand, feels like it's run the globe."

His blue gaze dropped to her chest. "I'll have to kiss it all better."

"Can it wait until I stop bleeding to death?" Annie plopped down a stack of towels.

"I guess." She patted the coffee table in front of her and got to work on her friend's arm.

"I'm going to call Winslow." Keen stood and made the call. When he hung up he smiled. "He said Lara's pissed she didn't get to end him."

"She's awake?" A stupid tear sprang to Ava's eyes.

Keen's sweat-darkened hair flicked moisture when he shoved some off his forehead and nodded.

"Seems I missed some stuff," Annie whispered.

"Nothing you need to worry about." Ava kissed her friend's cheek, and then turned to Keen. "Can you get us some ice?"

He disappeared into the kitchen. When he came back the blood on his hands was gone and he held a Ziplock full of ice.

It took towels, ice, and a chunk of time to staunch the bleeding on Annie's arm. While she held pressure Keen plucked five glass shards from her feet.

No one looked toward the body. No one even mentioned it.

The squeak of the front door swiveled their heads. Keen brought his gun around too and shifted in front of Ava. His back brushed her calf.

"What is it with you two and dead bodies?" Mason Beaumont stood in the threshold. He studied what was left of Rory Coghlan's face.

"What is it with you showing up around the dead bodies? It's taking ambulance chaser a little far, don't you think?" Keen held a bead on him.

"I just heard about it at the hospital and wanted to come see for myself that the piece of shit was dead."

"How'd you get here so fast?" Ava demanded.

"I ran all the lights." He said it as though it were a given, like it was something he did all the time.

She expected a twinge of unease at Mason's awkward timing, but something in his eyes kept the panic at bay.

"Why are you really here? You're a lawyer hired on to a case that no longer exists." Keen stood.

Mason's eyes closed for more than a second, and then he centered his gaze on Keen. "So that's two strikes against me? The lawyer being one and the case no longer existing the other?"

"No." Keen stepped forward. "You have three strikes and you're about to be out because you keep lying."

"I'm not lying about anything." Mason wrung the back of his neck.

He kept the gun trained. "Fine. You're hiding something."

"That's not lying." He shrugged.

"Lawyers," Ava scoffed.

Mason waved Keen off and retreated a step. "Look, you have enough drama to deal with for one night. We'll talk later."

"Spill it or I'll pry it out of you. You know they teach us," he shifted a finger between her and himself, "these really fun techniques."

"Electrocution," Ava chimed.

"Water boarding," Keen added.

"Too popular these days." Her head shook. "Even moms are trying it on their kids. What about sight deprivation?"

"That's a good one. There is always sodium thiopental." Keen used the gun to tick it off his fingers.

"Ooh, truth serum," Ava squealed. "I know a guy."

"Will you two stop?" Mason begged.

"When you tell us what we want to know." Keen's arms spread wide.

"Fine, but you're not going to like it." The lawyer's arms spread, mirroring Keen's.

Ava had a glimmer of intuition about what the man would say. She covered her mouth.

"We're all ears." Keen puffed out his chest.

Mason's arms dropped to his sides. He pressed his lips together, and then released them. "Your father is my father."

Keen's mouth opened, but no sound escaped.

"The asshole you call your sperm donor is the asshole I call my sperm donor." The lawyer pinched his chin, scrubbing his ten o'clock shadow.

"So," Keen dragged the word out. "We're brothers?"

He shifted onto his heels and stuffed his hands in his pants pockets. "Half."

Everyone was quiet for a long minute. In the distance sirens wailed.

"No shit?" Her lover's chin lowered.

"None," Mason whispered.

Keen rubbed the top of his head, and then let it settle there. His gaze found Ava's.

She let him see her smile. She let him see the love she had for him. She let him see the hope she had for their future. All of their futures.

Her fingers twined gently around his. "He's got to be better than my half brother."

ENEMY MINE
A BASE BRANCH NOVEL

When friends become enemies and enemies become lovers.

Born in the blood of Sierra Leone's Civil War, enslaved, then sold to the US as an orphan, Base Branch operative Sloan Harris is emotionally dead and driven by vengeance. With no soul to give, her body becomes the bargaining chip to infiltrate a warlord's inner circle. The man called The Devil killed her family and helped destroy a region.

As son of the warlord, Baine Kendrick will happily use Sloan's body if it expedites his father's demise. Yet, he is wholly unprepared for the possessive and protective emotions she provokes. Maybe it's the flashes of memory ... two forgotten children drawing in the dirt beneath the boabab tree... But he fears there is more at stake than his life.

In the Devil's den with Baine by her side, Sloan braves certain death and discovers a spirit for living.

VERSIONS
A BLACKLIST NOVELLA

The truth doesn't have versions. Or does it?

Rin Lee covered her childhood in dirt and danced on its grave. Only she pranced a little too hard and spent her young-adult life tiptoeing the straight and narrow. Things finally paid off in the form of a job with the Department of Defense, a home of her own, and a boyfriend muscled enough he put Zach Efron to shame. Until one text reveals a hideous truth that splinters her world.

Suddenly she can't trust Nate or their surrogate family of friends. Can she possibly trust Luck—the man who mirrors her soul, scares her beyond the neat confines she's erected around herself, and makes her scrutinize the versions she's always been too angry to see?

Luck turned to the streets out of necessity, while Rin slapped on blinders and ignored those willing to help her. A stupid move for a sultry young woman. But the skills she learned in the rough and tumble underbelly of DC will serve his latest assignment well. Because people like them have the instinct to survive.

ENEMY MINE
A BASE BRANCH NOVEL

When friends become enemies and enemies become lovers.

Born in the blood of Sierra Leone's Civil War, enslaved, then sold to the US as an orphan, Base Branch operative Sloan Harris is emotionally dead and driven by vengeance. With no soul to give, her body becomes the bargaining chip to infiltrate a warlord's inner circle. The man called The Devil killed her family and helped destroy a region.

As son of the warlord, Baine Kendrick will happily use Sloan's body if it expedites his father's demise. Yet, he is wholly unprepared for the possessive and protective emotions she provokes. Maybe it's the flashes of memory ... two forgotten children drawing in the dirt beneath the boabab tree... But he fears there is more at stake than his life.

In the Devil's den with Baine by her side, Sloan braves certain death and discovers a spirit for living.

VERSIONS
A BLACKLIST NOVELLA

The truth doesn't have versions. Or does it?

Rin Lee covered her childhood in dirt and danced on its grave. Only she pranced a little too hard and spent her young-adult life tiptoeing the straight and narrow. Things finally paid off in the form of a job with the Department of Defense, a home of her own, and a boyfriend muscled enough he put Zach Efron to shame. Until one text reveals a hideous truth that splinters her world.

Suddenly she can't trust Nate or their surrogate family of friends. Can she possibly trust Luck—the man who mirrors her soul, scares her beyond the neat confines she's erected around herself, and makes her scrutinize the versions she's always been too angry to see?

Luck turned to the streets out of necessity, while Rin slapped on blinders and ignored those willing to help her. A stupid move for a sultry young woman. But the skills she learned in the rough and tumble underbelly of DC will serve his latest assignment well. Because people like them have the instinct to survive.

Megan Mitcham was born and raised among the live oaks and shrimp boats of the Mississippi Gulf Coast, where her enormous family still calls home. She attended college at the University of Southern Mississippi where she received a bachelor's degree in curriculum, instruction, and special education. For several years Megan worked as a teacher in Mississippi. She married and moved to South Carolina and began working for an international non-profit organization as an instructor and co-director.

In 2009 Megan fell in love with books. Until then, books had been a source for research or the topic of tests. But one day she read *Mercy* by Julie Garwood. And oh, Mercy, she was hooked!

Megan lives in Southern Arkansas where she pens heart pounding romantic thriller novels and window-steaming erotic romance. For information on releases and giveaways subscribe at meganmitcham.com!

Facebook: @MeganMMMitcham
Twitter: MeganMitchamAuthor
Pinterest: MeganMitcham5
Website: www.meganmitcham.com

FOR INFORMATION ON NEW RELEASES &
GIVEAWAYS, SIGN UP FOR MEGAN'S
NEWSLETTER AT WWW.MEGANMITCHAM.COM.